HUNTED ON PREDATOR PLANET

BOOK ONE OF THE
PREDATOR PLANET SERIES

VICKY L. HOLT

EOS
PUBLISHING

To Hammond, my little monster

ABOUT THE AUTHOR

Website:
www.lovevickyholt.com
Twitter:
https://twitter.com/LoveVickyHolt
Facebook:
https://www.facebook.com/lovevickyholt
Instagram:
https://www.instagram.com/lovevickyholt

ABOUT EOS PUBLISHING
Website:
http://eos-publishing.com
Twitter:
https://twitter.com/eospublishing
Facebook:
https://www.facebook.com/eospublishing
Instagram:
http://instagram.com/eospublishing

SUBSCRIBE TO NEWSLETTER
https://eos-publishing.com/newsletter

1

"Wilderness is not welcoming.
It is the place where humans may be prey."
--William E. Glassley

As my Emergency Egress Pod burned through the ionosphere of a huge green planet, I shrieked so loud I couldn't hear the alarms blaring from within my vehicle, nor the calm vocalizations of the onboard computer. The life-support systems were going haywire, and I yelped in pain when the IV administering the cryodrug ripped from my sleeve port. At least my double five-point harness wasn't releasing; I would die as soon as we made it to the mesosphere. As it was, I might die anyway.

Were there heat shields? How many PSI could my viewing porthole withstand? By now, my screaming had abated to terrified whimpers. The flames outside my window glowed orange and yellow, but also white and blue and some shades of violet I'd never seen before.

Finally, I could hear the onboard computer through my flight helmet. "Sinus tachycardia detected. Remain calm and I will administer a tranquilizer."

"N-no! Negative! Don't do that!"

"It is inadvisable to come out of cryosleep during landing, K90-Miner 105."

"I don't even know how I woke up!" My panic had me in a hammerlock. My aptly named "EEP" continued to flame brilliantly out the window.

Coming out of cryosleep is supposed to be this soothing, lullaby-shrouded experience filled with aromatherapy, ocean sounds, and the gradual awakening of all systems. Welcome to my life.

"Sensors indicate minor errors occurred in the Emergency Egress Pod. I will reset to pre-flight settings."

"What? Don't do that now!" I started to hyperventilate. I closed my eyes and took a deep breath. The temp-control prevented my window from fogging up—a curse instead of a blessing, though I was mesmerized by the whooshing white-hot flames outside. "You can land us safely, right?"

"Landing in seventeen minutes. Hull intact; heat shields at one hundred percent. Please remain calm, K90-Miner 105."

"Just call me Esra," I said, willing my breathing to slow.

"Noted: Esra. I am called VELMA. I am the latest tech available to Intergalactic Mining Conglomerate, Machine Learning Division."

"Uh, okay," I said. "Any particular reason you're called VELMA?"

"VELMA derives from the Old German variant Wilma, meaning determined protector."

"Okay, that's cool." I could have used a determined protector a few years ago on Earth. I shook my head and expelled a sigh. Ancient history. "Nice to meet you, VELMA," I said, distracted by my view out the porthole. Mesmerizing. Hypnotizing. Terrifying.

"I have deployed the transospheric nanosatellite array," VELMA announced. Five minutes later, she spoke again. "Scanning planet's surface," she said. "Rotational axis at twenty-five degrees. Ionosphere particle atomization estimates planet's age at eighty-seven million intergalactic standard years." I listened to her narration with half an ear. "Probability of undiscovered ores at ninety-two-point eight seven percent."

Eventually, the pod broke through the atmosphere of the green world, and I watched in amazement as mountains, jaded hills, forest canopies and golden-yellow fields passed my porthole.

"What is this planet?" I said with awe in my voice.

"The Interplanetary Unification of Races has not yet charted this planet. When the mothership *Lucidity* was compromised, all EEPs were jettisoned into space. I scanned planet candidates until crossing the Pollack-Custer belt and traveled five light-years to this habitable planet."

I felt the EEP's thrusters engage and my belly did a roller coaster loop, and we landed upright. I closed my eyes and expelled a whispered breath of gratitude.

"Life support systems online."

I grimaced at the computer's announcement. Was there still some malfunction? They should have been online this whole time. I took steadying breaths.

Powerful vibrations under my feet must have been the landing mechanism engaging. We settled with a small bump, and I sagged in my tight harness. I was not dead yet. A tear rolled down my cheek, but I couldn't swipe it away through my helmet.

I looked out the window at a wide meadow filled with tall grasses and green flowers. Surrounding the meadow was a circle of tall swaying trees. Flying insects that could be bees or flies, if we were on Earth, dipped and soared among the greenery. It looked for all the world like a perfect day for a picnic.

The computer shocked me out of my reverie.

"The humidity is ninety-four percent. The ambient temperature is one hundred degrees Fahrenheit. There are no immediate signs of active wildlife," the computer announced, "however, there are numerous emissions of methane, indole, skatole and sulfur-containing compounds, indicating scat deposits of varying sizes and amounts."

"Gross," I said, making a face.

"The excrements I've located with my volatile emissions scanners indicate a large range of mammals, reptiles and amphibians, consistent with the tropical environment."

"Wonderful," I said. "You've got a poop-scanner."

"The study of excrement reveals many things about living organisms, including diet, health, longevity, its order in the food chain, the presence of disease and contagions, and also the chemical makeup of the planet, such as the minerals and vitamins that are bio-available for humans."

"Like I said, a poop-scanner." I sighed, the adrenaline spike abating and fatigue setting in. I looked out the window. It looked like a rainforest, minus the rain. I stared for a little while, trying to see if there were any monkey-like creatures swinging from the trees.

The pod shook. I felt the reverberation in my feet.

"VELMA, do you have a seismograph?"

"I am equipped with thousands of methods for analyzing environments, a seismograph among them," she replied. "There is no indication of an earthquake, though I have detected hundreds of microtremors, much like the activity found on your home world."

"Okay, great. Could you tell me what made the pod …"

It felt like the swell of a wave carried my pod up and down, yet my view out the porthole didn't change. That had to be an earthquake. Nausea gripped me, and I clamped my mouth shut. I was *not* about to vomit inside this pod. *In my helmet.*

Before I could relax, I felt something vibrate. "VELMA, tell me you felt *that* vibration."

"The vibrations are caused by a living organism. There are no signs of seismic activity. As long as you remain in the pod, you will be one hundred percent safe."

"Is there something you're not telling me about this so-called living organism?" I felt panic rise in my chest. The beeping escalated.

"Support systems are showing elevated pulse and shallow breathing. Are you injured?"

"No, VELMA. I'm scared out of my freaking mind. Don't you dare tell me to calm down either or I'll …"

A shudder rippled its way through the pod, and my view out the window shifted. I stared in awe as two huge, dark-green monsters attacked each other about thirty feet from the pod. I had a front-row seat out the porthole, and I was never so glad for a catheter in my life. They had muscular hind legs and giant talons that dug into the ground as they fought. They grappled each other with clawed front legs and snapped huge narrow jaws full of bright-white teeth so sharp that just a glance on their enemy's scaled skin drew blood. I noticed their throats had huge bulges that reminded me of frogs, but these were wrinkled and a deep-orange color. By now, black blood was oozing from several wounds. I noticed one had a pretty bad gash on its hind leg.

"VELMA, are you seeing this?" My voice was hushed in reverence or fear.

"Esra, I do not see the way you do, but using Augmented Reality Digitization, I have picked up the presence of two reptilian creatures fighting for dominance. Based on similar scenarios on charted planets across galaxies, the outcome of the battle will grant the victor rights to procreate with any available females."

"Uh, thanks for the wildlife lesson," I mumbled.

"The Machine Learning Division engineers were avid fans of the Mutual of Omaha Wild Kingdom, a nature program airing from 1968 through 1988, a half century prior to Earth's Accountability Years."

Ignoring VELMA's droning, I watched the "reptiles" clash, though their fight brought them in and out of view of the porthole. They were massive. If they were thirty feet away, and they looked as big as elephants, about how big would that make them? I saw serrated teeth. Brown shiny talons. Heavy tails. Massive jaws.

I whispered as if my voice could carry outside the pod, terrified they would see the pod and come investigate. "VELMA, how big are these reptiles?"

"The reptiles measure five meters tall. They are both males. The outcome of the fight will determine ..."

"Yeah, yeah. I get it. Also, from now on, could you use Earth's Imperial system? And can you make this thing invisible?"

"Very well. The reptiles are sixteen point four zero two feet tall. The escape pod is not equipped with invisibility; however, I have activated the counter-illuminative hDEDs," the computer reported.

"The *what*?" I wondered out loud, clueless. All my last-minute cramming before we reached the Custer system had been on how to use the IGMC's Galvanite Mech-Drill. I hadn't studied the EEPs at all.

"A standard camouflage feature equipped in all Intergalactic Mining equipment," it replied. "You are safe from detection for now."

In other words, the Galvanite Mech-Drill had these hDEDs too. Guess I didn't cram good enough.

"*For now?*" I repeated.

"For now, you will remain undetected by the local flora and fauna. I cannot guarantee it will remain so should a large creature stumble across the pod. As is true for wildlife on all planets, one cannot predict an animal's behavior."

Smack!

My heart stopped when my viewing window darkened. The living thing gyrated and then took a step with one of its jointed legs, and a gigantic wasp ambled into view.

"Oh hell," I uttered, my eyes wide. "I've landed in a freaking B movie." I resisted the urge to smack the glass so it would step out of the way. I was still trying to see the fight.

"VELMA, do you know how many other pods landed on this planet?"

"That information is not available."

"Do you know how the *Lucidity* was compromised?"

"That information is not available."

I took a deep breath. Closed my eyes and centered myself, like I did on all those preflight tests. And exogeology exams. And collegiate track meets. And field expeditions in the Gobi Desert. And right before I walked out on Chris, for the last time.

The Kerberos 90 oxygenated moon expedition was off the table. My job with IGMC? I guessed it was terminated now. The minute my pod reached this atmosphere, I was alone.

"Can you get me audio of the outside? And tell me more about this planet?"

I heard a slight static buzz, and then audio filled my helmet. I had expected growling and roars, as well as buzzing from the wasp. Instead, I heard the churning of dirt and the snick of sharp claws and teeth scraping across skin. There were grunts, but they weren't as loud as I would have guessed. An odd sensation crept over me as I watched the silent battle play out before my eyes.

"The emergency evacuation from *Lucidity* necessitated a long flight. You are now located on the equator of an uncharted planet. My algorithms and diagnostic scans chose this planet because it sits nestled in the Goldilocks zone of a binary star system. A yellow giant and red dwarf are orbited by this planet and one other. They share the same orbit, and the other one is visible from this planet's surface. In addition, I was programmed to choose a planet with a tilted rotational axis, so as to provide my passenger with the best chance at survival in a moderate climate."

I looked out the window once the wasp flew away, seeing an orange sky and what looked like a green moon but must be the other planet. I remembered the *Lucidity* experiencing a huge jolt and the onboard AI alerting everyone to enter the rescue pods. After that, I recalled nothing else until I woke screaming.

"Back up a minute," I said, rehearsing all the computer had told me. "Did you say *five freaking years?*"

"No," she replied. "I said five light-years."

My heart had recovered. But my soul felt the crushing weight of defeat. My plans, goals, dreams...lost. Maybe *Lucidity* would send out trackers. Maybe other pods landed here too. But something told me I should make peace with VELMA for company. I was going nowhere anytime soon.

2

NARAXTHEL

The smells of my hunting grounds on planet *Ikthe* flooded my senses before anything else. Musty soil and rotting vegetation odors were thick in the air, as well as the gases released by noxious plants and moldering corpses of beasts. My ship secured behind me, I activated my cloaking device and began my hunt.

Stealth, strength, savagery.

I hunted the rokhura: a giant carnivore with jaws large enough to snap me in two. And I was one of the largest males of the Theraxl race.

The rokhura spread across this planet, swarming around bodies of water where the smaller prey came to drink.

Fists filled with the hilts of my weapons, I maxed out every stealth setting on my body armor with the gesture of an eye-blink on my visor. Familiar with the terrain, I ran through the dark and sun-dappled *ikfal*, avoiding roots and brush easily, as well as dodging the branches that would slap my helmet. A grid overlay inside my visor revealed the clearest path through the forest.

I approached the nearest body of water, and even before my sensors lit up the screen, I felt the rumble in the ground beneath my boots. A grim smile lifted my cheeks and revealed my fangs. To find them this quickly was a good omen.

Soon, the bloody corpse of my prey would burden my ship's hold. Perhaps my name would be uttered in the halls of the Royal Court before the two suns set on my home world, *Ikshe*.

I stopped at an opening between the trunks and foliage of the shady and vast *ikfal* and observed my prey. Two giant beasts fought each other with vicious swipes of taloned limbs and lethal strikes of bladed teeth. Blood poured from the wound of one rokhura's shoulder. I scanned the perimeter. A third rokhura, camouflaged in the ikfal, looked on the battle with interest. A female. She and the victor would feast on the flesh of the dead one, after which, a mating ritual would commence, destroying the surrounding area with its violence. Trees would snap like twigs; holes would open up in the ground; soil and roots would be slashed into great gouges. I pitied any creatures within fifty veltiks of this place.

I must hunt the victor. And its mate.

Songs would be sung in the Court of my valor and strength. The meat of three rokhura would feed many females on *Ikshe*, my neighboring home world.

Now my prey was within range, I disabled my stealth settings: it would be a fair battle. My heart thudded in its casing, and my four lungs expanded in preparation for battle. I saw the gaping wound on the rear leg of one of the males.

If I moved too soon, I would distract the group. The three would unite against a common foe, forgetting their lust to mate in favor of hunting and killing the interloper. Me. If I moved too late, the viciousness of the mating ritual could kill me as their combined strength and bloodlust would be formidable.

I snuck a path through the ikfal to the rear of the female. I would leap upon her back from behind, severing her throat with double blades at the same moment the alpha male would offer his death-strike to his victim.

That was the easy part.

I tracked the weaker male's limp and estimated the moment the alpha male would go in for the jugular. Leaping with the help of my enhanced armor, I landed at the apex of the rokhura's spine, using a blade to sink into the hard skin and scale up her spine like climbing a mountain. The air pulsed with her rumble of rage. I felt her entire body shake as her throat sac expanded with her roar. The victor was at that moment sinking its teeth into the neck of his opponent and didn't respond to his prospective mate's cry. With eager strength, I climbed the final steps to the female's vocal sac and used a double stroke, crossing my blades to finish her off.

Now the victor released its prey with dripping maw and cocked its head in confusion as his mate fell to the earth. I obscured myself with her body as she fell, leaping aside at the last minute to avoid being crushed. When the victor came to sniff his mate, I would lunge at his head and blind him. Shortly after, I would sever his vocal sac.

I crouched in wait, the female's flank hiding me from the rokhura. It approached tentatively, perhaps curious, but more likely cautious. The rokhura were the top predators on this planet for good reason.

I watched its nostrils flare at the musky scent of her blood saturating the ground. Soon his curiosity would shift to hunger, and he would devour her without regret. Except my knives would be embedded in his eye sockets in a few short tiks.

The sub-sonic roaring, even dampened by my ear protection, shook me to my bones. I gouged and dug, removing his eyes, then severed his throat with a final stroke from my raxtheza. I howled in victory, allowing the shower of black rokhura blood to drench my armor. I sent the sight-capture to my home world, where the Royal Court could watch my performance. The sight-captures did nothing to sway the outcome of the Lottery draw, but it would prove gruesome entertainment for the females.

Now to summon my mechanical Tech-Slave to help me secure the corpses to take back to Ikshe. The females would be fed for months with this kill. My chest swelled with pride. Once again, I, Naraxthel, had proven worthy to be called Iktheka Raxthe, the mighty hunter.

3

"VELMA, zoom in on the figure fighting with the reptiles." I had been transfixed by the battle, while a third monster had been hiding in the shadows of the forest. From out of nowhere I saw the two-legged alien leap into the fray. Hope beat a tattoo in my chest. Another person within sight of my pod! I didn't want to be alone on this planet.

VELMA's camera zeroed in with surprising detail. I appreciated the EEP's tech.

The humanoid figure wore a reddish metallic armor from head to toe. Its helmet was huge, giving the illusion of a monstrous beast. What did I know? Maybe the head was that big. I accessed the control panel within reach and toggled the camera around, finding the best possible view of the figure's entire body. Massive arms and legs, huge torso, tapered waist. If I had to guess, that was a male.

I zoomed in on the hands. I was amused to see four fingers and a thumb on each hand, but the armored claws were less funny.

The armor plates were articulated where one might expect them to be. Elbows, wrists, knees, ankles. As a student of the Interplanetary Unification of Races College Academy, I had seen lots of videos of the most active alien races. The variety was astonishing and remarkable. But very few races had the same arm and leg configuration that humans did. I studied its helmet again. A dark rectangle delineated where eyes must be. A light-absorbing visor, perhaps? The nose and mouth shapes on the helmet resembled more of a snout. Scrolls and engravings on the helmet denoted art intended to frighten and dismay. Horns, eyes, teeth—all demonizing the helmet. With graceful but intimidating power, the figure dealt the death blows with efficiency.

I was top in my class back home. Salutatorian, star pole vaulter, most promising miner. And yet the sight of that armored figure taking down not one, but two, gigantic reptiles with a guttural howl—I gulped. It was the first vocalization I'd heard besides VELMA.

Taking classes about interplanetary exploration was one thing. Witnessing it with my own eyeballs?

Coming off the cryodrug, most sensation had returned to my upper torso. I had full range of motion in my neck and arms; I could even bend at the waist if I wasn't harnessed in. But I had yet to feel my feet or legs and had no control of my lower digestive tract. I was grateful my nausea had prevented me from craving solid foods yet.

I watched out the porthole as a hovering land-crosser arrived and what looked like a robot stepped off to assist the armored creature butcher the beasts. Together, they made quick work removing pieces, but then took their time to wrap the heads with care.

"VELMA, disable the camouflage on the escape pod."

"It is inadvisable you disable the camouflage at this time, Esra."

"I want that armored man to see it! He can help us."

"My scanners do not detect a human male in the vicinity of the pod."

Frustration battled with hope. I opened my mouth to argue, but she continued.

"My seismic scanners detect a pack of large predatory creatures headed in this direction. High probability present they have smelled the blood of the fallen beasts."

The hope and frustration leaked out of me like water from a sieve.

"Sensors indicate sinus tachycardia and fluctuating blood oxygen levels. Do you require assistance?"

"No, VELMA," I said. "What do I do?"

If I was discovered by more of those beasts, I would become a very tasty toothpick. And while the, um, hunter, had taken down two with what looked like minimal effort, I seriously doubted his ability to take on an entire pack.

I watched on pins and needles as the two beings worked methodically to dismember the parts and contain them in a metallic-looking tarp. Did they know what was coming? Should I warn them? Where were they taking the meat? Maybe the hunter had a home here.

I debated. Alert the hunter to my presence? Or stay hidden?

"It is advised you remain calm. The camouflage effect on the pod will maintain moderate safety."

Moderate safety. As opposed to my moderately safe Earth life? The old panic started to work its way up my throat, but I shut it down. That was light-years away.

I felt the tremors shudder through my small craft. I looked out the window at the two beings. The one covered in black blood stood at full height and looked in my direction. Could it see me? My heart spiked.

"Please remain calm or I will initiate cryo-sleep once more."

"I'm trying," I said through gritted teeth. "You can feel that, right? It feels like a freaking zoo is stampeding toward us."

I watched the armored figure gesture to the ambulatory droid and then draw its weapon. The big weapon. The one that dispatched the huge beast's head so easily.

"Oh my freaking geology," I said. "He's going to face the pack." Maybe it was stupid, but I wanted that guy to know he wasn't alone. "Disable the camouflage." I hoped I didn't regret this.

My heart stuttered at the sight of the lone figure, his knees slightly bent, his hands gripping menacing weapons, his entire posture evoking war and death. Was he even afraid? Because there was no way he was going to live through this. My throat was dry, and my eyes stung at the sight. I saw him raise his weapon high, and once again I heard his primal howl; it sent reverb across the meadow and amped up my adrenaline. I panted.

"Remain calm," VELMA intoned.

I swallowed and watched, the rumbling growing more powerful in conjunction with the feeling returning to my lower extremities.

"How strong is this pod?"

"The Emergency Egress Pod was designed to withstand temperatures exceeding six thousand degrees Kelvin upon reentry into a planet's atmosphere. Its internal structure was designed to contain zero to one atmospheric pressure, to prevent you from being crushed in space. You may have complete confidence in the EEP's safety."

Before I could debate the relevance of atmospheric pressure versus *prehistoric* pressure, the stampeding became deafening, and I was hermetically sealed inside something called an EEP for short. The view from my porthole became obscured by thundering feet and churned up greenery and soil. My last sighting of the tall being with bloody armor was of it facing the pack in a stance of complete aggression, sword high and an apparent field of electricity shimmering across its armor. What was that thing?

Then I felt the pod teeter—totter—and tip.

I couldn't help the scream, slightly louder than an *eep!* My head jostled against my helmet, and I blacked out.

4

NARAXTHEL

I sent the Tech-Slave to my ship with the racing speeder and watched as the pack of rokhura descended upon me. How odd they would migrate together this far from the rainy season. I opened my wrist panel and activated the lightning barrier and increased my armor's tensile strength. Combat shields at full—I let the sight-capture record the moment I became the most powerful Iktheka Raxthe of the Theraxl race.

With a mighty howl, I raised my *shegoshe raxtheza*, and prepared for my final battle.

Ferocity flamed through my veins as I tore through the pack with my sun-blade. When they attacked in a fury, they were less crafty. I crippled four by removing their front legs, and then climbed the back of a maimed one in order to reach higher on the scaly bodies of the advancing predators. Slicing through their vocal sacs, I determined to make my people proud.

I lost count of the number that attacked me, and soon I was over-whelmed. Roaring my displeasure, I wielded my raxtheza like one possessed by an evil spirit.

I would die without offspring, no thanks to the suspicious Lottery, but my name would live on as an eternal legend. Naraxthel Roika, the Iktheka Raxthe, Death Bringer to the Gigantic Predator.

5

I awoke to VELMA's voice. "Error. Error. Error."

Silence for a few minutes, and then it would repeat.

I cursed under my breath. At last I could feel my feet inside my sturdy space footwear. I could also feel the restraints holding my legs and waist in place.

I blinked away the final webs of confusion and peered out the window. A green field split vertically down my window on the left, and an orange swath on the right. My pod was sideways.

I had no idea if VELMA was functioning or if she could right the EEP by herself, but it seemed like maybe not.

"VELMA, what is the status of the EEP?"

"Error. Error. Error."

Oh schist. Now what?

I closed my eyes and tried to remember my emergency training protocols.

"Computer restart. Code one, white, red, green, yellow, five, three, sixteen."

Silence.

Then a beep. "Rebooting. Please wait."

I sagged against my restraints and let out a shaky laugh.

"VELMA, undo the restraints."

"Please standby. Reboot in progress."

I grumbled.

They released with a zipping noise into the walls of the pod. I held my hands out to catch myself against the wall-cum-floor. The inside of the pod was spacious considering it was designed for one person. I had room to maneuver even though it was tipped over. I was reluctant to open the hatch, preferring to wait for the computer's update. I lay down and looked out the window, finding my bearings.

In the distance, I could see a heap of scale-covered bodies. Two dinosaur-like monsters tore at the flesh, one with entrails dangling from its jaws. My stomach lurched. I remembered the armored hunter and felt tears prick behind my eyes. Whatever it was, man or beast, some alien race the humans hadn't catalogued yet, it must have died with glory. There was no way it could have survived that many monsters. I would never forget the fearless stance, the determination in the set of its shoulders and legs. It was magnificent to behold.

Until those beasts were gone, there was no way I was exiting. I took the time to inventory my rations and explore all the cubbies and panels. A beep sounded.

"Greetings, Esra Weaver. Congratulations on your safe landing. This planet is uncategorized in the Interplanetary Unification of Races, however, based on my readings, the atmosphere, gravity and bioavailable nutrients are compatible with human life."

"So, your poop-scanner still works, huh?"

"The study of excrement reveals—"

"*Reveals many things about living organisms*, yeah thanks."

I couldn't help but smile. Apparently, VELMA's short-term memory had a little hiccup. Or it had no imagination.

"VELMA, can you right the pod? It was tipped over by a pack of rampaging dinosaurs." I called them dinosaurs for lack of a better word. With their scaled skin and sharp teeth and claws, it was the best I could do. However, they were unlike any renderings of dinosaurs I'd seen on Earth. With their flat-top heads and bulging throat pouches, they were alien.

"Due to the specific nature of the EEP, I do not have the capability of righting a fallen pod. However, the exterior was designed to be manipulated by a single human. Your vital signs are cleared for safe egress. However, it is inadvisable you leave the safety of the pod until hostiles have left the area. When you exit the craft, I suggest wearing your communication helmet as you make repairs to the EEP. Receiving instructions will be more efficacious."

I looked out at the predators. They were slowing down, and their bellies were distended from gorging on all the meat. Maybe they would wander off. If they decided to stay and nap, then I was going to go bonkers cooped up in this pod for another twelve hours, or however long they slept.

Immediately, instructions for righting the pod scrolled down the inside of my clear visor.

I watched the instructional video a couple times. It looked like even an exo-geologist could do it.

"VELMA, can you communicate with any of the other pods and their occupants?"

"Negative, Esra Weaver. Running diagnostic scans. That information is unavailable."

I smacked a matte-gray wall with my gloved hand. "We traveled light-years through space without a hitch and this thing gets knocked over once, and now we can't talk to anybody?"

"My beacon activated upon entering this planet's atmosphere, and I will notify you of any pings. It is possible that other pods landed on this planet, however, I have not received any pings. Storms, geological formations or large bodies of water may make communication difficult," VELMA explained. "It is advisable when you egress to find high ground and place the auxiliary beacon. This planet's mass is less than that of your home world. You will find it much easier to navigate."

I paced the five steps inside the pod and back again. My mind raced, and my fists clenched.

"Sending instructions to your helmet visor for possible EEP repairs."

I fumed. I should have tried talking to somebody when I first came to. I was trying to find my bearings and was distracted by all the sharp teeth. I closed my eyes and took a deep breath.

As long as I stayed near the EEP, I would be safe until my rescue. Because I *would* be rescued. The *Lucidity's* damage beacon would have been activated as soon as the pods were jettisoned. Someone in the Unification of Interplanetary Races would receive my signal and send help. They would.

The toothy beasts ambled away, half-heartedly chasing off some lesser animals that resembled Earth's jackals. Other than the deep-purple fur and wide leathery tails. Okay, they had humped backs like jackals, but that was it.

I sipped water from the flexible straw inside my helmet. My suit had a small amount of stored water. After checking with VELMA it was safe, I disengaged the catheter with the press of a button on the side of my suit's leg. Then I disconnected the opaque bag and placed it in the designated cubby. The EEP recycled everything. Fresh pee-water!

Assured nothing bigger than a squirrel was in the perimeter, I entered the exit sequence on one of the doors. The EEP was equipped with more than one way to egress. Smart rocket scientists.

I needed to reorient the EEP, and apparently, I needed to go climb a mountain to place a beacon as well.

With the instructions playing on repeat in my visor, I found the exterior handles and rotational grips. A series of robotic arms and levers maneuvered until the pod stood upright on four stabilizer legs.

I stood back and admired my new home. With the push of a couple buttons, two panels expanded. I would have enough room inside to stretch out and sleep at night. It was like a two-man tent with some badass technology.

I climbed back in and found the locker with the auxiliary beacon. "So, where do I stick this thing?"

"I sent a map to your IntraVisor. The easiest route has been marked. Instructions will display when it is time to place and activate the beacon."

"Okay, thanks."

I took a deep breath and stepped out of the main hatch. The door sealed shut behind me. I didn't want any surprise guests when I came back.

The first thing I noticed was the torn-up ground surrounding the pile of dead reptile bodies. It looked like a war zone. Huge gashes in the meadow revealed the red dirt. Trees near the area had been uprooted. All the violence had transpired while I was unconscious. I paused, roving my gaze over the mass of bloodied carcasses. Was the armored being in there somewhere? If I dared to go closer, would I find it dismembered? My stomach roiled. Did I owe the creature anything?

I sucked my lips between my teeth. What about a decent burial? I took a step toward the fallen beasts. I looked out over the meadow. Dark birds descended upon the glistening bones to the east, but nothing else roamed. My charted hike approached a berm that fronted the vast meadow on the north. Dark-orange talus littered the bottom of the rise from a long-ago rock-fall, but now green and yellow grasses tufted up between the jumbled rocks. Rising up behind the defile of boulders was a hill topped with leafed-out trees. To the east, where the remains of the reptile battle lay, a hazy shimmer rose above the golden meadow grasses. There must be a body of water over that rise. The south to my right boasted an impenetrable forest of huge trees. It was that wood the land-crosser had disappeared into before the pack attacked. I should check it out later. I turned to inspect my EEP and the landscape behind it, the west. The meadow blanketed three hundred feet or so, and then low brush and bracken tangled the way until the swath of forest curved around to encircle the meadow. An outcropping of dark-orange boulders with black striations interrupted the smooth surface of the ground. The place appeared desolate.

I rubbed my hands up and down my arms, though they were covered fingertip to shoulder in my flight suit. Psychosomatic chills pimpled my arms.

I took another step toward the pile of corpses. I would just check. The dark birds circled above, maybe twenty-five feet in the air. The suns glared behind them when I looked up, so their silhouettes were all I could distinguish. Walking faster, I swallowed a lump. I tried to see past the carnage, into the future a million years when the pile of bones would be fossilized. It helped stave off the nausea. I stole another glance upward, at the dark birds coming to scavenge. I couldn't hear anything; it gave me chills up my spine. I reached the nearest carcass.

Its flank came up to my shoulder. I marveled at its size but shook myself from the reverie. I just wanted to see if the creature in its red armor was still ... alive. A shadow passed overhead. One of the scavenging birds drew closer, unafraid. I swallowed again and felt my face tighten and pale. The dripping slime from the dead reptiles slicked over the bones. Slender bones snapped under my boots as I climbed up the tumble. I cringed when the nano-sensors in my gloved fingertips allowed me to "touch" the mucous-membranes and severed sinews just waiting to be picked apart by the feathered friends congregating above me. I looked up again to see them hover, unsure now that they were close enough to see my eyes.

They resembled larger versions of the turkey buzzards back home, though their rust-colored wattles hung low and heavy from their necks.

Wary but determined, I peered through broken bones and torn scaled flesh, trying to detect the distinctive red armor. There, lodged between two huge but very dead reptiles, I spied a red-armored leg. Praying it wasn't *just* a leg, I straddled a limb and reached down between the heavy bodies and touched the ankle. No response.

I frowned. The being had been so *confident*. Another shadow passed over, and I looked up just in time to see the brisk brush of wings. I yelped and waved my arm at the black bird. Still no noises from them. I scrambled further across the mound and pulled at anything I could lift out of the way. If I could at least see the helmet and decide for myself if it was dead, then I could move on. I didn't think I would have the strength to move every dead beast off of him and bury him, but if there was the slightest chance ...

I maneuvered a bony limb out of the way and reached down into the sticky morass. A giant foreleg trapped the upper body of the being. Grunting, I yanked and pulled until a swath of skin peeled off and went flying over me. I watched with disgust as a bird swooped down and caught it between its purple beaks and flew off, two more chasing it for the treasure. I shuddered. At least I knew how to distract the vultures if they became a nuisance.

I reached down again and managed to scoot the leg off the helmet. The dull armor bore signs of abuse from the battle. Scrapes, stains and scratches told a story of a battle well fought. Even if I laid across the bloody remains where I crouched, I couldn't stretch my arm far enough down the well to pull the warrior from the pile. I turned on my helmet light for a better view and saw its helmet had what looked like dark solar panels similar to mine.

I toggled my mic.

"Hey," I said. "Are you alive?"

Nothing. It was a shame. I scrambled back down the mound and flung bits of gore off my gloves and sleeves, swiping at the smears as best I could. I blinked back a tear, not for the death of the armored person, but for myself. I was alone.

I followed the suggested route that lay in a digital readout across the view of the actual terrain. The exo-geologist in me wanted to stop and examine every pebble under boot, or every sharp rock jutting out from beneath the meadow grasses, but the sooner I installed the beacon, the sooner I would be found. Soon being the operative word. I frowned and stepped through the tall grasses, wary.

I let my gloved hands float above the tall weeds, their thistles and feathery spikes reminding me of foxtail barley back home. My suit was crafted from polymers and circuitry, stainless metals and carbon fibers, as well as concentrated pockets of nano-sensors. I was protected from poisonous stinging nettles or any other dangers this planet might have lurking in wait. The nano-sensors allowed me to feel the textures of every leaf or stem I touched while my skin remained unmarred.

My "picnic meadow" was idyllic until that giant wasp returned and started flying around my head. I tapped at my audio controls, because I still heard nothing other than the beat of its big, transparent wings. I tried not to panic. Back home, I wasn't afraid of bees or wasps. It was spiders that had me tied up in knots. But this wasp was as big as a crow. I ducked but tried not to make overt aggressive gestures. If it was protecting a nest, I would be in trouble until I left its territory. It continued to fly around me. My heart rate spiked. Okay, this was scarier than the half-inch hornets by my woodshed growing up. I cowered, making my way through the tall grass. In an act of desperation, the wasp curved in on itself when it attacked me, and I knew what came next. It was activating some nasty barbed stinger and coming in for the kill.

"Gah!" I shouted. It felt like a punch in the neck. I gasped inside my suit, thanking God, scientists, and carbon-infused polymers. At least there was no penetration and no venom infiltrating my suit. I dropped to the ground and covered my helmet, curling into a ball. The wasp stung my body repeatedly until it exhausted its supply of blue venom and fell to the ground. I was no entomologist, but I wondered if its venom and blood were somehow interconnected, that it would die like that.

I felt like I had been in a car wreck, but all sensors indicated I was injury free. I rose on shaky legs and looked down at the dead thing. It had a black carapace, transparent wings laced with orange veins, and four segments. Its head had mandibles and multiple eyes on either side. It had a bizarre orange sac thing under its head. Its stinger branched out from its butt like a grasping claw. I shivered. This planet was not a nice place. I considered stomping on it but decided against it. Anything could trigger death. Bent over with hands on my knees, I took a minute to recover.

The path I took wandered between gentle hills. The insects I'd seen before were flies, bright-red and obsidian black. They had long proboscises. I quivered at the thought of them sinking those things into my arm like huge mosquitos, but they used them to siphon nectar out of the spiny featherettes at the end of the grasses.

I trudged on, noting a gradual rise of the ground, and a thickening of the brush around me. I was headed toward a tall canopy of trees above the rocky talus, though possibly their height was the ground swelling beneath them. I had a hard time believing a beacon would be able to penetrate the thick foliage ahead of me, but I was a miner, not a SIG-INT officer. Maybe there was a break in the trees and a "small-ish" mountain behind. VELMA was right, though; it was much easier to move around here.

I accessed the calculator and discovered my weight was fifty pounds less on this green world. I huffed a short laugh.

Well, hell. I was here to stay.

6

NARAXTHEL

Shadows surrounded me. Was I in the afterworld then? *Maikthevelt*, the land of the last true embrace of the Goddesses, death.

If so, the fireside songs were true. The stench of this place was that of planet *Ikthe* multiplied by every stinking dead fish coupled with the contents of the bowel. The smell crawled into my nose like worms.

Worms.

Yes, I could feel the worms attempting to penetrate my dead flesh. My spirit was unable to leave the armored body, and I was forever trapped within it to suffer the pains of death.

My helmet stuttered flashing green lights.

My life signs appeared in a series of bars. My sight-capture was no longer relaying to the Royal Court. I was not dead. I was alive. I laughed. I was not sensing worms, but rather the tendrils of my armor re-accessing my veins throughout my body. Once again, my armor and I were one.

I realized I was buried beneath the rotting bodies of the rokhura. Their cannibalism knew no bounds, and once the latecomers arrived to attack me, their sensitive noses detected the rot of dead meat. They pounced on each other, and I fought my way to the center of the fumbling pack.

I couldn't move my limbs, but I used my eyelids to blink commands to my helmet-tech. The sight-capture must have stopped sending once a large rokhura fell atop my helmet. I was disappointed. The Royal Court would have seen my fierce battle, but they would then assume my death upon the ending of my feed. No matter. I would recover my ship and my trophies, and return to *Ikshe*, my paradisiacal home planet. I would feed the females of the Royal Court, and I would await the abysmal luck of the Lottery to bow in my favor. Though the last fifteen cycles no such luck had shone upon me.

But first, to extricate myself from the pit. The blackness was the overlapping hides of the carcasses. The weight was the enormous bones. My armor's defenses were depleted from the lack of light. The suns of *Ikthe* and *Ikshe* were powerful. Their radiation activated the cells on my armor and those of my ship. Much of my technology was powered by the life-givers, the hallowed Shegoshel.

But beneath the rokhura corpses, my sun cells were useless. The narrowest shaft of light penetrated a gap in the pile mounded atop me, almost as if the Goddesses themselves had poked a hole through the jumble. From that, my cells had livened enough to enervate my armor's tendrils. A rapid series of eye movements and blinks had my secondary power turning on. Soon, I would be able to push my way out from under the powerful bones of the great predators. Then to my ship, *Ikshe*, and the Royal Courts.

I heard the screeches of the filthy birds that feasted upon the stringy membranes adhering to the bones. They feinted toward me, but veered away, concerned with the meaty bones, and not my foul, dripping armor. I clambered out from the massive pile, and scanned the meadow noting prey signs. The living rokhura had feasted, mated, and left the torn-up ground to build their nests elsewhere. No other beasts approached the carnage. Once the suns set, they would arrive in droves to lick the bones clean.

I pulled an aching leg out of the hole I had created for my exit and stood at my full height, king of a hill of bones, and surveyed the damage. I had to dig through *kathe* to find one of my weapons. My satisfied smile told the tale of my victory. A glint off of metal caught my eye.

I leaped off the pile of bones and tough hides and loped a veltik before I could see the source of the glint: a vehicle. I approached it with my raxtheza raised. My scanners activated and attempted to identify the ship. It was small. A single *Theraxl* would fit inside such a vessel. It must have been designed to travel without passengers. I thought of the enemies of the *Theraxl* race. Would they have created such a machine to spy on the hunts of *Ikthe*? Burning flamed in my bowels and blood rushed through my veins. I would send a sight-capture of this vessel and send it to the Royal Court. Before I could press the comm, I spied the curve of a print in the ground.

I knelt and touched the imprint with my gloved finger.

It was the track of a boot.

A child!

What monster would send a defenseless child to *Ikthe*? Its very name denoted Certain Death.

My nostrils flared, and my lungs expanded. Whoever had done such a thing would pay with their entrails wrapped around their necks. But first, to find the vulnerable child before one of the hundreds of predators that lived on this planet found her.

The boot print was absent of smell. Very strange. I would have to rely upon my tracking skills alone, as well as the knowledge of Ikthe to find the child. The Royal Court would soon curse the damned bad luck of the Lottery. What female could deny herself the desire for *Iktheka Raxthel*? Bringer of death, slayer of predators and rescuer of a defenseless child? My incisors clipped my lip when my smile grew broader. The Goddesses would smile upon this Lottery. I would bring honor to my family name, and many offspring. I followed the tracks that led into the *ikfal*. If I felt uneasy, it was because I smelled like the limb-pit of a rokhura. I was sure to attract unwanted attention. The child couldn't last a tik in these woods. I should move faster.

7

"VELMA, how much farther to the drop-off point?"

"You are less than halfway to the drop-off point."

I chuckled. "Are we there ye—ah!"

I screamed all the way down the mudslide, but my screams echoed in my own ears. I had turned off my mic when I left the dead reptiles. My suit was designed for stealth on new planets.

As huge green leaves whipped past my vision, I noticed my super nano-infused carbon-polymer suit was now camouflaged by mud. Plant tentacles reached out to stop my slide, but they were ineffective against my top speed.

Indicators in my visor showed an increasing heart rate and blood pressure. I ignored the flashing symbols in favor of trying to steer my feet to avoid jutting tree roots.

The digital overlay was making me sick as the terrain flew by, so I disabled it with a voice command while simultaneously flailing for branches or roots to grasp. My gloves slipped with the viscous mud. I flew faster and faster, and I wished my suit had air brakes or a jet pack or something. The slide below me disappeared into lush green foliage. Was there a water fall at the end? Was I plummeting to my death?

With my heart in my throat, I resigned myself to almost certain death. What a crappy planet.

The greenery broke, and the slide disappeared from under my butt. I fell about five feet and plopped into a pool of bubbling mud with a loud slap. The impact took my breath away. I started to panic when I sank. I struggled against its pull, forgetting the first rule of quicksand: don't move. When my boots touched bottom, the mud was up to my chest.

Heart racing, I took as many deep and calming breaths as I could. It wasn't easy. I was terrified I might meet with some kind of prehistoric crocodile in the mud, but if I panicked, I'd get sucked down farther. The edge wasn't far, so I leaned back to distribute my weight over the surface into a floating position, grateful I weighed fifty pounds less in this place. Then, bit by bit, I tried to raise each of my legs. When I managed to pull them free, I kept them as flat as possible while I wriggled my torso and, inch by inch, snaked my way to shore and rolled onto dry land. I crawled as far away from the mud pit as I could, frequently looking back. No snapping teeth yet, but that meant nothing.

I looked around me at the thick shrubbery, tangled smooth roots and wide-fronded leaves. I was counting on VELMA to alert me to danger, but that didn't mean I wasn't going to try and see possible threats myself. A flat dark boulder with lighter stripes in it, gabbro with feldspar, was a good place to take a breather. I climbed up and tried scraping the thicker mud off my pants and sleeves. Once it dried, it would be harder to move around. Most fluids shed easily from my suit fabric.

Mid-swipe I realized I had dropped the beacon somewhere on my merciless slide down.

"Double dammit!"

I slumped on the rock and stared at the mud pit. The bubbles grew and popped. My suit was rated to 500° F, so even if the pit was 160°, I was fine. But when a lumpy head started to rise out of the mud, I realized just how precarious my life was on this god-forsaken planet.

It was tempting to release my helmet so I could experience the life on this world with all my senses, but odds were good I was missing the aroma of sulfur or other similar smells released from the fumarole. The set of four eyes blinked sequentially as it stared at me and continued to rise out of the mud. It was time for me to leave.

Without looking away, I backed off the rock and crept backward into the brush. When I felt obscured by leaves, I stopped moving. Maybe motion would set it off. Maybe it could run as fast as a cheetah and I was playing a dangerous game. I was hoping this planet's life was similar to the animal life back home. Anything that liked to hang out in a hot mud bath shouldn't be too quick on its feet, but this was Predator Planet. I didn't have much hope at this point.

The thing stopped rising, and looked as large as a hippopotamus, but its scaly skin was more like a crocodile's in its texture. It had a wide flat snout with four nostrils, all positioned at the top of its nose. It blew out a spray of dark-brown mud. It had a broad back and no tail. It looked to have four legs, but they were submerged in the pit.

Thank goodness I had landed in the shallow end, and not on this thing's back.

Before I could process this new species, a second one rose out of the mud. It was smaller than the first, but shared identical features.

While still staring at me, the biggest one took a lumbering step toward the opposite shore and yanked at some thick leaves growing at the edge. Its powerful jaws uprooted the entire bush, and it devoured it like the slowest woodchipper of all time. I watched in amazement as the leaves, twigs, trunk and roots, were consumed. It took a long time, and I had to shake myself out of the hypnosis. I was the first human to ever observe these creatures in their natural habitat, eating small trees like it was nothing.

Frustration at losing the beacon aside, I experienced a momentary thrill. I was exploring an alien planet! Everything I did here would be the first for humankind. Everything I saw or touched would be the first.

The huge mud cows chewed from side to side and slunk back into the mud. Bubbles rose from their behinds, and I had to wonder, was there an actual fumarole under there or was it just the mud cows' gas?

Relieved I wasn't going to be its next meal, I turned and looked up the steep tree-covered hillside. Somewhere in this mess was my beacon.

I hoped it had a signal of its own … a beacon for the beacon. Because as amazing as this all could be, I was still stranded with no feasible rescue in sight unless I planted and installed that thing.

"VELMA, can you ping the beacon? I dropped it down a hill."

"Locating auxiliary beacon. Beacon not found."

Dammit.

8

NARAXTHEL

The absence of the child's scent had me on edge. I knew every predator on *Ikthe*. With my shining blade tested, I had already killed a *scabika* and the venom-bearing snake we called *talathel*, "tasting many deaths." Its venom caused the victim to writhe in pain for weeks suffering wicked dreams. Sometimes the victim lived, but they were never the same.

With no scent to track, I couldn't be sure where the child headed if I lost trail sign.

I came upon a clearing in the meadow. Trampled down grass and a dead firefly. I gave a gruff laugh. How had a mere child killed the firefly? I examined its body. It had emptied its poison sacs. My head shot up. I scanned the vicinity, certain I would find the collapsed body of a dead child. Instead, I saw the grasses parted into a small footpath. What sorcery was this? I followed.

The tall grasses made way to the edge of the ikfal, and I crouched to enter the game trail. The crescent of a heel made in red mud was but one clue. Within the brush, broken branches and crushed leaves revealed the path of my prize. A wry smile crossed my features. The mighty hunter was hunting a child.

Making my way through thick foliage, I flattened one of the giant stinging insects against a tree trunk. They were a nuisance to my kind, but fatal to smaller creatures. My anxiety for the child increased with each step, just as the soil changed color the farther up the hill I went.

After many veltiks, I realized I had lost sign. No more broken twigs, no prints in the stinking black detritus underfoot. Still my sense of smell failed me. The child had no odor.

Another talathel slithered down from one of the great white-trunked trees, its shining green scales advertising both beauty and a spiraling horrific death. I grasped it by its neck as thick as my wrist and yanked it out of the tree. Its entire length fell from the canopy, and its coiled muscles wrapped around one of my legs. This was stronger than the last one; I needed both hands to wrench its jaws apart until it snapped. Lax in death, it fell to the ground with a thud. The scrabbling *jokapazathel* ran out from under the brush to scavenge it with their sharp teeth and claws. They were furious tiny scavengers, often not waiting for a creature to die before picking its flesh from its bones. They had dark-brown fur with yellow dappled spots, well-suited to life on the ikfal floor.

I had lost the child's trail. Backtracking, I found the last sign. It was a full boot print, perfectly pressed into the brown mud of the upper ground. Frequent rains on Ikthe washed the lighter red-orange dirt from the tops of the hills down to the valleys. Black and brown mud shown through the brush the higher up one traveled. There sat the print, outlined in fine detail. There were odd geometric shapes pressed into the mud, like a language. Who would inscribe a language onto the bottom of one's boot? What did the shapes mean? Perhaps this was not a Theraxl child. But a child from where? Only our enemies, the Makathel race, knew of our sister planets. They attacked Ikshe once a century, but never touched Ikthe. Who would do so? And even our mortal enemies loved and cherished their children.

The longer I thought on it, the more troubled I became.

Was this a child, or a spirit from the afterlife? Tales of spirits tormenting the hunters of Ikthe were often told on the space stations orbiting Ikshe. I dismissed them as the stories of the bored and lazy. But I must wonder now. Had I been following the trail of a lost spirit?

I circled the last track, careful not to mar its shape. I puzzled over it when a glance to my right revealed a gash carved into an ikfa trunk. Inspecting more closely, I almost stepped off the invisible ridge. A mudslide.

Ah. I remembered this slide now, having fallen down it many hunts ago myself, as I frequently haunted new game trails; a hunter never overhunted a prime area. The pit at the bottom hosted elder sister and younger sister mud-beasts that smelled of scabika dung. They ate plants. Unless one was unfortunate enough to stumble across their brood of younglings. Then they would grind one's bones to dust with their teeth.

This was not the brooding season, so the child would be unmolested. But had she survived the fall?

Some of the trees of this planet were carnivorous. The long tendrils of the forest-teeth tree would grasp an unsuspecting creature and curve it into itself. The bole of the trunk would split to accommodate its prey, and then close inch by inch as its juices digested the animal while it yet lived.

I decided to take the slower descent down the hill. The child had the luck of the Holy Shegoshel to find this mudslide. With no scent to lure predators, and now to be covered in a layer of mud-beast slime, she would be invisible to at least half the animals of the planet.

Perhaps she was an emissary sent from the Holy Sisters of Shegoshel. Perhaps my long delay in winning the Lottery was being investigated by our deities, and my chance to create offspring for the Mighty Hunter line was at last due.

I stepped gingerly down the hill, letting the claws of my gloves gouge trunks to steady myself, and letting the weight of my heavy boots crush the seeking tendrils of the forest-teeth tree. My boot knocked against metal. I stooped to pick up the object. Turning it over in my hands, I studied the metal cylinder.

Its design was sleek and clean. Its heft spoke of several internal components. I ran my scanner across it, and a message appeared in my visor.

"UNABLE TO IDENTIFY."

I looked for seams and found a thin line dividing the cylinder in half. Using my claws, I pried it apart. Wires and green chips with silver lines inscribed in strange shapes filled the cylinder. A glowing red light shone from one end. I fiddled with a gray button on the top, and the light switched to green. It brought to mind the communication devices I had on my ship. They blinked to show when they were working properly. This was a beacon!

Anger erupted from my heart-home. It was a spy! Some enemy of small stature would send a beacon and alert others to the location of my hunting planet? *Raxfathe* to the enemy, after we battled together.

I took a random handful of wires and ripped. The green light died. As would the spy who dared to reveal the sister planets to the universe.

9

As expected, some of the mud dried on my suit, making it harder and harder to move. I ached to remove the foul thing, but something told me my polymer suit was probably the only thin layer standing between me and death. A number of menacing plants and insects with about six too-many legs snatched at me.

The flora on this planet was breathtaking in its beauty. Huge fronds, so green they were almost black, offered cool shade. Yet glowing red orbs peeked out from the shadows—eyes unblinking and ominous. I was afraid to inspect them closer, but they didn't appear to be animal eyes. No, the plants had eyes here. I shuddered, shaking off the memory of Chris staring at me over an open bottle of liquor.

The bluff grew steeper and I panted as I struggled to find purchase among the bracken. I grabbed tree roots and the thick stems of bushes to pull myself up. Even missing fifty pounds, it was becoming more and more difficult. I grabbed onto a beautiful green root but noticed my error too late.

That was no root.

My suit stifled the scream that would have echoed throughout the forest when the snake's huge head circled around and faced me. I let go of the snake only to flail for something else to grip, but my hand found crumbling rust-colored dirt and rotting plant life. With my right arm socket burning, I held on to the other tree root with all my might.

The snake's eyes were jeweled with red and gold striations, and it wove a slow dance before me. I shook myself from the hypnotic movement and fixed my bearings. I looked down to see the tail of the snake wrapping around my ankle and working its way up my leg. Even through the suit I could feel the long muscles beneath the scaly skin as they squeezed tighter and tighter.

Oh no. I was not being crushed by some overgrown garter snake. Not on an alien planet no human had ever seen. If I was going out, I was going out big. Like by one of those big-ass dinosaurs I'd seen overtake the armored figure. With my right shoulder aching, I used my free left hand to access the tool belt around my thigh. I had a multitool in my grasp. A good thing, because the ambitious snake's body was now wrapped around my upper thigh. It was putting pressure on my femoral artery.

I lifted my head to meet the gaze of the dancing snake. Its head was as big as my helmet.

"VELMA, what is the threat assessment of the reptile?"

"I do not sense the presence of a reptile."

Oh schist.

"VELMA, use your scanner thing. I'm staring at a freaking snake, here."

"The lifeform has a minimal heat signature and should pose no threat."

"What the...?"

I was on my own.

With a frantic jab, I sunk my tool into the snake's thick body now coiled around my waist. I stabbed it again and again, and it grew tighter and tighter. How was that possible? The reptile's bright-red blood made the scales slippery. What if I could dislodge it? But I couldn't let go of my tool, and I couldn't let go of the tree root.

Then an idea came to mind.

I was on a steep bluff. If I let go, the snake would have to readjust its leverage to prevent my dead weight from pulling it down with me. I took a deep breath and quit fighting to hold the branch. I released my grip and let gravity take over.

The snake uncoiled its wounded belly to grasp around other stationary objects, and its tight hold of me relaxed. I exhaled to make myself smaller by a degree or two, and let myself slip through and tumble down the bluff. I already knew what was at the bottom, and I preferred to take my chances with the ugly hippos.

The snake coiled and uncoiled, trying to regain its, uh, footing, but the wounds I inflicted must have been bothering it more than I realized. It slithered off into the dark foliage, leaving a trail of blood in its wake. I had fallen a few feet, and I was now cradled in a large bush. That one didn't have eyes, thank goodness.

My heart rate returned to normal.

"VELMA, did you not notice I was fighting for my life here?"

"Your escalated pulse and O2 levels indicated a state of beneficial exercise."

I opened my mouth to argue, then shook my head. She needed to be recalibrated or something.

I resumed my climb, more careful than ever of which branch I grabbed hold of. Some of the roots resembled the twining smooth limbs of mangrove trees back home. But they were larger. With plenty of hand and footholds, I made progress, though I was wary of the dark tunnels, one of which the snake had disappeared in to lick its wounds.

Hand over hand, I climbed back up, keeping an eye out for the beacon. It had to be around here somewhere.

"VELMA, any sign of the beacon?"

"My scanners are picking up low levels of both solar and electric power nearby."

"Excellent!" I climbed. "Give me the location of the beacon."

A red light glowed on a superimposed grid.

"Okay," I said, wheezing. "Almost there."

Left hand, up. Right hand, up. Left hand, up. Then something grabbed my calf.

"What?" I looked down. A thick vine was tangled around my lower leg. "Oh, it's just a plant."

VELMA was silent. I looked back down and tried to kick my way out of the tangle. It grew tighter. It wasn't the snake, was it? My helmet bumped the bank as I tried to peer down at the tendril knotted around my calf. It yanked again.

Okay, that was not normal.

I pulled up with all my might, trying to dislodge the vine. It pulled back.

Oh, hell no.

I wrapped my left arm around a jutting root and reached down with my right hand to yank at this octopus plant. Every tendril I ripped away was replaced by two. Soon, it looked like my leg was sprouting its own greenery.

I grabbed my multi-tool again—the pliers this time. I snapped the vines in two and worked my boot through the tangle as fast as I could. Once I was off this horrible hill, I was running back to my EEP and locking myself in permanently. This was ridiculous.

I kicked and fought, snapping off thin ropes and trying to break free. It gave up after several minutes, and I reached out to grab another handhold. I pulled with all my might, panting with the effort and wanting to maneuver my feet as far away from that vine as possible. My head came up past more shrubbery, and then my eyes fell upon a pair of huge armored boots. I froze.

Oh. Wow.

10

NARAXTHEL

My ears picked up the sounds of snapping branches long before I saw the enemy. Still no scent came to my nose, but no matter. Nothing on Ikthe was as loud as this intruder.

I followed the sound; it arose from the side of the hill. My enemy was climbing back up. I drew my weapon, the raxtheza, and readied to grant this spy its due battle before receiving *raxfathe*. It would be a mercy on such a planet as Ikthe.

While I heard the snap and strain of branches and leaves and scuffling boots, I could not hear the pants of breath or gasps of effort. What a strange enemy the Goddesses of the Shegoshel had brought to me.

There. The leaves trembled. And parted. I saw a muddy gloved hand grasp onto a root. The other came up. A helmet joined them. It rose, and within the clear helmet I saw the delicate features of—a female. Her eyes were the color of the great Waters of Ikthe, many veltiks away from here. Green and blue, shifting with the waves. The moment the female's wide eyes met mine, her face contorted into a scream, though I heard nothing. The gloved hands clawed for handholds, and all the while she stared at me through the brush.

Spy or no, I could not perform *raxfathe* on a female. But what to do?

She lost her grip and disappeared into the thick green leaves as she fell.

My lungs churned for breath and my heart-home stuttered. I felt the chill of the Great Mountain of Shegoshel, several veltiks to the north, as if I were sitting in its shadow. Shards of ice ran through my veins. A quick scan of my life signs revealed all to be normal. Why this icy cold?

The enemy spy was a female. With eyes like the oceans teeming with death-swimmers.

The Goddesses of the Shegoshel were laughing at me today.

I had no choice but to follow the enemy down. I must protect my people, my people's planets, and my people's customs. The enemy must die. But like the jeweled talathel serpent, sometimes it was a shame to eradicate a thing of beauty, though it would kill you without a thought.

I sheathed my raxtheza and jumped down the side of the bluff. The enemy's soft-armored suit might disguise its breaths and voice, but it couldn't mask the loud bumbling through the foliage.

The spy would be my newest trophy within a matter of tiks.

11

Snakes. Human-eating plants. Hippos that ate entire trees in one gulp. Reptiles so huge they might as well be dinosaurs. And I couldn't forget the mud. So much mud. The rusty goop slipped through my hands and made my gloves too slick to hold on to any of the huge leaves or bendy branches I could reach.

I yelped, trying and failing to stop my fall. It could be argued the mud was saving my life as I slipped and slid right back down the embankment. Different trail, same destination. I calculated how long my suit could provide air under the boiling mud pit. If those *things* down there left me alone, maybe I could last a while.

Well, it wasn't much of a plan, but it was the only one I had. Some of the other choices were following the bloody trail of the jade death snake or letting the aggressive octopus plant haul me to who knows where. Yeah, no. Mud pit it was.

Momentum gave me an edge, as well as the fact I was sliding out of control. That huge guy, the hunting alien who took out all those dinosaurs? He was a lot bigger standing. He could snap me in half with one hand. While I had cheered him on from safe inside my EEP, he had been far away. And when he was buried by dead dinosaurs, he hadn't seemed quite so … large.

As my gaze followed his legs up and up, his size became apparent. His armor plates surrounded powerful thighs. He had a tool belt, like me, but with unrecognizable items. Emblems on his chest plates were punctuated with black metal embedded in the red material of his armor. Broad shoulders and weapons strapped to his back revealed him to be not just a hunter, but a warrior. And when I saw the hint of glowing eyes through his black visor and massive war-like helmet, my mouth went dry and my heart punched a hole through my sternum. He was alive! But he hadn't looked happy.

For a second, my body felt weightless, then I plopped into the pit.

With a prayer I was nowhere near its ugly hosts, I sank all the way down, satisfied I would be invisible. I had plenty of oxygen in my suit. Pressure gauges, temperature controls. Heck, I could watch a movie down here.

It was nothing but blackness. I could activate the light in my helmet, but it would just show me my terrified reflection. I wasn't in peak form. Crash landings did that to a person. Oh, and also almost dying by several different creatures in one day.

Speaking of creatures, I felt something brush against my leg. I cringed and moved my leg away. Something brushed against it again. I was immersed in mud. Nothing could see me, but I could see nothing either.

It was just one of the peaceful, tree-loving beasts. That's all. I could probably reach a hand out …

The computer beeped.

"Heart rate accelerated. Are you injured?"

"No. I don't think so?"

"Please remain calm. Environment sensors activated."

"Environment sensors?" I asked VELMA. "You mean like, you could tell me if I'm in a mud pit or something?"

"High levels of bio-matter indicate the rich presence of bio-available nutrients. There is also a large amount of methane and excrement indicators."

I shuddered and grimaced. Better to be buried in a massive pit of liquid excrement than to be drawn and quartered by that hulking alien out there.

"VELMA, sleep mode."

I needed radio silence. It had some kind of electric armor. It could intercept my radio waves. I predicted it had thermal vision and night vision and so on. Honestly, I didn't know why I wasn't already discovered. Mud, maybe.

I felt another bump against my leg. Shivering, I reached toward it. My tentative gloved fingers found a large limb. The mud creature! It was in no hurry, and my touch didn't faze it at all. I moved through the mud and sidled myself so close to the hippo thing that we should write up some wedding invitations. I had a wild idea, and I prayed it would work.

I just kept petting the beast's huge belly. As long as I knew where its legs were, I couldn't be stepped on. I hoped his smaller friend stayed back, too. And if the alien did have some kind of life-form sensor, my little life-sign should be obscured by these big HipCow things.

I waited. And waited. When two hours had gone by, my oxygen sensors indicated my stores were at half capacity. I was still alive. My heart had even returned to its normal pace. And if that thing hadn't found me by now, that meant it lost my trail.

With careful movements, I made my way around the huge beast; it was even bigger than a Clydesdale. I debated going around the back or front but thinking about those huge teeth had me risking the bubble-maker in the back. Better to be farted on than chewed up. With one hand resting against the rough hide of my new best friend, I reached and stretched until I felt the shore. This was a huge risk. The armored figure could just have been having a smoke and waiting for me to come up for air. If that was the case, it would have the advantage, because I needed to wipe the mud off my visor before I could see anything.

Sidling close to the HipCow, I wiped the front of my helmet. My gloves smeared away a thick layer of goop. I looked around the entire pit, searching the shoreline for the dark-red armor of the dino-hunter. Nothing.

"VELMA, scan for life-forms or for the beacon."

"Scanning."

I recalled seeing the busted beacon in one of the armored dude's gloves. VELMA had sensed either the beacon or the dude. It should still work.

"Two amphibious creatures are within one meter. No other life-forms detected. Beacon unavailable."

I sighed. One meter, huh? My hand still rested on one of their flanks. At least the AI narrowed the distance down. It picked up the large creatures fine. Although it had given me no warning about the snake. None.

I just had to be extra cautious.

With no sign of the hunter, I crept out of the mud pit. I was now on the shore where the HipCow had eaten that small tree. I needed a game plan.

I squatted and used a hand to wipe away mud from the back of my helmet where the solar panels were embedded. I would need to discover an area with more sun. The recharging warning alerted me I had thirty minutes to charge the panels.

While climbing the hill had been difficult, it wasn't as hard as it would have been on Earth. But falling for my life and all the near-death alien animal encounters had taken their toll. I needed rest, some food, and a stiff drink. Recycled pee sounded great about now.

The problem was, I couldn't go back to the EEP.

Assuming the hunter was, in fact, the same one I had witnessed nearly die in a pack of dinosaurs, then it had to have found my vehicle. And then my tracks. It was tracking me. Hunting me. Those eyes ...

His gaze sent a shiver through me that started from the base of my spine and ended up firing from every nerve ending in my body. His helmet said, "I'm going to kill you and enjoy it." I was fine to never see those glowing red eyes again.

And his sword! It was serrated, a shiny purplish-silver color, and emblazoned with weird symbols that glowed with the light of the two suns shining on this planet. I shuddered at the mental image of him using it to disembowel me. Okay, I wasn't hungry anymore.

I sat, my haunches complaining from overuse.

If I couldn't return to the EEP, then where could I go? What could I do?

My suit protected me from poisonous barbs and was impenetrable by those wicked gigantic wasps. I hadn't noticed fangs on the snake, but that was because I'd scrambled away before it could open its mouth and show me. I didn't know if my suit would work against fangs, teeth, and claws—I was beginning to sweat under my suit. This planet might have oxygen and water and *bioavailable nutrients*, but just about every living thing on it was out to end me. I couldn't wear my suit forever. There were things that could only be managed *without* it.

I needed shelter. Water. Food. A, uh, facility. Otherwise, my suit could protect my skin and control the temperature.

And I needed to launch off this planet. The beacon would have been nice. I stared at the bumpy back of my newest friend and considered the broken beacon. Did the hunter leave it up there? Was it irreparable? Would he be waiting for me to come back for it?

I lay back on the muddy shore with a groan. I was not cut out for this. I was a freaking exo-geologist. I could tell you why the topsoil on this planet was rusty orange-red; if IGMC knew I was here, they'd have me taking samples of the iron that had to be everywhere and searching for galvanite veins. But I knew nothing about strategy or evasive maneuvers or staying alive. If it wasn't for my suit, I'd have been dead four or five times by now. I paused mid-thought. I *did* know about evasive maneuvers and staying alive. *Thanks to Chris.*

I stared up through the canopy, watching the streaming light filter through tiny cracks of green and yellow leaves. How many times had I thought it was the end? Now I was here. When I wasn't fighting off hungry predators, it was peaceful, hearing the slow munching of the HipCows. I wanted to name them. I barely passed Latin in high school, so it wouldn't be a scientific name. More like Fred and Mabel.

I watched the leaves above me tremble in the wind. Except the humidity according to VELMA was 100%. There was no wind. Schist.

It was time to stand up and face whatever death had in store for me now. I closed my eyes and took a quick breath.

I opened my eyes and saw a huge butterfly. Well, not a butterfly. It was a long insect with great wings, but they weren't in that four-lobed shape of the butterflies on Earth. There were three lobes on each side, and the edges were feathered. Shimmers of blue and green rippled across the wings. It fluttered along, descending closer to me until it landed on a huge yellow-green bush with tiny white flowers. The winged insect with eight legs, (Lovely—an arachnid butterfly. Cruel, cruel planet.) had a tiny proboscis. It fit into the white flowers and danced along the leaves of the bush. I sat up, but it paid me no mind, so intent on feeding from the blossoms. I was dying to smell this planet, but again, not brave enough to remove my helmet just yet.

I crouched and crawled a little closer. The blue-green butterfly was as big as a bicycle tire. It was so beautiful I could almost cry.

I watched it until it had exhausted the nectar of the entire bush, and then it floated away between the foliage.

My eye caught sight of an odd-colored rock, and my heart rate picked up. I bent over and retrieved it, satisfied when I hefted it in both hands. It was exactly what I thought it was. Not rock—clay. Back home I once found a huge clay deposit in the bed of a stream. I had realized with growing excitement it was everywhere and had collected tons to sculpt with. Finding this clay by the mud pit meant something specific to this exo-geologist today. Now.

A fumarole meant there was a subsoil fissure. Blue clay indicated sedimentary deformation. And where fissures and deformation met—water created vast tunnels of streams and rivers. Basically?

It meant there were caves nearby.

12

NARAXTHEL

I stared at the mud-beasts for a long time. They were not known to eat meat. But other than the flat rock where my enemy must have rested earlier, there was no sign of her. I scratched at the dried mud on the rock. It flaked easily. She would have sat here after her first fall into the pit. I could mark the path she took up the bluff. Broken branches and swaths of flattened brush where she struggled.

This spy was not equal in ability to the Theraxl.

Considering her pale skin and bright eyes, I wondered what she was. She was not of the Makathel race. We had enough trouble with them, I knew they resembled Theraxl. I had seen the flesh of her face. From her trail sign I deduced she had two arms and two legs, as did Theraxl. Yet, she was so small. How had one so defenseless come to be on this planet? Were there other races trying to find the Sister Planets? A trembling stirred in my chest.

Ikshe was too desirable. Too perfect. Other races would see it and want to make it their own.

A flash of her eyes came to mind. How they widened in terror just before she fell.

It stirred something inside me.

I felt the crease form between my brows beneath my helmet. The

Goddesses were toying with this Theraxl, so long had I been waiting for the Lottery to show me favor.

Theraxl's greatest honor was to have many offspring. It was bestowed upon those mighty hunters who'd earned the privilege of having their name put in the Lottery. Fifteen cycles I had brought generous portions of meat to the Royal Court. Fifteen cycles my name had gone into the Lottery. And fifteen cycles I had not been chosen to mate with one of the unattached females of the Royal Court.

My disappointment had hardened to resolve.

This cycle was already different in so many ways.

A large bubble popped in the pit, startling me. Shame, fleeting and sharp like a sting, brought me to attention. I had been lost in selfish thoughts. I had a spy to discover.

I traced the path of her fall thrice. I knew the spot where she would have fallen in. I stepped into the pit, but it was shallow where I stood.

She couldn't stay down in the pit. It was filled with noxious poisons. Yet I couldn't detect a spot where she had left the pit. I circled it, noting the vegetation at the shore. The only place where there was evidence of her tiny hands climbing out was the place where she had made her way back up the bluff after her first fall. She couldn't have passed me. I would have seen her.

I climbed halfway up the embankment. I paused at the blood. I had seen it before. Touching it and bringing it to my nose, I smelled the blood of the talathel. She had maimed it. The fatally wounded talathel would retreat.

It was a dark tunnel. The vegetation was thick. Its trail was fouled with bones and excrement. Could the talathel have lain in wait and snatched her from the fall?

For once, my size was a liability. I could force my way into the game trail, but a wounded talathel cornered in its lair was not something I wanted to meet.

I had a sinking feeling my enemy had met her end. Either suffocating and dying in the pit, or being mauled by the mud-beasts, or devoured by the talathel.

When I looked up at the green canopy, another possibility came to mind. One of the rodaxl could have snatched her.

I rubbed the spot above my heart-home. An unfamiliar ache pinched my soul.

Frowning, I left the mud pit and headed to my ship. I needn't have worried about an alien spy. Ikthe could take care of herself.

I would send word. The Royal Court must think me dead. How they would crow to hear of my triumphant survival!

When I broke through the ikfal, I felt the Shegoshel smiling upon me before their spheres sunk below the horizon. But I had no smile for them in return.

13

The first sun went down. According to VELMA, I had thirty minutes before the second sun went down. So far, no luck. I'd been attacked by five more of those damn black wasps the size of ravens, but I discovered they cannibalized their dead. How convenient for me. I used my multi-tool like a tiny machete, but it was worthless in that application. I had been scouring the muddy banks for hours and now the light was waning.

Considering the predators that came out during the day were ruthless, I couldn't wait to see what the night had in store.

It was a shame the beefy dinosaur killer looked like he wanted my head on his wall. It would have been nice to have an ally on this world. I wondered about his robot and if his vehicle made it to his home.

Who would choose to live on this planet?

"VELMA, are there signs of civilization on this planet?"

"The transospheric nanosatellite array shows no traces of civilization. The absence of pollutants in both the air and water, in addition to the lack of architectural features on the planet's surface indicate a Class B planet."

I remembered from my interplanetary studies that Class As were habitable planets that had not been visited by sentient life. Class Bs were habitable but uncolonized and had been visited at least once. By definition, as soon as any EEP landed on a Class A, it became a Class B. But then again, the presence of that armored hunter also classified Death Planet as a B.

My teeth worried my lip as I thwacked away at a stubborn low bush. No signs of civilization or architectural features meant the armored hunter didn't, in fact, have a house here. That meant he had a ship.

If my cave plan didn't work out, maybe I could bring a peace offering to the hunter. Of course, he was probably long gone by now. "I come in peace," wouldn't have worked anyway. He looked angry the last time I saw him. With *my* beacon.

I reached down to grab at the thick branch and twist it off, when a gust of breeze eddied out of a small dark opening. I held my breath as the dead leaves whirled around me. I longed to feel the air on my face. Entering a cave or animal den was at least as dangerous as traipsing around the lovely picnic planet, so the suit was going nowhere. I could imagine the dank smell and cool air. I loved spelunking when I was a teen.

I crouched down and activated my helmet light. Using the broken branch, I poked in front of me. I scanned the tunnel that was maybe twice as wide as I was. One of those snakes could fit inside, but it looked like an arboreal reptile. The floor of the opening was dry and littered with a lot of brittle old brush. No scat. A very good sign so far.

I continued my slow crawl and exploration. My solar panels had been charging when I was scoping the area around the pit, so I had plenty of air. VELMA's volatile emissions scanner showed breathable air outside my suit as well. I tried not to get my hopes up, but having a safe place to strip off my suit and take a seat sounded about like heaven.

I noticed a widening of the tunnel as well as a gentle decline. I could stand up here. The topography was confusing me. This low, the floor of the cave should be damp with puddles scattered about. I proceeded, lighting the walls for signs of any visitors.

Not even a handprint.

A wave of loneliness swept over me, and I had to lean against a wall for a second. I could not think about the facts right now. I needed a simple place to disrobe and rest. That was it. I was not going to dwell on the crash landing, the bazillion ways I might die here, or the fact I was completely and utterly alone. Nope. And that wasn't a tear at the corner of my eye, either.

I stood back up and walked deeper into the cave.

My visor screen lit up.

"Sensors indicate a large life-form nearby."

Oh *schist!*

Nearby for VELMA was like—

Something hit me from behind and I fell onto my knees. I rolled and brought up my multi-tool. Pliers would work in a pinch against whatever was …

I screamed.

A spider the size of the family dog waved its front two legs at me while its mouth parts opened and closed menacingly. I couldn't sniff the air, but I had perfect hearing. Its mouth clacked together in a sickening crunching noise.

I held my tool forward, mimicking the leg-waving with my two arms.

All the wasp attacks gave me about eighty percent confidence in the strength of my suit. But that didn't mean I wanted those mandibles anywhere near me.

I turned on my mic.

"It's okayyy, little spider," I said in a soft voice. "I won't hurrrt you."

That might have been a lie.

It backed away the tiniest bit.

"Um, want to hear a song?"

"Sinus tachycardia detected. BPM 120 and rising."

Not now, VELMA.

It backed away again. It was working!

My voice shook. "The itsy-bitsy spider went up the waterspout!" My tool handy, I did the motions.

"Down came the rain and washed the spider out!" The spider cocked its super ugly head and stared at me with a million eyes. Okay, spider was just the approximation for whatever this thing was. It was furry and had a lot of legs.

"Out came the sun and dried up all the rain." I hitched out with tears streaming down my face.

The spider bent its legs.

"Increased activity in your amygdala," VELMA said in my ear.

Not now, VELMA.

"So the itsy bitsy spider went up the spout aga—?" I screamed when it jumped toward me. I held my tool straight out with a rigid arm. The tool glanced across its body, then the creature grasped my arm with several legs, and I thanked God and the rocket scientists again and again for my magical suit, and especially for my helmet, because even though I could see every single gooey eyeball smashed against the glass, it wasn't touching me. It was trying every angle it could to snap its teeth into my neck, my shoulder, my arm, and it wasn't happening. Its mandibles slipped against the material; it couldn't manage a grip. My heartbeat spiked. I didn't need VELMA to tell me that.

As much as I recoiled at the idea, I used my free hand and arm to try and wrestle it off. Shudders of revulsion coursed through me when I grabbed at legs and tried to pry them off. I could hear the crunching and squelching noises. Just like the bugs I was used to, its limbs snapped with pressure, and soon I could also hear its cries of pain. I adjusted my grip on my tool, and squeezing my eyes shut, I jammed it up. I felt its legs release, and I opened my eyes to see it scrabbling away from me. Panting, I jumped after it and, with a primal yell, stabbed it in the head.

It curled up on its back and died.

"Sensors indicate a life-form nearby."

The tears continued to pour down my face. I hated everything about this place.

I stood over the thing and involuntarily shook, imagining its creepy legs crawling all over me again. I did a herky-jerky dance, waving my arms like a maniac and shivering, reliving the horror.

I kicked the corpse against the wall. I needed to set it on fire because my imagination was, without question, going to resurrect it a million times if I tried to rest in this cave.

I retrieved matches from one of my pockets. It took several tries for my shaking hands to cooperate, but the corpse eventually went up like a Molotov cocktail, and I backed away from the flames.

I felt a shudder beneath my feet as I stared at the fire. I cocked my head. Was that a scrape of something against the cave wall?

Still panting, I turned. Emerging from a huge opening I hadn't shone my light on yet, was the granddaddy of my little campfire. It was as big as a horse if it was an inch. Just like the small one I killed, it was covered in hairy fibers. It had a dozen legs; its head was made up of eyes. I could see my headlamp reflecting back at me from a hundred of them. We paused, measuring our lives against the background of a flickering flaming bug.

I froze.

The thing about these spiders was they didn't have webs in this cave. They had their mandibles. The ends of their legs had sticky pads instead of claws. I still hadn't seen waste, so while they roamed these caves, it wasn't where they digested their meals. All of these thoughts ran through my mind while I tried to make my body move. Outrunning it wasn't an option.

Gripping my bloody tool tighter, I bent my knees in a crouch. The big daddy mimicked me. Oh yeah, he was going to pounce.

"Risk of malignant hypertension present. Tachycardia 180 BPM. Please remain calm."

"Spider," I croaked out.

The big leggy creature cocked its head at me. I forgot my mic was still on.

"The itsy-bitsy spider went up the waterspout," I started again and then jumped. Too late, I saw the big spider had an appendage the little one lacked.

A huge curving spike rose out from the back of its head and rushed at me before I could dodge out of the way.

I was a dead miner.

14

NARAXTHEL

Nightfall on Ikthe heightened my hunting instincts. While my ship would be waiting for me with the Tech-Slave, several animals stalked the lands between here and my ship.

I felt the rush of my holy calling, and unsheathed my raxtheza.

I smelled the night-time cousin of talathel, agothe talaza, nearby. I crouched amidst the grasses and waited for her to show her black tongue. She slithered into a coil, hissing and readying to make me her meal. The agothe talazal were crafty serpents. I heard her sister behind me. They thought to corner the Iktheka? I pulled a deep breath into my lungs and knew the moment they struck.

I rolled, slicing the raxtheza upward, disemboweling one, and then I jumped to my feet, bringing my blade down in full circle. I beheaded the first one.

The blood would bring numerous animals to this site. I ran through the field, using my nose to alert me to the dangers. Every creature, every glade, every creation on Ikthe released a unique smell. Theraxl could detect changes in a creature's body—such as the moment a snake would strike. I could smell the crushed grasses beneath my boots, their spicy tang reminding me of a special soup my mother used to cook. The smells were a tapestry for my mind, teaching me, reminding me, warning me.

That's why it was so odd to track the female enemy without her scent. It shamed me to admit that without a smell, I could not hunt as effectively.

I recalled the sight of her eyes through the strange helmet. It was not a warrior's helmet like my own.

It held in the sound of her scream when she fell.

It held in the sound of her scream.

It … held … in … her scent!

If the helmet and clothing she wore were so effective as to conceal her scent from my nose, what could it keep out? Could it protect her from the poisons of the mud-beast's home?

Fury flooded my heart-home, and I exulted in it.

She yet lived! The clever traveler outwitted the Mighty Hunter by obscuring herself in the pit with the mud-beast.

I turned around, running back to the ikfal and back to the pit. I felt flush with hot blood in my face and chest, and for the third time in many cycles, I laughed.

I found the path down to the pit and slid, letting my weight speed me along. With the diurnal setting in my helmet, I saw her muddy prints tracking all around the pit. She hadn't bothered to hide her tracks at all, so confident was she I would never return.

The corner of my mouth turned up. She was worthy prey, indeed.

What had she been doing? At first, I thought she had been collecting fuel for a fire, or perhaps brush to form a shelter. The shrubberies and foliage surrounding the pit were hacked to bits. Her tracks and muddy handprints littered the entire area, surrounded slender trunks and smeared across rocks. I found a lump of blue clay almost obscured from her muddy hands. Why would she hold the clay in her hands and then drop it?

The odor of the mud was thick in the air. Pleasure tightened the skin of my face. Now I could track her by scent.

I found it concentrated by a thick overgrowth of bushes and small trees. I found the hole she entered.

Heart picking up pace and breaths escalating, I ignored the size of the hole. I would cut my way through if need be.

The sounds from within the cave reached my ears. I heard the crackling of a fire and a female voice—singing? I smelled the stench of the night-walkers, and a fire, and the mud.

The stupidity of the female spy knew no bounds. Entering the cave of a night-walker, at night. With no vial of the Waters of Shegoshel.

I felt less ashamed of losing her in the pit. It had been dumb luck. Now she was mine, provided I could capture her before she died from the night-walker's strike. If she did, I supposed I could revive her with my vial. If I wished.

The walls of the tunnel pressed around my girth. I inched my way forward until it widened and the light from the fire and her helmet lit the entire room. I broke free of the tight tunnel just as the night-walker struck.

I had no time.

It struck her chest and she collapsed. The agothe-fax turned to face me, and I threw my raxtheza at its head. It cleaved in two, and its striker fell limp beside its body. I noted the fire was the younger sister agothe-fax.

At least the spy had drawn out the last occupant of this cave. The night-walkers lived two-by-two, elder sister and younger sister, much like the serpents that had attacked me a rotik before.

I stood over the female's body. There was an absence of blood, which surprised me. Perhaps her suit contained that, as well. If I were to resurrect her with the vial, then I had to remove her helmet. I knelt and lifted her head, using my other hand to trace around the neck. There was some sort of seal connecting the helmet to the suit, confirming my suspicions about its ability to protect its wearer from the poisons in the mud pit.

I checked the place the striker hit. There was no hole in the suit. I nodded with approval. Whatever the female's race, her people had designed a powerful armor. The venom didn't penetrate the suit. If the powerful strike didn't kill her, then she would survive.

I observed the female's chest, to see if her heart and heart-home worked together, to see if she still lived. There was no movement of breathing. I frowned. I had seen her small vehicle and the tracks leading away from it. Her short expedition had ended in her death. I didn't know if the air of Ikthe was compatible with her race. Perhaps that is why she kept her helmet on. There was not time to determine. I frowned. Removing her helmet could kill her. My gaze strayed to her chest again. Still nothing. Perhaps she was already dead. I growled in frustration.

I rolled her small body to the side, facing away from me. I spied a small latch. I filled my lungs. I tried to detect a heartbeat from her back by pressing my hand to her spine. Nothing. I let out a somber breath.

Using a claw, I pulled it out and heard a hissing noise. If her race's technology was similar to mine, then that was the air pressure releasing.

The first thing I noticed when I removed the helmet from her head was the scent rising from her hair. It washed over me in layers. First, the sweat, then the musk of female exertion, and last, the faintest aroma of the cool season when Ikshe burst with flowers and the jodaxl laid eggs. My heart-home released my heart for two tiks before resuming its natural order. My lungs gasped for air, my nose sank into her hair to repeat the joyful experience. My throat dried up. What sorcery was this? My heart-home would never release my heart. I jerked away from the scent of her hair.

A noise chimed in my ear.

The Royal Court summoned my comm.

I retreated from the body. Confusion replaced the momentary joy. My heart and heart-home should remain as they were, separate. They parted briefly for all adolescents, then joined once more, never to be parted. The myths of the heart escaping its confines were silly fables. Nothing more.

"Iktheka, we received your sight-capture," Younger Sister Kama spoke. "You are still alive!"

"Yes."

"The drawing for the Lottery is tomorrow night. The Royal Court extends an invitation to you to sit on the dais when the names are drawn."

"I am honored, Younger Sister," I said, hoping she couldn't detect my reluctance. "Please give my regards to the Ikma, Elder Sister."

"We look forward to the many meals provided by your hunt," BoKama said. "May the life of Shegoshel shine upon you and your offspring."

I closed with the traditional ending. "May the death of your enemies bring peaceful slumber."

The younger sister and ambassador of the Royal Court ended the communication. I turned back to the body.

Cleansing the memory of her hair's scent from my mind, I resumed my work.

I found fastenings and puzzled over them until I had opened the suit at her chest. I was not surprised to see a massive purple bruise blooming from under a cloth breast covering. The covering obscured half of the bruise, but what crossed the pale skin was enough to see the damage inflicted by the agothe-fax's strike. A slender scar ran from above her sternum to her navel. It gave me pause, but it was an old wound. Still the female did not breathe. My eyes lingered on the curves of her chest a tik too long.

The creature's strike had the force of five Theraxl hunters. If Theraxl survived the venom after taking the vial of Shegoshel Waters, he had chest pain for many moon cycles thereafter. I had little hope for the fragile body that lay before me.

Ignoring the temptation to devour the fragrance of her hair, I instead removed my clawed glove and placed my hand upon the bruise and the old scar. Her smooth skin was cool to the touch. Scowling, I pondered how to revive her. My race had a bone cage surrounding the heart-home and lungs, as well as other vital tender organs. Her skin, stature, and teeth were like that of prey: weak and fragile. Had her body no bone-cage to protect her heart?

I removed my own helmet, placing it beside hers on the cave floor, and bent to listen to her chest. At first, I heard nothing, but her chest formed a soft pillow for my head. I rested it there, to see if her heart-home sang the song of echoing death. Still nothing. That meant she lay in the valley between the land of the Shegoshel and the mountain of eternal death. The smooth texture of her skin sent my heart into a gallop. I pulled my hand away.

How odd the Goddesses of Shegoshel placed this enemy in my hands. Not fifty iktiks ago my plans were to remove her spirit from her frail body. And now I contemplated calling it back.

I was no *maikshe*. I didn't carry the healing oils or mystical recipes that manipulated the spirits of Theraxl to both enter and leave their bodies. But I had the vial. Perhaps it would work, even though her body did not absorb any venom. At times, the Waters of Shegoshel were called upon in other healings.

I lifted her head with one clawed hand; I cradled it as if it were a large tree-fruit. I used the claw on my other hand to open her mouth. The softness of her lips jolted my concentration. Shaking my head, I retrieved my vial and flicked the lid off with my thumb-claw.

My brows clashed together. I shook my head. Risk after risk.

Perhaps our air poisoned her lungs. Perhaps this vial, intended to preserve her life, would kill her. But she already lay dying. That was only permitted if it had been by my hand. I held the vial in preparation to administer the healing drops. I stared at her lips, dry and pale. I hoped the vial could revive her. Yet …

I pocketed it instead. She was not Theraxl. Generations of my people would spin in their celestial orbits were I to dose this stranger with our sacred Waters. Maybe the Waters would have revived her heart and heart-home. Maybe they would have sent her spirit to the afterlife.

If I was not going to gift her with the Waters, I must do something else to help.

She had little breath. I had breath aplenty. Perhaps I could give her mine.

I leaned down, letting her unique aroma flood my senses. I filled my lungs and pressed my lips against hers. I blew a measured breath for the count of several tiks, then removed my mouth from hers. I placed my hand on her chest, but felt no motion. I would try once more. I made certain to create a seal with my mouth, that no breath would escape. With my hand on her scar, I blew until her chest rose under my hand. Once more. And once more. And once more. I breathed for her, willing her to breathe on her own with my every attempt.

For several tiks, my breathing filtered through the cave air, mocking me when it echoed. Then her chest rose under my hand. I pulled it away and watched, fearing it was my imagination. It rose again, high and full. I rested on my haunches and let my arms and shoulders relax. Moisture gathered at the corners of my eyes, but it was a dry cave. I wiped them without further thought. Never had I studied someone's sleeping form with such care. Her chest rose. Again. And again. I believed she would live. But I wouldn't know until I returned from Ikshe.

Time would reveal the answer. Goddesses willing, perhaps they would answer my next question: why did this frail creature cause my heart to try to leave its secure chamber? It was an abomination.

15

ESRA

I dreamed I was running across the picnic meadow with my hair flowing behind me. Ahead, I saw a huge mountain and just as dreams go, I was suddenly at its base.

I looked up, but the top was obscured by clouds. I climbed and noticed I was wearing a flowing white dress and no shoes. My fingers and toes grasped the ridges in the rock. I climbed and climbed, and when boulders rained down upon me, I dodged them effortlessly.

Fresh mist hit my hot face, and then I was sitting in a lotus pose at the top of the mountain. Two beautiful women—no, not women—females, mimicked my pose.

I felt as if they were observing me.

"H-hello."

"Hello, little sister."

I looked around, but they were addressing me. The larger of the two had hair as bright as the sun. Her facial bones were angular; her eyes slanted. She had a slender nose and thin lips. Her skin was luminous, but also had an unusual texture and greenish tint. The smaller of the two had identical but smaller features.

"What am I doing here?" I said. "I mean, up here. With you."

"You came to us. But now we know you are here, we are judging your worthiness."

I cocked my head at them. *Worthiness for what?* "I didn't know you were here when I climbed the mountain," I told them, "and as to my worthiness, I don't understand why it's necessary?"

My life flashed before my eyes. Oh Mica. Was I dying? Dead? I couldn't remember what I had been doing before. Something like a safari. A hippo. I couldn't remember.

"She'll do," the younger one said.

I spared her a grateful glance, but again, I didn't know what they were judging me on. Then one of many scenes I worked so hard to forget played across my mind's eye. I knew they could see it as well.

My heart raced. I panted in shallow breaths. I felt the impact again, like fire, like knives, and the shame was as fresh as the day it happened. I flung my arms in front of my face, as if it were happening again. I looked between my arms at them. They both shed tears for me. I lowered my arms, looking around as if Chris would be there.

"Yes," the larger one nodded. "She is the one." Then she smiled, and flanking somewhat human-looking teeth, were two very long fangs. Fangs?

16

NARAXTHEL

I closed my eyes and concentrated on my own breaths. I leaned over her chest once again to listen. The tiniest of breaths expelled. She yet breathed on her own.

As gently as I could manage with clawed fingers, I lifted her eyelids one at a time to see her eyes. They were rolled back. I couldn't see their beautiful color, but I remembered them.

Unlike my own eyes, hers had a central black dot. Her eyes reminded me of the *awaafa,* the giant winged blue-green butterfly native to Ikthe.

I found a clean cloth from my pack and folded it upon the stone floor as a pillow for her head. I allowed the back of my knuckle to caress the tender skin under her eye. So pale. I could see the tiniest network of veins beneath her skin. What race sent a fragile female to do the work of a spy? Someone whose bones could snap if I squeezed hard enough? Suspicions raced in my mind. What would an alien race desire from Ikthe? We valued the meat and the challenge of hunting here. We valued the healing Waters of Shegoshel and a single prized metal. Ikthe was sacred in its violence. Out of death, sprang life.

Attuned to her breaths, I could resist the call of her hair no longer. I lifted her head enough to pull the length from under and combed through it with my claws. Every stroke wafted the scent of it to my nose. I reveled in the fragrance. I plaited her hair into a hundred braidlets. When she wakened, she would have the woven hair of the women of the Royal Court, the symbol of victory over death.

The Royal Court!

In my worry, I had forgotten the invitation.

I looked around the cave. The light from her helmet faded. The burning agothe-fax was embers now.

I must leave to attend the Lottery drawing. But she would awaken in the dark.

I bent one last time, my ear to her chest. Another breath.

I could not bring her to Ikshe. It was forbidden. I could not hide her in the hold of my ship. It was overflowing with the meat for my people. And the orbit guards inspected every ship bow to stern anyway.

I was obliged to leave the female here.

With the deaths of the agothe-faxl, it was the safest location at the moment. I placed her helmet upon her chest. When she awakened in the blackness, her hands would find the helmet. It was the best I could do.

I would hasten to return to Ikthe after the Lottery. My name hadn't been drawn in fifteen cycles. Auspicious hunting expedition aside, why would it be drawn this time?

I felt the ache return when I left the cave behind and ran many lengths to my ship. It did not abate when my ship entered the orbit of Ikshe. I suspected I would find relief once I returned to the surface of Ikthe. The Goddesses were playing with Naraxthel today. I imagined the Sisters tittering at the thought of the Mighty Hunter eager to return to Certain Death to gaze upon the face of a pale dead female and inhale the fragrance of the valley lilies from her hair.

17

The back of my head throbbed, but the most urgent pain belonged to my sternum. I had yet to open my eyes, choosing instead to inventory my aches. "VELMA, what is my health status?"

I heard a mumble.

I frowned and opened my eyes. Complete blackness surrounded me. Then a powerful, dank smell assaulted my nose so heavily I almost gagged. What the—where was my helmet?

Ah, the weight on my upper chest. I must have put it there ... I grasped it with both hands.

I remembered the monster spider coming at me from the shadows. I yelped and scrabbled backward until my back hit the wall, my helmet rolling away from me with a clatter as I crab-crawled with my hands. I gasped and whimpered, fearing for my life. I looked everywhere, but the darkness was complete. And now I didn't have my helmet, unless I crawled around looking for it.

What had happened to the spider? I wracked my brain, trying to remember the last thing. The spider came at me. Was I singing that song? I couldn't remember. Why had I taken my helmet off? My suit was saving my life on an hourly basis.

Without the barrier created by my helmet, I smelled a strong musty odor with a slight sour tang to it. I could smell clay and water and salt. And something burnt and stale.

There was also the trace of something earthy and peppery. But it was fleeting.

I listened. Was there anything else in here with me?

I put a hand to my thudding chest, discovering my open suit. My sternum and surrounding area was numb. I must have been losing my mind, because I did not remember taking off my helmet or unfastening my suit. Maybe I inspected my injury and passed out.

I needed my helmet. I refastened my suit and then groped my way along the floor of the pitch-black cave. Frantic to find my helmet, I patted the gritty ground with each crawling step, reaching around to try and find it. My hand fell on something hard and angular—my multi-tool!

I pressed on until my hand met something furry and I yelped and jerked away. My squeak echoed against the cave walls. Snap. I needed my helmet before anything came after me. I reached forward again. Petting the fur, I pressed my fingers into it and felt the hardness beneath. Gulping, I tried to wrap my fingers around the limb. They didn't quite reach all the way around, but I knew what it was. It was one of the many legs of the giant spider beast. Lifeless, it still had the power to send my breathing into spasms. Especially in the dark.

I had heard the clattering of my helmet, but noises echoed in here, and I had no idea where it could be. My frustration grew as I continued to crawl around. I had no way of knowing if I was canvassing the exact same area or what. And why the hell was my helmet light not on? That only happened when I'd been without solar power for over twenty hours. *Oh crap.*

"VELMA, activate auxiliary light."

Its light pierced my eyes and gave me an instant headache, even though it was a soft orange glow. "Ow." I closed my eyes against it, then squinted between my fingers until I was used to it. It was feet away from me, the light emanating from interspaced LEDs around the neck ring and inside at the top.

Using the glow, I looked around and stutter-stepped when I saw the humongous corpse of the spider-beast. At least it was dead.

Moving my arms hurt the bruising on my chest. I bent to retrieve my helmet with care. I was used to the odor in the cave now, but I needed a medical assessment. I put it on and ran a diagnostic.

"Esra Weaver, you have suffered a concussion, as well as blunt force trauma to your sternum, resulting in a large area of contusions and a subdermal hematoma just below your sternum. Please return to the EEP to receive emergency medical treatment."

Oh schist. What the hell happened in here? I looked back at the huge spider. I walked closer to inspect the dead body. I couldn't tell which was the head-end and which was the tail-end. I shined the light on its many-eyed head and realized it had been split in two. I didn't do that, did I? I leaned in closer. Gooey junk clotted the huge wound, but it was clear something sharp had cleaved it in two. My multi-tool wasn't large enough to have achieved that.

I looked back around to the small pile of ash. Then I looked in all the dark alcoves of the cavernous room and the offshoot tunnels. Did some other terrifying animal, maybe the natural predator to the spider thingies, come in and …? No, the corpse wasn't eaten. Or even picked at.

Something, or rather, someone, had split its head open. Killed it. I placed a hand on my chest. Prevented it from killing me.

Double schist. That armored alien had found me.

Then I remembered my suit had been opened and my helmet off. What had he done to me? I took off my helmet again and reached up to the sore spot on my head and felt heavy locks of hair. What in the Sam Hill? I placed the helmet on the floor beside me and felt my head with both hands.

My head was full of tiny braids. I threaded my fingers through the braids, marveling at the patience it would have taken someone to do. And the time. How long had I been out?

Okay. I blew a breath out. It couldn't have been the hunter. Based on his helmet alone, *he* would have split me in two. There had to be another sentient being on the planet. It was the explanation that made sense. Some kind of benevolent, aboriginal, compassionate female.

I cocked my head, the flicker of a benevolent female's visage coming to mind. Then it fled before I could capture it. Did I dream…? Shaking my head made it throb more. "Ow."

I cringed at the pain. The adrenaline rush was wearing off.

"Please return to the EEP for emergency medical treatment." VELMA's voice was muffled.

"I know. Give me a hot minute, will you?" I replaced the helmet, made sure everything was right and tight, and asked for a map back to the EEP.

Maybe my benefactor would meet me on my way out. Maybe it was the braids or the cloven head, but I suspected their medicine wasn't as advanced as mine.

Using the cave wall for support, I made my way through the tunnels. Each step jarred the ache in my chest, and each sway of my arms caused a deep throb to pulse at my sternum. The map overlay was taking me in a different direction from where I entered. This could be good, or very, very bad. Although my breathing was labored, I was pretty sure my ribs weren't broken. Thanks to Chris, I already knew what that felt like. The tunnel I was in narrowed. I lowered to a crawl, aching with every movement. I had to stop frequently to rest.

I tried to imagine the female who braided my hair. I hadn't had anyone touch my hair since Earth, and I paid them to do it. A cut and style by a girl in a hurry. I remembered feeling disappointed the head massage didn't last long enough. Once again, the hazy memory of a woman's—no—a female's face, crossed my mind. She wasn't human. There was another one, too. I paused and squeezed my eyes shut, trying to catch the image. It wafted away. My chest hurt. I had to take another rest.

I laid my head back for a minute. Everything pulsed inside me.

"Return to the EEP for emergency medical treatment."

I am, VELMA, I am.

18

NARAXTHEL

I stood still and naked as the eunuchs removed all the *fakathe* from my skin with large amounts of scented water and rough cloths. Gritting my teeth when they scraped the filth off my skin with pieces of bark, I closed my eyes.

My thoughts turned to Ikthe again and again. More to the point, to the female lying on a stone floor in the dark. Had she awakened? Would she stay within the safety of the cave once she did?

I cursed aloud. She would not.

The eunuchs jerked away from me, alarmed at my use of the profane word *kathe*. Some words were not to be used in the Fortress of the Royal Court. I ground my teeth together and submitted to their ministrations. Hunting was a filthy work.

Next came the arm bands denoting my kills. The eunuchs welded the bands around my bicep, the heat from the closing tool burning my skin. I glimpsed their curious glances when I endured it.

I closed my eyes and frowned. The female showed strength and bravery, as well as determination. She had a hunter's spirit. I wondered how extensive her injury was on the inside. I heard no evidence of a heart-home. Did her race not have the sacred chamber that held the heart? Should not a species as delicate as hers have the heart cage?

From my palpations, I only detected a few bones one such as I could snap with little effort. Perhaps her Goddesses gave her strength elsewhere to protect her heart. I could not work out a logical explanation, but then the Goddesses were seldom logical. Only consider the old tales that told of Theraxl hearts leaving their solid cage upon finding the proper mate after a turbulent adolescence. Such ridiculous nonsense. The heart would be forever vulnerable were such a thing to occur. The eunuchs flinched when I snorted.

Now they layered royal clothing upon me. A swath of green fabric around my waist, a thick belt of animal hide, and metal plates on my chest. A headpiece made of orange rodaxl feathers flared out from my brow. Gems were pushed into my temples, small barbs working their way into my thick skin. I chafed under their hasty treatment of my hair fronds and their constant touching. I hadn't been touched this much since I was tripping around my mother's skirts.

The eunuchs frowned incessantly, as they had to work twice as fast. I had arrived late. Their green skin showed the faded marks of past beatings. A flare of guilt threatened to consume me, but I tamped it down. We were all enslaved by the Queen, in one way or another.

Another eunuch poked his head in the doorway, looking around the smooth floors and tapestry-covered walls as if searching for something. At last his eyes fell upon me. He frowned.

"They are ready for their honored guest," he said, his eyes slanting up and down my body.

I lifted a brow. None of them addressed me as Theraxl, but spoke as if I wasn't in the room. It was as I suspected. My sight-capture had been shown across the planet. That would have resulted in Theraxl researching my lineage and my history. The fact I hadn't created offspring since I was inducted as a hunter for Theraxl meant there was a subtle distrust of me and my parentage. I growled at the two fussing with my headpiece, and they slinked away from me.

"Take me to the dais," I said.

The third eunuch dipped his head, and I followed him out of the bathing room, the steady dripping of water echoing off the white clay-smeared walls with a lonely sound.

My heart was back at the cave, even as I strode through the halls of the Royal Court, annoyed by the pomp. To think yesterday I would have sung the song of *raxshe raxma*, in preparation for the Lottery draw, and have been satisfied to sit on the dais with the Elder Sister and Younger Sister puzzled me. For today, in this tik, I wanted out of the ceremonial clothing, out of this Court, and off Ikshe.

19

Dim light woke me from a sleep so sound, I thought I was in my childhood bedroom. I stared at the gray wall across from me, trying to figure out where my lacy white canopy was. Then I heard VELMA's synthesized voice.

"Auxiliary battery charged," she said. "Return to the EEP for emergency medical treatment."

I blinked twice, and everything came back to me. I had a hematoma that needed to be treated, among other things. My suit lost some power, but the light from the distant exit was enough to charge its emergency stores to full. Exhaustion had caught up to me.

It was just as well. I could imagine the kinds of delightful nighttime creatures I had missed by sleeping one off in a cave tunnel. Upon further reflection, it was a lucky break I lost consciousness. I was in no shape to fight off anything tougher than a butterfly. Correction: an Earth butterfly.

I also realized my fairy alien-godmother hadn't returned in the night. Maybe she turned into a pumpkin. Shrugging off the mysterious source of my braids, I stood up, feeling every bruise across my chest and reaching down to my abdomen. What had that thing done to me? Its mandibles hadn't pierced my suit since its integrity was at a hundred percent. I'd been hit.

I couldn't force the memory to return, so I used the wall to help me stand, and made my way out of the cave.

The exit opened out to a meadow. Was it the same one I called the picnic meadow? A breeze rippled across the green and yellow spikes with their salmon featherettes, and once again I was captivated by the beauty of this primeval place. I scanned for those crow-sized wasps. I didn't think I could handle an attack by them today, suit notwithstanding.

I looked at my map and dropped to my knees. I would crawl there. I was wiped out and it hurt to stand.

I gripped my multi-tool and gritted my teeth. I needed to reach the EEP.

I fell in and out of consciousness. I was in the picnic meadow but running through the grasses. Then I was crawling again. Then I was climbing a mountain. Everything felt like a distant dream. The pain grew stronger. But according to the map, I was almost there. Such as it was, the EEP was my home now, and I longed to be within its safe confines.

I felt rumbling through my hands and knees.

No.

Oh, please no, don't let those huge reptiles be coming back here.

I had to run to the EEP. I would not survive unless I did.

I hitched up to my knees and tracked the area.

"VELMA, locate the nearest lifeforms."

"A pack of large reptiles is approaching from the northwest."

Wonderful.

I looked around but still couldn't see them. Ahead I saw the shiny cone of my EEP. I had to run, even though my entire chest ached with every motion.

I started running, and seven steps into my sprint I saw the beasts at my ten o'clock. They were massive. I was a dead woman unless I ran like hell.

I pulled it out, sprinting faster than my pole-vaulting days, and soon I couldn't hear my own gasping breaths over the roar of the galloping reptile feet and growls. I didn't know if they could see or smell me, but I didn't want to find out.

I made it to the vehicle and slammed my palm on the reader. The opening shot up with a hiss and I dove in, screaming at VELMA to shut the door and go into camo mode.

I curled into the fetal position when the reptiles hit the pod, and I felt it tip and roll. I bashed around inside, frantic to grab a handhold. It felt as if they were playing soccer with my EEP. Praying to God and any dead rocket scientists, I squeezed my eyes shut and whimpered throughout the ordeal.

After what seemed like forever, the movement stopped. I was holding onto a long rail so hard my hands cramped. I opened my eyes and looked out the window. I saw dirt.

There was no way in hell I was *egressing* this vehicle until ambassadors from *Lucidity* dragged me out. I would just sit here in the dark and live out my days.

I anchored my helmet to its spot and crawled into my alcove. The EEP was set up for the passenger to sit in a semi-reclined position for its flight, but the seat could also adjust to standing. While the beasts had knocked the pod around, it was still functional. I strapped myself in and relaxed as much as I could, considering the pod was tipped. Again.

"Running medical scan. Please attach all nodes and bio-mechanics for a complete evaluation."

I grumbled but did as asked. The IV port on my sleeve squeezed my arm, and I felt the sting of the needle.

"Please remain calm. Scanning. Your results will arrive momentarily."

It hurt to breathe. That spider-scorpion did a number on my breastbone. I hoped it wasn't cracked or broken. My ribs could be broken, too. I groaned. It just got better and better.

"Scanning complete. Administering anti-inflammatory medicine through the port. Bruising found on your ribs. Recommended treatment is eight to ten weeks of rest with no heavy lifting. Standard doses of anti-inflammatory medicine will help the swelling and discomfort," VELMA said.

While it felt good to be back in the pod, I questioned the necessity of coming all the way back here for what amounted to a couple ibuprofens. But what did I know?

"You also have multiple contusions from the erratic movements of the EEP."

I closed my eyes and sighed. Cringing—I could imagine life with Chris again. The bruises. I shook my head.

"Results of your blood screening as follows:"

My head snapped up. I should have known it would do a blood test as well.

"Abnormal amounts of antibodies indicate the presence of a possible infection. Trace amounts of an unknown substance are present in your blood. Did you ingest anything on this planet?"

"No. I haven't even had time to take a pee!"

"Your blood has been tested for hundreds of substances. The unfamiliar chemical resembles the chemical makeup of Salvinorin A, a hallucinogenic." Images of a flower my mom called Salvia flashed on the screen in my pod. "If you see something similar to this, it is recommended you do not ingest it."

"I haven't hallucinated," I protested. Flashes of my dream came to mind, but that didn't count. "And I didn't eat anything. In fact, I'm starving!"

"Please choose an MRE packet and drink at least three pouches of water," VELMA responded. "Your blood shows some signs of mild dehydration."

"Anything else?" I said, dreading pretty much whatever VELMA was going to spout.

"Low-grade fever of 99.9° F."

I groaned. I needed to eat, rest, answer nature's call, oh, and find the busted beacon and launch off this cursed planet that somehow was drugging me. All while lying on my side.

"VELMA, are there signs of life outside the EEP?"

"There are no signs of animal life within a thirty-foot radius."

Okay. I needed to right the pod again. What a pain in the ass. Didn't the stabilizers do anything?

"VELMA, I need to egress and stand the pod up again."

"Detaching bio-mechanics."

I grabbed my helmet and secured it. Took a deep breath and groaned. "My chest." I opened one of the hatches, wincing when I raised my arm. I poked my head up, ready to retreat immediately. In the distance, storm clouds were gathering in the dusky sky, and a gust shook the feathered grasses. One of those snakes could be hiding in there. I watched for a while, looking for movement that was out of sync with the wind.

Satisfied it was all clear, I struggled to climb out and initiated the same process I had done yesterday, rotating handles and adjusting mechanisms. It took longer this time, since one of the stabilizer legs had been damaged.

I was no mechanic. VELMA sent instructions to repair it, but I ended up finding a flat rock with gray and black striations in it and putting it under the leg. I stood back to admire my work. "Gneiss." With a quick scout around the area, I scrambled back inside and shut the door.

Now I could use the bathroom!

It was the simple things in life.

Since it was an emergency vehicle, there wasn't a shower. I had to use recycled liquids stored in pouches with super absorbent cloths to clean up, careful of the awful bruises found everywhere on my body. I reached up both hands to massage my scalp, *ow*, and that fragrance of soil and pepper wafted into my nose. I closed my eyes and inhaled deeply, realizing it came from my hair. Whoever had braided my hair had left a lingering scent upon the braids.

Tears welled up without warning, and I hiccoughed on a sob.

Was it worth it? Leaving Chris and everything he did to me behind, only to be stranded here?

Just like old times, bruises covered a lot of my body, but the most enduring pain was in my soul. For some reason, the braids triggered my tears.

Who did it, and why? I couldn't even begin to guess at the why, but weirdness aside, it was a tender gesture for someone who lay unconscious and dying on a cave floor. VELMA could give me medicines, but as far as I knew, my EEP didn't have a cure for a broken heart.

20

NARAXTHEL

"Iktheka Raxthe, welcome to the Royal Court," said my revered queen. The Elder Sister's white braids were woven with strands of purple *woaiquovelt*, the prized metal of Ikthe. It was soft and malleable, yet rare. It caught the light from scattered torches throughout the great hall.

Hunters who had been able to retrieve the metal were rewarded handsomely. I had never been chosen for such an expedition, but I had no regret of it. To extract woaiquovelt, hunters must travel *by two* into the mountain. If my death came during a hunt, I preferred it came by no one's fault but my own.

My musings were not missed by the Elder Sister. "Something troubles you, Iktheka Raxthe," she whispered. I cocked my head as I looked into her light-ringed, blood-colored eyes. Her textured skin glowed from the application of a scented oil mixed with the crushed pearls found in the oceans of Ikthe. The jewels embedded at her temples glowed orange. Never would such a privileged Theraxl have had occasion to speak to a lowly Iktheka such as myself. Before today.

"I must thank you for the esteemed invitation to join you on the Dais," I said as I bowed my head. "An honor so high is not soon forgotten."

I hoped my manners were suitable, for my heart ached to be somewhere else. Elder Sister fixed her shrewd, calculating eyes upon me.

"We at the Court enjoyed your sight-capture very much," she said with gleaming white fangs. "The Younger Sister and I were most delighted to see the blood spill upon your armor."

A deep crease formed between my brows. A thought occurred to me. While I hadn't noticed the small vehicle until much later, could it have shown up on the sight-capture? I perspired.

"Such violence and power. It is what Theraxl thrive upon, is it not?" She let her hand linger upon my arm.

The Elder Sister wasn't … wooing me, was she? Such things were whispered about in hushed tones behind the tapestries. The rituals dictated who mated with whom. The Elder and Younger Sisters had consorts. I slid my eyes around the room casually, trying to locate them. They were absent. And yet my nose did not deceive me. I smelled arousal and lust from her skin. An image of the soft traveler's naked stomach flashed in my mind. I frowned.

"Hunting is a filthy business," I said. "It took your eunuchs many rotiks to wash the fakathe from my skin."

"We know," Younger Sister said from behind me. She rested her claws upon my arm, where the black metal rings circled my upper arm. "The Royal Court admires the dirty work of all of our Ikthekal." She rubbed her bare stomach with her other hand, the claws making lazy circles around the dip of her navel. "The Sisters of the Royal Court grow hungry, and the Mighty Hunters sate our many hungers."

I looked from the greedy eyes of Younger Sister to the cold ones of Elder Sister. I smelled conflicting scents between the two females, yet I couldn't distinguish between them. Arousal, but also hatred and … trepidation? My mouth turned down.

For a moment, the growling eyes of the rokhura crossed my mind.

"It is both a duty and an honor to feed the Sisters of the Royal Court." I could think of nothing else to do but dip my head again, my hair fronds brushing along my cheeks and brow.

I was a hunter. I was not familiar with the intrigues of the Court. I did not know the games or the words or the strategies. I bowed, not wishing for their shrewd eyes to witness my discomfort.

The Elder Sister tittered.

"Come, Iktheka Raxthe," she said as she stood. "It is time for the Lottery." She took me by one hand.

Younger Sister handed me my tablet, a circle made of stone with my family lineage symbol etched upon it. Many of the other Sisters of the Royal Court had guests they led by the hand to the large drum in the center of the hall. We dropped our tablets into the funnel at the top, and they wheeled down the drum with a deep rolling sound.

I met the eyes of my fellow hunters. Most of us hunted alone. I saw expressions of yearning and hope on their faces, as well as boredom and restlessness on others.

The counters would draw the names after the great feast.

Eunuchs hastened into the hall and removed the drum, while mechanical Tech-Slaves entered with tables and stools.

My discomfort grew as the Elder and Younger Sisters insisted I sit with them on the dais for the feast. I was accustomed to sitting at the long table near the doors. From that less-esteemed position, I could scout the room for those females who might join me in raxma and raxshe, blessing me with posterity. From the dais, the entire room was visible, but gazing upon any females other than the Elder and Younger Sister would be considered rude.

Not for the first time, I marveled at my poor reception of the grand invitation I'd received. As if some fragile spy from another world had more clout with me than the rulers of my people. It was nonsense.

Yet throughout the meal of roasted rokhura meat, organ pies, spiced entrails and other meaty delicacies, I found myself anxious for the meal to end, for the Lottery to end, and to be dismissed.

The Sisters sat on either side of me, sharing smiles and looks, and touching my arms and hands, and my thighs, as well.

They offered me the fruited wines of Ikshe, strong drinks made from the fruit of the flower meadows at the peak of ripeness. They plied me with so much drink, I felt I might float away.

They drank as well, and with the flowing wines, their words tumbled about my ears.

"You are so quiet, Iktheka Raxthe," Younger Sister teased me. "Do you miss the adventure of the Hunting Grounds?"

"He misses Certain Death!" Elder Sister crowed.

"Yes, he misses Certain Death frequently," Younger Sister agreed. They laughed at their double-speak. "Lucky for us!"

"Indeed. We are quite lucky," Elder Sister said. "Tell us stories, Naraxthel."

My head shot up. I had not given leave for anyone to use my true name. All evening they addressed me as Hunter or Mighty Hunter, as was proper. Hearing my name on the lips of a beautiful yet powerful female, the Ikma of our people, caused a deep shudder in my body.

When I didn't smile, Elder Sister frowned at me. I saw anger flash in her blood-red eyes.

"Do you have any stories?" Her voice was quiet, her stare unflinching.

My left fist clenched and unclenched, my claws digging into the flesh of my hand. But I nodded. "I have a story."

The Sisters clapped their hands together and my Ikma whispered into the ear of one of her eunuchs. He blew a horn, and everyone grew quiet.

My mind ran through the stories of my hunts through the last fifteen cycles. None would compare to finding the spy. Yet something held me back from revealing her presence on Ikthe.

"Last Cycle, my ship crashed just short of the Mountains of Ikfal."

Some in the crowd nodded. They knew the terrain there; it was difficult to navigate.

"My Tech-Slave lost its comm ability, and I was left alone near the nesting grounds of the rodaxl."

Some of the females crooned. They were a bloodthirsty group.

"As expected, the rodaxl flew out to discover what caused the disturbance in their forest. One swooped down and grabbed my useless Tech-Slave. Now I wouldn't even be able to fix it. They would tear it apart once they realized it wasn't meat and scatter its parts throughout the ikfal."

I took a swig of my fruit wine. I'd had so much, I lost its flavor on my numb tongue.

"The rodaxl hunted me," I began. "I ran amongst the trees of the ikfal, dodging their talons every time they swooped. The great one, the one with the largest wing span, dove for me. The rodaxl are very intelligent. I knew I couldn't outrun it, but I would need my wits about me to outsmart it."

I looked around the hall. The older hunters nodded.

"I decided to climb a tree."

The Younger Sister gasped. "You would be too close to them. They could snatch you so easily!"

I smiled at her. "That was my plan."

Elder Sister had yet to smile at me since requesting the story. It made me uneasy.

"The rodax snatched me up, and when it tried to tear me limb from limb, I gave it pieces of my armor instead. In frustration, it lifted its head to yowl, as they do, and at that moment, I lanced its vocal sac, spilling its blood like rain down on the ikfal."

The room broke into applause and shouts, and goblets of wine clanked against each other, the red wine spilling like rodaxl blood.

The din grew louder as the other hunters regaled their table companions with stories of their own hunts. I downed the rest of my fruited wine and tore into a great chunk of meat on my charger.

Elder Sister watched me with shining blood-red eyes. "And then you survived the fall from the sky, when the dead rodax fell?"

I smelled her distrust. "I landed in a tree and climbed down."

"Bed me tonight, Naraxthel," Elder Sister commanded.

I spewed food out of my mouth. Younger Sister burst out in a deep laugh.

I bowed my head and wiped my mouth. My mother never taught me of Royal intrigues. My next step took me out over a chasm. Perhaps I would land on a slender ledge.

"You honor my family and my name, Ikma Scabmal Kama." I stood from my stool and bowed deeply, my headdress dipping to the floor. "A humble hunter must refuse such condescension."

I waited for her to say it was all in jest. The Consorts would demand my death if I accepted her invitation. Would they not? I had yet to rise, waiting.

I heard her clap her hands together.

"Let us draw the Lottery!"

More shouts and clapping and laughter. I remained bowing to my queen Elder Sister.

Younger Sister placed her hand on my shoulder. "Rise, Iktheka Raxthe." A waft smelling like curiosity tickled my nose for a jotik, then it passed.

I rose, schooling my features. I had still to learn if I passed whatever test my Ikma had given me. I snuck a glance at Younger Sister, who regarded me with narrowed eyes and a folded brow. But she said nothing.

Five names would be drawn from the drum.

The five hunters would wander the room, talking to females until suitable matches were made. The couples would leave the Royal Court and begin the earnest pursuit of producing offspring. The remaining hunters were welcome to eat and drink or leave at their leisure.

Recreational mating was not discouraged, but no offspring would come of it, by Royal Edict. Without the sacred raxma and raxshe rites, it was not biologically possible.

Eunuchs pulled five tablets out. Younger Sister read the true names. It was one of the few times when a hunter's name was heard aloud in public.

"Raxkarax."

A burly hunter with a long mane of hair fronds stood proudly. His friends clapped him on the back and cheered. Someone proclaimed he had eight offspring already.

"Natheka." The hunter who joined me on my first hunt. He had two offspring now.

"Raxthezana." I had heard of him. His father died on a Shegoshel Waters expedition. He had one child.

"Hivelt Matheza." A very large hunter stood at the end of the long table. He would make a mighty foe. I was glad he was not *maikthe*, the enemy.

The fire pit behind the Dais burned hot with the hard wood of the ikfal on Certain Death. I felt sweat slide down my spine. One more name, and I would make my excuses and leave for Ikthe. Perhaps I would make it back before the traveler awoke. Perhaps she still lived. If she had perished from her wound, I would bury her in the cave where she slew the younger sister agothe-fax. Not a small kill for a frail soft traveler, a *yasheza mahavelt*, from another world. She was a good little hunter, too, a *joiktheka*.

"Naraxthel Roika."

My heart stopped, and my heart-home readied to open, to release it. How could this be?

Younger Sister nudged me forward. The crowd burst into song, the *raxshe raxma*, the song of sex and offspring. Two years from now, the mothers would bring forth their baby hunters and sisters, the results of tonight's ceremony. Those whose names had not been chosen would be entered into another Lottery in three moon's time, and so on.

To say I was unprepared was an understatement. I had no female chosen. I had no retreat prepared for the ritual of raxshe, the creation of my first child. My mouth was dry, but my goblet was empty of fruit wine.

I felt claws dig into my arm and pull me away from the Dais. Elder Sister took me to an alcove behind a tapestry.

"You will mate with me, Naraxthel."

I stammered. "M-my Ikma. What of my Ikna? I would not dishonor your Consort." This I said, once again bowing my head. I need not remind her offspring between us was forbidden, her position as Queen and Elder Sister notwithstanding.

A clawed hand brought my face close to hers. "You will deny your Ikma?"

A thousand thoughts raced across my mind. Offspring, Consorts, making an enemy of the Elder Sister. There was no right choice. And yet one thing brought peace to the echoing chamber of my heart-home: the thought of the dying traveler on Ikthe.

"I will deny my Ikma the mistake of mating with a lowly hunter." I bowed, then rose and looked into her raging eyes.

"I give you one more chance, Naraxthel," she ground out her words.

Anger, bright and hot, flashed in my own face.

"You would deny me offspring?" I said. "I never imagined Elder Sister would be such a selfish female." I bit out the words and grasped her wrist, yanking her hand from my face.

Excitement flared in her eyes for a second, then dimmed to hatred. Without leaving my gaze, she shouted for her guards.

They flanked me. I stood tall, staring at her.

"Naraxthel Roika," she said, her slow smile revealing her sharp teeth. "I desire you will go on an expedition to the Mountains of Shegoshel."

The rumble of conversation in the room lulled. Several hunters turned to listen to the Ikma.

"Every name drawn tonight will join in the expedition. Ready yourselves to leave before the younger sister sun sets."

The occupants of the room gasped. Elder Sister strode from the room, her dark-green skirts and cloak flying behind her.

Phrases such as "unprecedented" and "preposterous" were thrown about, as well as many whispered "kathes."

The queen had just sentenced the five Lottery winners to death before they even had the chance to further their lineage.

I looked around the room, finding the faces of the four other hunters. Did they suspect I refused her advances? The celebrating died off. One of the females threw the contents of her goblet in the face of Hivelt Matheza before walking out of the room.

Inwardly, I cringed.

Had I not taken the righteous path? The holy path? For hundreds of courses, these had been the ways of Theraxl.

The Ikma was not who I thought she was.

Younger Sister, BoKama, stood to the side. She did not look at me, but rather stared at the gleaming molten images of the Goddesses that adorned the great hall. Her lips moved as if in a silent prayer. My brow creased.

I looked around the room again. This time my eyes met those of the Ikma Scabmal Kama's Consort. I steeled myself for his censure, yet instead, he bowed his head so slightly I might not have noticed had I looked away. His mouth was a grim line. He knew. And with his begrudging respect, I feared I was the first and only to tell the Elder Sister no. In spite of this awful turn of events, I felt a gentle thrumming in my chest. Realization caused my heart-home to nudge my heart. I was returning to Ikthe.

I passed through the great hall, my fellows and sisters parting before me. Anxiety for the soft traveler hastened my steps to the ship hangar. I heard scuffling behind me, and just as I crossed the threshold, the sharp tang of anger filled my nostrils. I spun in time to get hit in the face with a huge fist.

Blood dripped from the cut on my cheekbone. I swiped it away with my knuckle but stared at Hivelt until he looked away. "Tell me you would have accepted her proposal," I asked him.

Hivelt growled and looked over at the three other Theraxl. We stood in the housing where our ships waited, scowling at one another.

"You would have?" My voice rose, and my burning eyes met those of my companions. "Every one of you would have?"

I took a step back and spat on the floor.

"It is the way of the Court," Raxthezana grumbled. "It has been for many cycles."

Raxkarax spoke up. "You would have known such, had your name been called cycles ago."

I turned my back on them all. Heaved a breath. Felt a fire low in my belly. Shame. Disgust. Embarrassment. I couldn't puzzle out my feelings.

"You were honorable to tell us the reason she did this to us," Hivelt muttered. "The suns have set on this day."

I turned back again.

"We will survive this quest," I told them. "All of us. Then we will end the corruption of our ways."

Their eyes grew large, but they said nothing.

I was returning to Ikthe, as I had wanted, but now I had an audience. A duty to return them to Ikshe alive. A mission to preserve the rituals of my people. Preserve the ways of Theraxl? Which included killing defenseless females if discovered in unexpected places? There was no room to worry about some unknown female, but I did. I could never reveal her presence to them. If she had lived through the night, she wouldn't survive Theraxl warriors.

I smashed my fist into a wall then stalked to my ship.

A headache pounded inside my skull. "My ship is ready," I said. "I had my Tech-Slave prepare to leave."

"You didn't expect your name to be drawn, did you?" Raxkarax questioned. "You truly know nothing."

"Naraxthel is a hunter with honor," Natheka broke his silence. "I hunted with him on his first trek to Ikthe." He took a step near me. "He saved my life, when he could have saved his own and received great glory."

I absently rubbed my shoulder, a long-ago wound forgotten until now.

All the while, Raxthezana never said a word. He stared at me as we ran the ship through its protocols.

Of them all, perhaps he deserved to hate me the most. His own father had died on a woaiquovelt expedition. Theraxl lineage requires a single male member to make an expedition every one-hundred cycles. He should have been spared the ordeal.

I spoke no more, choosing instead the stony silence of our forced camaraderie. With the green jewel of Ikthe in the view screen, we fired our engines and left the housing that orbited Ikshe. Many such journeys were made, a well-worn path between the stars, as the sister planets continuously joined in paths that intersected with death.

#

21

"VELMA, what time is it?"

I rubbed sleep from my eyes and felt mild achiness when I took a big breath. Three cheers for modern medicine.

"Which unit of time measurement would you like me to use? Interplanetary General Time, Earth's Greenwich Mean Time, or Class B Planet Modified Time?"

"Uh." It was too early for this nonsense. "Using general Earth terms, when did the suns rise on this planet?"

"The second sunrise was completed twenty minutes ago. The ambient light from this sunrise alerted the melanopsin photopigments in your eyes to begin the awakening sequence."

That was VELMA. Better than coffee.

"I'm awake, alright. Good ol' melanopsin," I grumbled while I unfastened everything. "VELMA, mark the last ping you received from the beacon. I'm going to find it today and set that damn thing up."

"Last known location marked and saved to your files."

"Thank you."

I had a big day ahead of me. Survive. Fix and plant the beacon. Survive some more. Return to my homey little EEP. Punctuated by several more bouts of fighting for my survival. Speaking of survival, I squatted on the ground outside my pod using heavy-duty tape to attach a plate-sized mesh screen to the opposite end of an IGMC-issued machete. It looked like a fly swatter. Er, wasp swatter? Now I could whack them away from me like tennis balls, and if they came back for extra helpings, I'd introduce them to the blade end.

As I trudged through the meadow hefting my weapon, I cussed. My life had come to this.

I left a wake of dead wasps and a blubbery, brown lump. There wasn't even something on Earth to compare it to. Nevertheless, it stopped blubbing after I was through with it.

"It is inadvisable you kill every form of life you come in contact with."

"Yeah, well VELMA, it sucked itself to my foot and wouldn't let go," I said. "You clearly never saw the movie *The Blob*."

"*The Blob*, a cult hit out of the twentieth century featuring a slow-moving red mass that collected unsuspecting humans as it made its way through town."

"That's the one," I said. "Thanks for the reference."

"The last known location is found to your right; please avoid falling down the ..."

"Gaaaahhhhhh!"

I used my fly-swatter to stop my wild career down the mud-slide. I remembered it was there. I did.

Hanging by the swatter, I found purchase with my boots on some brown branches. I steered clear of the green roots. I recalled they had minds of their own.

"VELMA," I gasped out. "How close am I to the beacon?"

"Eight point eight five feet to your right."

"So, like, at my ten o'clock, or what?"

"O'clock refers to the Earth time construct—"

"Stop! Just, never mind. Show me on the map."

The readout popped up in my visor. I climbed hand over hand and a bit sideways to reach my destination. As expected, the beacon was not there. But it should be in the vicinity ...

I combed the area, using my big fly-swatter like a rake.

I was about to give up and go take a dip with my favorite HipCow when my swatter hit something.

I crawled and peeled layers of greenery away and found one half of my beacon.

"Yes!" I bashed it against my helmet when I tried to kiss it. "Oops."

I inflated my magnetized pouch and stuffed the part inside. After another hour, I found the second half. Inspecting the wires, I could see my good friend Mr. AngryPants had simply ripped them all in half. Ha. Joke was on him. All I had to do was solder them all back together again.

I earned an A in my electronic components class.

With my parts stowed away, I grappled my way back to the top of the hill.

Okay, I could check some stuff off my list. Surviving. Found the beacon.

I was down the hill and halfway to my sleek triangular pod when something tugged at my ankle and pulled me backward. I screamed on the way down, my swatter falling as I reached to catch my fall. My helmet hit the ground with a thud, knocking my head in the process. I saw stars for a second but shook my head and groped around for my weapon.

"VELMA, what is this?" I felt a tremendous squeeze around my right ankle and another tug on my left arm. A blur of brown slid beside and over me. It was scaly and long like a snake, but it had dozens of lizard-like legs all along its sides. I tried to clamber up, but its muscular body twisted around my arms and knocked me flat on my back. "VELMA?"

"Scanning. Two reptile-like creatures are within one meter."

Frantic, I slapped the ground around me, wincing whenever my glove made contact with the creature. By the grace of God, I found my swatter and gripped it with all my strength. I brought it up beside me and sawed at the thick muscles holding me down over and over again, until the brown snake writhed and came to a rest. I hoped it was dead. Something still had a powerful grip of my ankle. I heaved and pushed my way out from under the dead thing only to see its bigger cousin trying to swallow my boot.

"Heartbeat approaching 135 beats per minute. Do you require assistance?"

"Yes," I grated, trying to use my other boot to kick the snake's mouth off. "This thing is trying to eat me."

"The IGMC Explorer Suit X8 is graded up to 8.3 psi," she replied. "The crocodile of your home world has 3700 pounds per square inch pressure in its bite."

"Not," I grunted while hacking at the "snake's" head. "Helping."

"However, your boots are graded to withstand 4500 psi," she continued. "If you can prevent the reptile from reaching your calf, your suit will maintain its integrity."

"Thanks," I said and swung my erstwhile *fly* swatter at the beast. The machete-end flayed open its skin above the eye. Its length crept around itself, coiling and approaching my other leg. If it got a hold of my other leg or my waist, I was a goner. I hit it five times with my weapon and kicked at its jaws with my other boot. Huffing, I kicked it hard, and felt its jaws slacken. Again! I timed a kick and a hit at the same time, sweat pouring over every inch of skin inside my suit. The liquid cooling system couldn't keep up with fight or die perspiration. I felt heat start to grow in my belly and flare up to my pounding head. Ringing in my ears and a rush of energy burst through me.

Its jaws tightened a bit, and I erupted. "Freaking piece of schist snake!" I roared at it and kicked both legs furiously. "I've had enough of this freaking stupid planet! Freaking stupid monsters!" I screamed and yanked at my leg and pulled it free. With all my limbs free, I attacked the giant millipede-salamander-snake with my weapon and boots, sparing not a single scale in my flurry of limbs. Its coiling stopped, and its head lolled to the side. A flash of drunk Chris pummeling me haunted my memory, but I shut it down.

My fury abated, and I stood over it, shoulders drooping and spit flecking the inside of my helmet.

I panted and shivered, staring at the blood and the wrinkled bag at its throat. It seemed like every horrific creature on this planet had that ugly throat sac. I shuddered.

A hand on my hip, I looked toward the pod. I was about fifty feet from my EEP. No more reptiles spotted. *If I could just have a little rest.* A low droning buzz sounded at my left.

"Oh, heck no," I said, swinging my swatter in a roundhouse and making contact with the insect. Two more followed, but I knew their weakness now. Drain their venom. The injured one under my boot stung until it died, and the other two followed as I knocked them out of the air.

Gasping for breath, I realized I had tears coursing down my cheeks. I would be damned if I was going to let this planet get the best of me. If I wanted to die, I would have let Chris finish me off.

Glancing at the dead bugs, I was starting to feel capable. Other than the recurring chest pain from that beast spider. Fighting B-movie monsters to the death didn't count as resting. VELMA would remind me of that any second now. I trudged toward the pod.

I gulped. I wondered if the armored fellow was going to come back. Chills ran up and down my spine. What a specimen of unimpeachable power. I had to admit it might be cool to meet him, I mean, if he didn't kill me first.

Shivering, I limped the last feet to the EEP. Sealed myself inside.

"VELMA, activate counter-illuminative hDEDs. Also, we need to work on your reptile alert system."

"I am not familiar with that alert system."

"I know."

I stowed my helmet. I was staring down at my boots with distaste. "VELMA, where is the nearest fresh water?" I pounded on a panel that released a silvery pouch. I sucked down its contents.

"There is a large lake one hundred forty-seven point three feet to the east. However, it is inadvisable you visit the lake," she said. "Compiled data of over six thousand inhabited planets in a hundred different galaxies suggests such a habitat to be prime hunting grounds for dangerous predators, including the large reptiles you classify as dinosaurs."

I slumped into my seat. I needed that water.

It had been a few days, and I could feel my health depleting. Bio-vac shots notwithstanding, the human body was not meant to live on

MREs and recycled water for any length of time. So, I also needed to skin and butcher those dead snakes.

I had a few hours before the two suns set.

"VELMA, scan for life-forms," I said. Then I remembered being double-teamed by the snakes. Heat signatures didn't work for them. Or for the spiders. Or for the wasps, now I thought about it. I thought about the gross wrinkled bags of flesh under all their jaws. They reminded me of turkey waddles. I wondered if they had a purpose beyond vestigial like in Earth animals. Maybe they inflated with air? Maybe this planet flooded in cycles, and they used their throat pouches to float? I shook my head and replaced my water pouch in its cubby. I needed a biologist to consult.

"No signs of animal life within thirty feet," she said.

I grunted. It echoed deep in the tin can I was calling home. It gave me an idea.

"Scan for infrasonic and ultrasonic Hertz," I told her.

VELMA illuminated several creatures denoted by a fuzzy blue shape overlaid on an image of the surrounding area.

"Bingo," I said with a big smile. I stepped closer to the screen.

I studied the shapes. "Zoom in on that tree," I said, touching the screen. VELMA zoomed in. "Holy schist, those are some big monkeys."

I hadn't seen these yet.

"The arboreal vertebrates do not match the scientific classification of simian."

"Thank you, VELMA." Smart ass. "Do they not give off an infrared signature?"

"Negative. Infrasound signature has revealed several more life-forms than previously recognized. The larger creatures of this planet use sounds below 20 Hz."

I laughed. "You're welcome."

I watched the creatures in the tree. Using the augmented reality digitization tool, I calculated their size to be that of chimpanzees back home. I tapped a few buttons and dispatched one of the EEP's drones. Within minutes, I had a clear video capture of the animals in the tree.

My heart jumped to my throat.

These were not monkeys. They were gigantic birds. They had the leathery wings of bats. Naked long necks attached to bald scaly heads with a ring of orange feathers sprouting from the back. They had two eyes on each side of their heads. Huge talons gripped the thick, smooth branches of the tree. A group of them surrounded some bloody mass and tore membranous pieces off. I controlled the camera to zoom in on their heads. Their throats had huge bulbous protrusions. The infrasound! They used those protrusions to rumble at each other and communicate.

I felt tingles of fear creep up the back of my neck. I would never hear one of these coming.

I retracted the drone. Its housing was outside the pod in a hatch that opened and shut automatically. My whole operation was solar powered, so on a planet with two suns, we were set. I was using the "royal we" rhetorically. You know, since I was alone.

I exited the EEP. It was time to forage.

A smear of bluish-purple smoke streaked across the sky trailing behind a red ship in the distance. I stopped cold. Was that—? Was it a rescue ship? But then I remembered the beacon sitting in pieces inside my pod. Chills shot down my spine.

"VELMA, did your sensors pick up that ship streak across the sky?"

"Nanosatellite array net was breached. Nano-drones deployed."

I watched it disappear into a great bank of dark-green trees. It had to be over six hundred feet away.

"Sensors picking up electrical signals from the UFO. Possible life signs."

"Human life?" Hope the size of a small balloon inflated.

"It is not probable." My balloon made a fart noise.

"Oh my gosh. Aliens?"

"By definition, you are an alien," VELMA reminded me.

I scoffed as I hustled through the grasses. "I was here first," I said. I had a new item to add to my checklist. Evade an alien invasion. On my planet.

I cursed. I had planned on an expedition for some vegetation I could eat, as well as to collect the reptile meat, which is why I searched for animal life in the first place. And found it. But now I needed to find that ship before whoever flew it found *me*.

"VELMA, track the landing of the red ship."

"Scanning. According to my calculation, the landing site is six hundred seventy-four feet west. It would take you thirty minutes to reach the destination, putting you at risk of predation during nocturnal hours."

I bit my lip. "VELMA, patch into the camera feed of one of those nano-drones but keep it under cover."

"Patching into feed."

As long as I kept the hDEDs activated, whoever flew the ship wouldn't be able to find me. Unless, of course, they had superior tech.

"Destination reached. Thermal imaging engaged."

Even in the gloom of twilight, I could tell it was the red ship. Its charcoal hull was sleek, almost reminiscent of a bird's beak. The back bulged up like a whale. I couldn't see the landing gear. Without a frame of reference, I couldn't tell how big the ship was. I didn't see its passenger or passengers anywhere. I took over the controls for the drone and circled the area, trying to find a path into the woods. There was no trace of anything. I wished I could maneuver closer, but I didn't want the drone to be detected.

I hovered for a while but saw no signs anyone was in or around the ship.

"Would you like to deploy an off-board camera to surveille the landing site?"

"Yes." I could feel an urgency as my heart hammered and my lungs couldn't find enough air. It had to be him. He was coming for me. Prickles of sweat beads made my armpits itch.

The drone retreated into the foliage. I couldn't see what its little robotic arms were doing, but soon, another video feed patched into my screen.

"Gotcha," I said, eyes fixed on the video. "Thanks, VELMA."

"You may watch recordings from the off-board camera at any time."

Now I had to hustle.

With limited sunlight left, I hiked to the dead snakes and cut off a few strips. I wasn't prepared to make a fire and attract the rowdy nightlife or the ship's occupant, but I could adapt a heating element to cook the meat. After checking the feed once more and finding it quiet, I foraged around just outside the pod. In minutes, I had a variety of strange-looking vegetation from which to choose. Secure inside the pod, I sat samples on the scanning surface. A clear acrylic enclosure snapped down, and various tools erupted from inside the enclosure to test the fruits. One by one, VELMA spat out reports on the bio-availability of the items and their likelihood of poisoning me. One plant was marked as poisonous to humans. Its fruit was an obnoxious orange color with red spots, and it grew in the shape of a banana. Hey, it was a long shot.

Everything else was deemed safe for me to eat.

Every few minutes I inspected the video feed. Its stillness gave me eerie shivers.

Rubbing my hands together, I sat down to my first real meal in a while.

The viny green tendrils tasted like heavily peppered grass. It wasn't horrible. The green balls from the yellow-leafed bush burst in my mouth when I crunched them. They were so sour they made my eyes water. "That's gonna take a while to get used to."

The long, dark-green seed pods were next. I pulled them from the low-hanging branches of a black tree. I had high hopes for these things. They reminded me of my grandma's heirloom pole beans.

I cracked open the pods and let the purple peas drop into my hand. I sniffed them and recoiled. They smelled like stinky socks. "All in the name of science ..." I plugged my nose and put them in my mouth. I liked the texture at first bite. Cautious, I unplugged my nose and let my taste buds experience the delicacy. Okay. They tasted a bit like a strong cheese. There was just the right amount of saltiness and bite. I could almost imagine I was eating a cheeseburger. I ate some cooked meat along with it, satisfied to have a hot meal. The purple beans from the dark-green seed pods were my favorite.

"VELMA, please locate every black tree in a half-mile radius."

A map sprang up on the screen. I was set for life here.

Movement on my little drone's off-board camera caught my eye. Oh crap.

It *was* the armored guy from before. My purple burger turned to coal in my mouth. He had brought reinforcements.

22

NARAXTHEL

"We are not enemies," I announced to the quiet group. Grunts and growls met my ears. "The *Makathel* come from far away. *They* seek to steal our planets. *They* seek to subjugate our women."

Raxkarax met my eyes. He would listen. Natheka sprawled in his seat in the ship. He had already shown loyalty to me. Raxthezana refused to acknowledge me since we landed, instead sharpening his blade with a clump of black lava rock. His name meant blade-male. I would do well to remember that. I turned to Hivelt Matheza. I still felt the sting of his strike to my face. My strength had held him back from administering his death blow.

"I do not wish to be *your* enemy."

Hivelt snorted when I emphasized "your." He laughed.

"You have felt the wrath of Hivelt Matheza. And now you want to be friends."

I offered him my hand. He considered it a long tik. Then he grasped it, and we pierced the rough textured skin of each other's palms with our claws.

"We will return our wrath upon those who deserve it," he said. "Whomever it may be."

He squeezed my hand. I felt his promise and warning.

"I noticed you landed too far from the Mountains of Shegoshel," Raxthezana spoke up. "Have you no intention of obeying the queen?"

I licked my blood from my palm and faced Raxthezana. "You know better than any hunter. Why do the Ikthekal die so easily on this trek?"

His face colored from the usual moss green to a yellow hue. His armor creaked as he stood. "Do you dare to insult the death of my father?"

I must step with caution around this chasm.

"Never. What do the stories say?"

He bowed his head.

A low voice sang the song of the Mountains of Shegoshel.

"They invited us to kiss the faces of the Suns
We climbed and fell
The slaves to the Sisters
The weak at the feet of the strong
Every step closer to death
Every step closer to life
May our deaths bring life to the Sisters
May the Sisters bring life
Out of our deaths
As we kiss the faces of the Suns"

Natheka's voice echoed within the metal walls of my flyer's cabin.

"If Theraxl hunters will not admit what is right before your eyes, I will tell you!" I stood amidst them, my chest heaving as I shouted. "Our Ikma thrust a blade through the ritual of Raxshe Raxma. And when I refused to submit, she broke the oaths. Sending us to our deaths, because she did not receive what she demanded, like a petulant child!"

The hunters were silent until Hivelt spoke. "The expedition to retrieve the Waters of Shegoshel is supposed to be after a solemn cere-mony," he said. "The females send the warriors off with lilies from the fields wrapped around our necks."

"And twined in our hair fronds," Natheka added.

I stalked away from the hunters and observed the green ikfal through the window of my ship. The suns were setting, bringing the cloak of night to Certain Death. My eyes caught a tiny light.

My heart stumbled against the walls of my heart-home for the briefest of moments. Using the sight-capture in my visor, I homed in on the light. It was green and flashing in rhythmic beats. It was a small machine flying above the trees. Then it retreated deeper into the ikfal.

My little traveler lived. And sent her spying vermin ship to see my power. Challenge and fight flooded my veins in a thick rush. If I didn't have to keep the other hunters away from the female, I would hunt her down and—

A flash of her scent came to mind, along with the sensation of her hair spilling through my large fingers. Even the taste of her lips held my thoughts captive. My head bowed. What would I do to the slender willow branch? Flay her skin and disembowel her for the jokapazathel to devour?

My head shot up to observe out the window, but the small flying machine was invisible now. It was just as well. Raxthezana stood at my elbow. He spoke. "Perhaps you are the Mighty Hunter your sight-capture showed you to be."

I said nothing.

"We must show the Ikma we will not be toyed with," Raxthezana continued. "All five of us must return. We must bear the vials of the Waters of Shegoshel, as if it were a fountain. We must bear the cold lava metal in bushels and baskets. We will bring Theraxl wealth untold."

"They will sing songs of our valor in the halls and in the Court," said Natheka. "And by our deeds will they see the error Ikma did commit. Let the tribunal decide her fate."

"May the life of Shegoshel shine upon us and our offspring." That from Hivelt.

"May the death of our enemies bring peaceful slumber." And Raxkarax finished the salutation.

"We will plan now," I said, and there were no more arguments as we exited my ship into the clearing of the ikfal.

23

With steady hands and clear eyes, I soldered each wire painstakingly to its mate late into the night. "I've got you now," I muttered. The camouflage feature was engaged, my porthole closed. They wouldn't be able to find me.

I used a tweezer implement to pinch the last two wires together and touched the soldering iron to the melting puddle of metal. A satisfying thread of smoke rose into the air.

"A-ha! Take that, alien bully." I jumped up and thrust my fist into the air.

Sitting back down, I snapped the two cylindrical halves together, pressed the buttons and it lit up with a steady blink.

I sat back and stretched, popping my back. "A in electronic components class."

I put my hands on my hips and stared at the beacon. Someone was going to find me. Warm showers. Hot chocolate. Candy bars. Popcorn. Bacon. Actual cheeseburgers. Okay, why was food the direction I was going here? How about people? How about my job on Kerberos 90?

I sighed, and my smile dimmed. *Chris*. How excited should I be to go back to humanity? I shook my head.

My celebratory mood dampened by the reality of a sucky past, I put my tools away and made up my little bed. Turned off all the lights. And lay there, wide awake, thinking about the alien specter that haunted my mind, as well as the crotchety old woman who braided my hair. At least, I liked to imagine some bent old alien lady with long white braids of her own. She mixed up herbal remedies in a stone mortar and pestle. She had a humped back. And she had to have some kind of badass weaponry, because that giant spider's head was *in two*.

"Awaken, Esra Weaver. My calculations and scans show your path to the hill will be unencumbered by dangerous carnivores."

I blinked several times and rubbed the crust out of my eyes with a finger and tried to remember that last tendril of a dream. Two green-skinned aliens? Then it vanished.

"Excellent," I answered and climbed to my feet, stretching out the kinks. "I assume you used the subsonic scan?"

"I did. Upon further study, I am compiling a list of biological features of the wildlife you have encountered thus far."

"Wait," I said, cocking my head. "You did say Machine Learning Division, didn't you? Cool."

"It is most helpful you have survived each of these encounters."

I opened my mouth to speak, but what could I say to that? You're welcome I didn't die? I chuffed.

"Let me scrounge some breakfast, and I'll start my day." I put my suit on over my sports bra and jockey shorts. Last night, I had wiped down the inside of my helmet with disinfectant wipes and used an aerosol spritzer to sterilize the inside of my suit. Even after my thorough sponge bath, let's just say I was about ready to battle it out with a dinosaur or any one of those huge aliens over some fresh water. I fastened, zipped, buttoned and snapped, and clicked my helmet into place.

I checked the infrasound overlay on the screen. All was quiet this morning, just minutes before the second sun rose. I inspected the landing site of the alien ship, but it was also quiet. Did my red guy like to sleep in? Outside, I allowed myself ten minutes to gather more of the items I knew were safe to eat, and a few more unknowns for testing. I had a handful of gigantic flowers that reminded me of zucchini blooms, but they were a little dirty. If only there was a stream or something. And with my helmet on, I couldn't scent anything. In the cave, when my helmet had been removed by a mysterious being, I could smell everything. The dead spiders, the dirt, moisture ...

Yes!

I scurried back inside the pod and scanned the unknown vegetation. Took off my helmet and breathed deep of the produce. I needed to move fast. I popped the sour berries by the handful. It was like sour candy without the sugar. I used the veggies to supplement my rehydrated eggs and potatoes. It was almost like sour tomatillos salsa. Yeah, I was going with that. I put the beacon in my inflatable pouch and fixed my helmet in place.

After I set the beacon, I was going to pay my HipCow a visit, and then the cave. I bet two handfuls of purple burgers and a bundle of pepper grass there was fresh water down there, and I was going to find it if it killed me. Correction: it could kill me. And if there were more spiders down there? Maybe I should wait ... But no. It was a matter of time before the alien found my camouflaged ship, and I didn't want to be trapped inside when he did. I sniffed my armpits and grimaced. I hoped I wouldn't die for the sake of clean laundry. But it was kind of worth it.

24

NARAXTHEL

"Raxthezana noticed I landed far from the base of the Mountains of Shegoshel." I drew a map in the red dirt with a stick. "Here are the mountains." I pointed to the triangles. "The common paths up the Great Mountain are treacherous. Only think of the song."

"We climb, we fall," Natheka whispered.

"Chasm after chasm and crevasse after crevasse," I said with a nod. "There are not enough ropes on Ikshe to support a safe crossing of the mountain canyons."

"We cannot land our ship on the Great Mountain," Hivelt said. "It is forbidden."

"Why is it forbidden?" I asked the group. They were silent. "Is it tradition to do it the hard way?" I pushed.

Raxthezana spoke up. "No."

He drew our attention away from crunching into the bones of our breakfast meal.

"I have studied the mystery of the deaths of these expeditions."

I swallowed my bite and hid my surprise. The hunters, the Ikthekal, were not a curious lot. We hunted. We killed. We ate. We mated when allowed. And we did it all again until we died.

"If you knew my father, you would know he was a brutal warrior who showed no mercy," he said. "His bones were like rocks. His skin like the hide of the scabika." He plucked at his own hide. "He couldn't be killed easily. I disbelieved his death for many years." He frowned. "And so, I began studying."

He picked up my stick from the ground and drew another map.

"This is the path to the Great Mountain. This is the Great Mountain. These are the gases that spew from its mouth." He drew wavy lines. "These gases will explode the fuel of our ships. We cannot land nearer the Great Mountain."

We nodded, pleased with this information, even if it meant a more difficult journey.

"The paths will surely kill all of us," Raxkarax complained. "How does anyone survive the quest?"

Raxthezana smiled, his fangs clipping his bottom lip. His thick brow shadowed his red eyes, and his strong jaw clenched.

"I have spoken with every survivor of the past fifty cycles."

This time, I couldn't hide my surprise. "How many are there?"

"Eight," he answered. "But I tracked them all down. I wrote down every tale. Every clue. Every sign."

I nodded, as did my brethren. The Goddesses of Shegoshel were indeed with me. With us. I considered sharing my *little* discovery with them in that moment. I wondered what their reactions would be?

"The Goddesses of Shegoshel have prepared you for this journey, Raxthezana," I offered. "Do you not see it?"

He frowned. "I prepared myself."

"Oh, and did you know the good Ikma was going to select you to die on the Mountain on the same night you were selected to mate?" Natheka growled.

I held my hands out. "This is not the time for squabbles. Raxthezana has much to teach us. I will sit at his feet and learn."

I brought my frame low to the ground, adopting the pose of the young student. My companions followed. Raxthezana was taken aback but recovered with a shake of his head. He smirked and puffed his chest out, meeting our eyes one by one.

"We will not be crossing any canyons," he said with a crafty smile. "We go under the Mountain. That is the way to survive the quest."

He drew a different map of curving lines and circles. "Here are underground passageways. Caves. Water tunnels. Veins of rich woaiquovelt. The predators we need fear are the agothe-faxl. But there are five of us, and those black sisters take large areas for their own." He drew exes over drawings of the many-legged creatures. "With two per large area, we will have to kill five or six pair, total."

"Unless it is the mating season," Natheka said.

"Not for another month, at least," said Raxthezana.

"From where do we begin our trek?" Raxkarax asked.

"There is an entrance not far from here," Raxthezana answered. "Maybe thirty vel tiks."

Ah. The cave of the mud-beasts. Where I left the little traveler to die.

The Goddesses of Shegoshel were sending me very clear messages this cycle. Sadly, I was a poor interpreter and an even poorer follower. My breakfast churned in my gut. I should tell them now. For our people and for our planets, we must find the female before we do anything else.

But she is mine.

I stood at once, the thought causing my heart and heart-home to tremble against one another, as if I were an adolescent.

My brethren watched me as I retreated to the ship with no explanation. I hid in my quarters and scowled. I must tell them. I must tell them now. I took a deep breath, filling my lungs with the stale air in my ship. If I put my trust in the Goddesses, would they catch me once I fell?

25

The beacon's ready-light flashed in tandem with its invisible pulse. Strange to think it sent waves out into the reaches of space just sitting there. I gazed into the permanently tangerine-tinted sky, as if I could see anything—the *Lucidity* in orbit, for example. Nothing up there but wispy gray clouds and distant flying creatures. Still, the silence of this planet gave me the shivers.

I hiked back down to the tree line and found the game trail that opened up to the mud-slide. Hands on hips, I regarded the opening. Deep breaths. I bent over and pushed aside some foliage that hadn't been thrashed by my earlier panic. Sunlight didn't pass through much of the canopy. Layers of deep-green and a variety of possible deaths lay ahead of me. The jade serpent and the hungry plant could be the least of them. I swallowed, but it proved difficult. It felt like my throat was sticking to itself it was so dry. I didn't want to, but I needed to do this. I needed a fresh water source, and I preferred one *not* populated by giant flesh-eating reptiles. The cave was my best bet.

My heart in my throat, I squatted to a sitting position. It was time for the mud luge. This time, I was going down on purpose. Taking predator planet on my terms was how I would survive.

I grimaced. Refusing to tumble down like before, I used my boots for leverage in a controlled skid. I was lucky it wasn't raining, because the rust-colored slop was viscous enough. I held my machete-swatter with both hands, ready to impale the first beast that tried to eat me, as I made my way down in short bursts. I expected to find Fred and Mabel in their usual spot, but as I came closer to the bottom I swallowed hard and prayed I didn't run into anything else.

When I arrived, I was slathered in almost as much muck as the two large mammalians. I trudged my way around the bog, side-stepping Mabel. Fred turned and measured me in a way that made my skin prickle. I hated feeling like prey. I gulped, gripped my weapon tightly, but lowered it as I raised my free hand in a gesture I used to approach a spooked horse back on Earth.

"Easy there, big boy," I cooed, trying to reassure him. "I'm not after your girl."

He huffed out a heavy snort, reared back and lowered his head with his four eyes locked on me. I could feel the bottom of the pit quake from his movement. Copious amounts of sweat poured off me in waves. I laser-focused on him, watching for any sign he was about to charge.

"Shh," I hushed him. "I'm backing off now…" I inched away from Mabel, but Fred kept eyeballing me. I made it around to the mouth of my cave after a solid ten minutes. I breathed a heavy sigh and relaxed my muscles when Fred's disquieting stare returned to the studied indifference I had come to know. I turned toward my cave and crawled in.

I gave a humorless laugh. My planet. My cave.

Once inside, I made my way through the tunnel and came to the cavern where the dead spider was. Something was off. It still looked as fresh as the day it was killed. The wound cloven into its head glistened like new and the tissue and meat inside was still … juicy. I wanted more light.

I fished the torch out of one of my pockets and hit the high beam. Shining it around the walls, I felt like smacking myself in the head. Of course.

The beam caught crystalline sparkles everywhere. White walls, bumpy stalactite ceilings, dried rivulets of salt crystals covering the floor in a classic rimstone dam. This was a salt cavern. It was antibacterial, so this spider body would never decompose. I stepped away and took it all in again, shutting off my flashlight and pocketing it once more.

"Wooow," I whispered as I made my way further in. My helmet light shone all around. I could see the ash from the little fire. The walls were pristine, webs of white sillimanite crystals glittering like diamonds under my helmet light. If I was hoping for signs of ancient alien hieroglyphs, I was disappointed, but the untouched beauty of this place was a jewel in and of itself. "VELMA, can you do an echolocation and create maps of all the tunnels? Maybe find a water pool?"

"Scanning."

I walked over to the spider beast again and inspected its carcass. Even dead and crumpled, this thing was the size of a small car. My mysterious god-mother would have to be over six feet tall to have the advantage. I rubbed my sternum, the pain returning to remind me of how close I had come to becoming its last meal. There was a long appendage draped over its bulky remains. I leaned down for a closer look. It had a glossy black spike on the end. Like a scorpion tail, fifty times bigger. Lovely.

I stared at it. Imagined it stiff. Imagined it propelling its way toward my chest.

"You dirty bastard," I said. "You tried to stick me with that, didn't you? Come here." I held up the end, confident my gloves and suit were still protecting me from venom or poisons. I spied an orifice at the end of the spike. "VELMA, what's he packing in there?"

"A cursory volatile emissions scan detects proteins consisting of seventy-five cross-linked amino acids," the computer said. "For a more precise analysis, you would have to collect a sample and—"

"No, that's okay," I said. "Let's just call it 'instant death' and be done with it."

I tossed the spike away from me with a bad case of the jitters, and my gaze dropped to the cavern floor.

My heart stopped. My mouth dropped open, and a roiling in my stomach battled with a need to hyperventilate. I could see all my boot prints clear as day. Scuffs from when I'd crawled on my hands and knees searching for my helmet. And a boot track so big, both my feet would fit inside it.

I could feel my hands sweating inside my gloves.

I knelt and toggled the IGMC-issued camera. I placed my hand next to the boot print for reference. "VELMA, can you estimate the weight and height of this being based on the boot print?" My voice squeaked.

"My scan of the cave tunnels is complete. Do you wish to access it?"

"After," I said, still staring.

"Scanning print. Based on the depth of the print, the being weighs one hundred fifty-eight kilograms, or three hundred fifty pounds. This is adjusted to the current planet's gravitational pull. On Earth, the male would weigh one hundred eighty-one kilograms, or four hundred pounds. The male is two point thirteen meters, or seven feet tall."

"How do you know it's a male?" I said. "I mean, it could be a female, right?"

"There are scattered prints that match this one around the cave floor. I was able to judge its stride and weight distribution. It is ninety-eight percent probability it is a male."

The prints and the dead spider told the story. I let my eyes roam all over the room again.

I had been lying on the floor, unconscious. I glanced over at the huge mandibles on the spider beast. And that huge alien I saw on the hill had come in here and slain the monster. He used that blade I saw him wield when the horde descended on him.

I unfastened my helmet with haste and placed it on the ground by my feet. The salty but dank air hit me with force. With trembling fingers, I unfastened my gloves. I ran my shaking hands through the braids in disbelief. He touched me. He checked my wounds; that's why my suit was undone but my underwear unmolested. He braided my hair. My brows drew together.

I quaked on the inside as I let the silky braids slide between my fingers. I kept them because they made it easier to wash. One question tumbled around in my brain. *Why?*

"Esra Weaver, your heart rate has increased," VELMA announced. "Are you in danger?"

"I don't know," I said. "I really don't know."

I'd seen the emotionless glowing eyes when he spied me in the brush just before I fell. I'd seen what he'd done to my beacon. Why would he go to the trouble to defend me? Why would he...show me mercy?

"Sinus tachycardia detected. Are you—"

"I'm *fine*, okay?" But I wasn't. My eyes darted around the cave. The alien warrior could've been anywhere. The cold chill from glowing eyes flashed through my mind again, then him running me through with that massive blade. I felt a sudden coldness hit me in my core, and my mind screamed at me to flee. But to where?

His planet. *His cave.*

Then another notion crossed my mind. If he wanted to find me, I'd have been found. If he wanted to kill me, he could have done it ten times by now. Unless ... he was toying with me. Was he playing with his prey? I swallowed in spite of my dry mouth. Was the hunt more fun for him than the kill?

I squeezed my eyes shut and took some calming breaths. I had to stop this. Panic wouldn't get me anywhere. I placed my hand over my chest and tried to slow my pulse. I told myself if that giant, *whatever* he was, had plans for me, I'd find out soon enough. For now, I had a job to do. I needed *water*.

"I'm fine," I repeated, expelling a breath. "I'll study those tunnels now."

A map of the tunnels appeared in my screen. VELMA marked two areas that had water. I chose the closest one and trekked through the caves. The walls sparkled with minerals. I used my multi-tool to scrape some off into a small vial. It was magnetite or hematite. A streak test would confirm.

A hundred-sixty-five feet into the cave, I rounded a bend and stopped dead in my tracks.

Glowing bluish orbs floated in a small pool of water. The glowing balls revealed the edges of the pool. It bubbled gently.

"VELMA, check for noxious gases."

"The air is composed of twenty-one percent oxygen and seventy-eight percent nitrogen with harmless gases making up the residue. It is safe."

"VELMA, run that subsonic scan and a, uh, the Geiger Counter."

I wasn't taking any chances in here. This was too good to be true. The glowing lights had to be bio-luminescent life-forms. It further asserted my theory this was a salt cave. At least on Earth, there were no fresh water luminescent animals. But there were plenty in the salty oceans. This pool was super-saturated with salts. I examined the room, noticing several elaborate salt crystal shelves and stalagmites. If the orbs weren't poisonous "jellyfish" then this little spot was a paradise on death planet. I stepped closer.

"VELMA, what is the temperature of the water?"

I crossed my fingers.

"My scans did not indicate the presence of any vertebrates in the vicinity. I also took the liberty of scanning for excrements. The area is clear. The temperature of the water varies from 38 Celsius to 40 degrees Celsius."

I did the mental math. Holy halite. It was a freaking hot tub.

"VELMA, can you determine if the glowing orbs in the water are life-forms and if they are poisonous?"

I wasn't about to luxuriate with radioactive jellyfish. But it was tempting to take my chances.

"The spheres are invertebrates. I need a sample to determine the molecular structure of any excretions from the life-forms."

Oh my gosh with the excretions. VELMA was obsessed with feces.

I deliberated for six stinking minutes. Yes, it was unwise. Okay, it was tactically insane, considering every new environment produced something horrifying and deadly. But I was up to my eyeballs in all kinds of smelly filth from the moment I was dropped into this green and rusted hell, and I was sick and tired of sponging it off with my own *pisswater!* I wanted—correction—*needed* a hot bath, and it would've taken *way too long* to harvest a sample of the orbs and then hump them *all the way* back to the EEP! I stood there another six minutes, staring at the hypnotic pulsing orbs in that bubbling bath that called my name. *What about the spiders?*

I had VELMA run yet another scan. "No other lifeforms detected."

I had taken a lot of twists and turns since the spot where I lay dying. I filled my lungs. And I stripped, leaving my helmet with its opening to the side so I could hear VELMA. The cavern's air was much chillier than on the surface. Goosebumps prickled every inch of my sticky skin.

"It is inadvisable to enter the water under these conditions."

"Do you have a nose, VELMA?" I asked, gathering my undies in a bundle. I planned on scrubbing them on the rocks.

"I can detect some chemical compounds using the mass spectrometer, but I do not smell as you do."

"*Exactly* my point," I said with a dry smile. "Enable your sensors and alert me if something's coming. If I don't hear from you in the next twenty minutes, we'll call this mission accomplished, and if you don't hear from me, I hereby bequeath my effects to ..." My voice trailed off. To whoever found me first.

Maybe it was fear, more likely shock, but I was shivering from the inside out, a chill so deep in my bones I felt like I would never be warm—or clean—again. With shaking limbs, I dipped a naked toe in the water, my ears tuned to the slightest rustle of noise. Still utter silence. The spheres floated away from me at first, but I didn't care. I had the machete-swatter close in case they tried to start something. I also kept my ears open for any warnings from VELMA, and shuffling or sneaking, and loose pebbles scraping. Any sound that didn't come from me or VELMA resulted in me streaking out of the bath and swinging my weapon like a crazy woman. As much as I wanted to enjoy this little taste of home, I couldn't allow myself to relax. I knew if I did, something would appear out of nowhere and try to swallow me whole. Still, the water felt amazing and was as clean as it could've been on this planet, though a bar of soap would've been nice. I tilted my head back against the basin's edge and allowed my eyes to close. I had some soap in the EEP. If this ended well, next time I'd bring it.

No matter. I could feel the water detoxing my pores. I dipped my head and scrubbed my scalp. The water sluiced off my braids. After a few minutes, the orbs floated near me. I reached for my weapon and watched as they approached, almost like curious puppies. They "sniffed" me out, determined I was not a threat I guess, and joined me in companionable silence.

When I was convinced they weren't trying to hypnotize me with their pulsating light, or merge into some kind of gooey blob to smother and digest me, or lull me into a false sense of security with their cuteness, I placed the machete-swatter aside and scrubbed my underthings before laying them out on the flat ground. In this cave, they would dry in no time.

I gave some thought to my alien neighbor, wondered what his motivations were. I couldn't figure him out. He was a savage beast-slayer. He could have carved my liver out and ate it, but instead he tended to my wounds, and braided my hair better than Jheri back home. All I could do was shake my head in wonderment and trepidation.

With regret, I eased out of my hot tub. Okay, so it wasn't fresh water for drinking. But that was what my auto-filter canister was for. I retrieved it from its large pocket and filled it halfway. I didn't want to inundate the filtration system with the salt content. In every other way, this waterhole was near perfect. I'd call this mission accomplished, though it may have felt far more successful if I had had a towel, a virgin mojito, and didn't have an overriding fear for my life.

I dripped dry, wrung out my underwear and slipped everything back on, all the while cocking my head or turning an ear to detect sounds or movement.

"VELMA, what's the quickest route back to the EEP?"

"Inserting map now."

"Thank you." I collected some glowing remnants into another vial I had. It was too late if they were deadly, but it might be nice to know what did me in.

Honestly? I hadn't felt this good since before I "landed." I had a semi-positive outlook, and it had nothing to do with the fact a certain gigantic alien *maybe* didn't want to kill me.

26

NARAXTHEL

I was unfamiliar with the emotion swirling around inside my entrails. I was Iktheka Raxthe. I did not fear. Yet the feeling in my gut seemed to be a close relative. I did not fear for myself. I had battled an entire pack of rokhura. I considered the hunters gathered in the clearing. I thought of those bright, frightened eyes, and then the broken body, so small, on the cave floor. No, I did not fear for myself.

"I have a story to tell," I announced. They all peered at me, curiosity blazing in their yellow-ringed red eyes. "It goes no further than your ears."

Hivelt leaned forward. Raxthezana scratched his chin. Natheka cocked his head. Raxkarax gestured with his hand for me to continue.

"When I awoke from beneath the pile of dead rokhura bodies, I caught the reflection of suns' light off metal. It wasn't my ship."

Their attention was mine.

I told them of the boot print, no bigger than a child's. I told them of the beacon I destroyed. And finally, I told them of the female wrapped in a powerful suit that protected her from almost every foe on this planet.

"But where is this female now? Did you not kill the spy?" Raxthezana asked.

I met his eye. "She hid in a cave of the agothe-faxl. Even the one you have suggested we enter the tunnel system by." They nodded as if it were the end of the story. What weak creature could survive an encounter with the agothe-faxl? And yet ... "I believe she lived."

Raxthezana jumped up. "What? Nothing smaller than Theraxl lives after confronting the agothe-faxl."

"I know. I followed her in the cave. I found her just as the agothe-fax struck her chest," I said, replaying the image in my mind, that moment she collapsed to the ground before I could see her eyes one last time. "I slew the agothe-fax. Then I tried to revive her."

Natheka frowned. "You didn't use the Waters of Shegoshel?"

I pressed my lips together. Their faces contorted in anger. "I did not," I said. "But if she had been envenomated, I would have."

They gasped. Hivelt stood to his full height. "Natheka. You said this son of a *kathe* was noble."

I growled. "You would have done differently?" I challenged them all. "You would have done the ritual of *raxfathe* instead? On a female no bigger than one of our children?"

Hivelt backed off, his frown a deep groove, and turned his head away. He spat on the ground and then spoke to me. "You impugn my honor? We abide by the same beliefs. Even the spies of *Makathel* earn the privilege of fighting to the death before receiving *raxfathe*."

"Perhaps I should have told you earlier," I said. "However, I will allow no one to touch her."

Raxkarax gaped at me with horror. "You are not going to mate with her?"

My eyes widened. "What nonsense do you speak? I have a ship and a piece of prime land on Ikshe!" I shook my hair fronds. How could I make them understand what this soft traveler was to me, when I didn't understand it myself? "She bested the younger sister agothe-fax."

Raxthezana cocked his head, surprised.

"I wish to make peace with her," I said. "She may never leave Ikthe now. But she will become a mighty hunter. I will teach her."

Hivelt snickered.

I ignored him.

"Well then," Natheka said. "Where is this legendary female?"

I felt my skin darken with warmth. "I have to find her."

Their laughs rumbled the ground beneath my feet. Hivelt doubled over and guffawed. "The Mighty Hunter has lost his prey!"

I growled and stalked off into the ikfal. Let them be eaten by a rokhura.

27

I was lying to myself if I said I didn't want to meet him. I wondered about his face without the terrifying helmet. He had two arms and two legs, so I couldn't imagine his face would be that different. I saw two eyes. Maybe he had like, six nostrils or something. Or a mouthful of shark teeth. Musing about the way death planet evolved had me thinking about the creatures I'd met so far. The spiders hunted in twos. So did the snakes. I never counted the wasps. When they swarmed, it was somewhat pointless. Maybe with the two suns, Mother Nature decided to pair stuff up. Eh, I wasn't a biologist.

Now, the rocks? That was a different story. An antibacterial cave pretty much meant high salt deposits, as well as the presence of halite and sodium. In fact, I bet that pool was mostly salt, too. A water wash must run through the cave every so often. Maybe every fifty revolutions around the sun. That explained the rimstone dam, a formation that looked like rippling rock, but was, in fact, outgassed water leaving mineral precipitate behind to crystallize. The water carved out the walls and shot through the tunnels. There was high probability the source was not that far away.

I had seen the black mountain range in the distance. There could be obsidian in those mountains. If I could find more basalt, then that meant there was a huge tunnel system underneath. I'd have to sic VELMA on some seismic readings closer to the mountains. If any of those were active volcanoes, then using the cave systems could end up a deadly exercise. I was almost itching to study the rocks here. Now the beacon was up, I didn't have much time. Two weeks, tops. I knew the computer told me we hurtled through space for five light-years. But I didn't believe someplace like this wasn't charted by somebody. There had to be someone out there. Maybe not the *Lucidity*, but what about other Interplanetary Unification ships? I hoped.

I scraped my lip with my teeth as I walked through chest-high grass. I'd come out of another tunnel, still thinking and staring at the distant mountain range. I mean, I didn't have time to do an all-out geological dig, but I could at least gather some samples. I could put together a little prospectus, too. Some kind of a, I don't know, likelihood of profitable rocks present. Something Intergalactic Mining Conglomerate could use. They needed me. Enough to come find me. *Keep telling yourself that, Esra.* Speaking of rocks, it felt like I swallowed one. I blinked away a tear.

I stepped in something super smooshy.

"Aw VELMA!" I yelled. "You could have used your poop scanner to warn me about this!"

"I was told the excrement scanner was itself a piece of excrement."

"I was mad, okay? Oh my gosh, seriously! Yuck." I tried wiping my boot off in the grasses. It was a sticky mess. "That's it. Where's that lake you told me about?"

By now, both suns were up and judging by their angle, it was about eleven-ish in the morning.

"After compiling thousands of data hits from charted planetary systems and their supported life, I insist it is inadvisable for you to visit the lake, as it is eighty-nine percent probable it is a gathering place for several different creatures, many of which could be fatal to you."

"I know, but I just stepped in this stupid pile of crap you *could* have told me about." I grimaced, inspecting my boot.

The lake appeared in my visor map. It was a good two hundred feet away.

"Thank you."

I changed course, dragging my foot to try and rub more residue off. Thank goodness I couldn't smell anything. I shuddered.

"VELMA, activate the infrasound scan."

The lake came into view. I stopped short, just gazing at the teal water. It was so clear I could see the smooth rocks beneath the surface. The variety of colors hinted at a flourishing geological history. I detected unakite and granite just at a glance. Many water-tumbled rocks were orange, suggesting either rust-corroded iron, or perhaps a member of the garnet family. A wide sandy beach stretched for a half mile. The rusty sand shifted to the multi-colored pebbles of wave-crashed stone. The lake stretched as far as the eye could see with the tufts of trees or brush showing on the horizon, forming either an island or promontory from the other side. My brain fired with the possibilities. Beneath the sky that changed from blue to orange on a whim, the lake was striking in its beauty.

"At the moment, there are no vertebrates nearby. It is advisable you complete your task post-haste."

"Gah! VELMA, give me a minute," I said. "That's why AI never took over the world, you know. You're not curious enough." I took in one more panoramic view, then activated the ballast mode of my suit. I walked straight out into the water, filling my auto-filter canister as I went.

The water sloughed off the dirt and residue and grime from the last few days. I walked deeper and deeper, enjoying the gentle slope downward. With the clear water, I could see where the drop-off was, and I stopped. The fish were disappointingly similar to Earth fish. I guessed when an evolutionary edge worked, Mother Nature used it. They had dorsal fins and eyes on either side of their heads. They darted in schools and shimmered in the dappled sunlight underwater right in front of my helmet.

I stared out into the darker part of the lake. I was curious to the point of hoping nothing waited for me in ambush. I didn't know if my suit could withstand stomach acids, after all. I turned around and walked back up to the shore, breaking the surface of the water with my helmet.

"I sense the presence of several reptiles of enormous size."

Schist and Galvanite.

The dinos were back. They scuffled. I grabbed the telescopic monocle at my helmet's left and zoomed in to see a huge herd of grass-eating animals. It was the first I had seen them. They were monstrous and so numerous the reptiles weren't even making a dent. The dinosaurs were harassing one edge of the herd, driving the herbivores into a panic. They stampeded. Straight for the water.

"Oh crap!" I turned and dove back in, toggling the boots' ballast switch so I could swim underwater instead of sinking to the lake floor. I needed to go a bit over the drop-off. I hoped some nightmarish version of the megalodon was not in the lake. I swam fast and turned around to see the hairy beasts churn up the rocks and sand, muddying the water. They were so thick; I could no longer see the shore. How long was I stuck here? I searched behind me, fearing any moment some death planet form of crocodile or shark or Portuguese Man O' War was going to bite me in the butt. Or swallow me whole. I treaded water and gulped air a little irresponsibly.

"Please remain calm to avoid hypoxemia. Deep, even breaths," VELMA said in my ear. I took a deep breath.

I could get trampled underwater ahead of me or face an unknown death behind. I didn't like my choices. I couldn't see into the abyss. If the spiders here were as big as our personal electric cars, how big were the whales? "VELMA, what does the subsonic scan say?"

"A large mammal is swimming toward the herd from the drop-off."

"I don't see anything," I said, looking in all directions, but hindered by the parts of my helmet that weren't clear.

"A large mammal is approaching at a rapid rate of speed."

"I'm not seeing it, VELMA," my voice rose in panic. My eyes flashed everywhere, still nothing. "VELMA, help a girl out."

"Sinus tachycardia detected," VELMA announced. "Remain calm to prevent neurogenic shock."

"Tell me something I don't know! Like where in the hell is this so-called …"

There! A blur so big it created a huge shadow in the water. I couldn't make out a color. There was no color. It was every color. What the hell was it? I gasped for air, even though there was plenty in my suit. It was mammoth. It was silvery one minute, clear the next. The camouflage on this thing was incredible. A huge maw gaped open and grappled with one of the shaggy animals.

"Oh. Mica. Galvanite."

Flashes of dappled sunlight revealed a torpedo-shaped snout the size of my pod's nose cone. Yeah. And then white sabers snagged the back legs of an unfortunate land animal. I watched with gaping mouth and wide eyes as the legs snapped and blood clouded the water. Then the animal was gone, and the lake creature disappeared before my eyes.

"Oh, hell no," I muttered. "That was devilry. I'm leaving."

I had to take my chances with the stampeding herd. I was not getting sawed in half by that shark demon from hell.

I swam toward the fumbling legs of the beasts.

"It is inadvisable you approach the nervous herd. Given time, all will disperse, opening a safe passage to the emergency egress pod."

"Patience is not my strong suit," I argued, and pressed my way between huge limbs.

"I have witnessed this to be true," VELMA responded.

No time for talking. I needed to be farther away from the drop-off. The animals were as large as elephants. The pristine water was a muddy mess now. There was no room to navigate between the huge bodies. I puzzled it out. What if …?

I made my way to one of the submerged beasts and grabbed hold of the long hair. I pulled myself up and up until I was balancing on its back like a surfboard. I could see across several backs, all the way to shore. The muddied water swirled around the mammoths as they jockeyed back and forth, trying to avoid being eaten. I didn't blame them.

The screams of the prey summoned even more of the dino-beasts. They tore into their victims with relish, feasting without prejudice.

I sat with both hands grasping clumps of animal hair and both legs straddling the beast. I could sense its muscles bunching beneath me. She was jostled on either side by her frantic neighbors. The dinosaurs were lost in their frenzied eating. I counted around fifteen dinosaurs and estimated four mammoths down. It was hard to see them through the tearing claws and teeth of the reptiles.

If I used these hairy elephants like stepping stones, I could make my way to the north side of the meadow, right by the cave entrances. I could go back to the cave and wait out the buffet.

"Heart rate stabilized," VELMA said. "I have learned this indicates you have a plan."

"You could say that," I said between breaths. "Thanks for noticing."

A big beast rammed into the side of my ride, smashing my leg between their two bodies. I shouted and yanked my leg out. I had to stand on the broad back if I was going to do this. But I needed help. The IGMC Galvanite Mech-Drill was outfitted with some amazing tech. I wondered if my suit had anything like it.

"VELMA, does my suit have a gyroscope?"

"Engaged. I hope your plan works."

I found my balance and tried to stand. A little green indicator light showed my orientation on the upper right side of my visor. So far, so good. I would have to let go of the animal's fur now. With an eye out for the reptiles, I let go and held my arms straight out to shift my center of mass. The furry beasts were restless but starting to calm. My weight didn't seem to register with the beast I was perched on. I would have to jump about four feet to reach the back of the next one. And so on.

"VELMA, tell me when to jump so I land on the back of the next animal." I didn't give her time to argue with me; I took a couple small steps.

"Now." I landed with a whoosh, almost overcompensating but windmilling my arms. I took a couple more steps. "Now." Yes! Landed it. I kept going, jumping closer and closer to the side of the meadow. Behind me, the dinosaurs were still occupied. "Now."

Three more jumps. "Now. Now."

I looked back. And the biggest, meanest dinosaur of them all was looking straight at me. "Aw shit."

"I take your reference to excrement to mean your plan has failed."

"Nope. It means Plan A just morphed into Plan Haul Ass."

28

ΝΑRΑΧΤΗΕL
& COMPANY

We entered the agothe-faxl cave one by one, our armor shaving the inside of the cave walls. Hivelt did not fit. He dug the floor deeper using his raxtheza. The rest of us said nothing, valuing our appendages.

We came to the cavern where the dead agothe-fax lay, not far from her sister's ashes.

"Idiots," Hivelt said once he joined us in the larger room. "You have tramped about all over the tracks. We will be lucky to find one print of the female now."

I frowned. In my haste to see her again ... "We will wait for you, Hivelt."

He shoved between us without ceremony and scoured the ground. We were silent, as if noise would also disturb the tracks left by the female.

"She knelt by your boot print and placed her hand next to it. She would do well to be frightened of Theraxl."

My heart trembled against its cage once more. I willed it to stop. With little success.

"This way."

Hivelt bid us walk as close to the wall as allowed, that we might not disturb her tracks further. I noticed where she scraped mineral off the wall, yet there was little dust upon the floor. Why would she collect it? The passage led down into the darkest part of the cave. But when we turned the corner, we saw a pool of water with the *johohishe Shegoshel,* little water suns.

"She bathed," Hivelt announced.

Raxthezana snorted. "The Mighty Tracker pronounces a bath near a pool of water!" Hivelt took a step toward Raxthezana who bowed deeply. In mockery or apology, I couldn't discern.

I neared the water's edge and crouched. "She has strange feet."

The others joined me, careful not to step on the tracks.

"She is no bigger than a child," Raxkarex noted. "I can see why you would refuse the flaying and disemboweling ritual."

I swallowed bile but said nothing.

"Very small," agreed Hivelt. "Perhaps she is a child of her race."

"I thought so at first," I said. "But there was maturity in her eyes. She is adult."

"Let's find her then," Natheka announced. "We will discover her business on Ikthe."

"Indeed," said Hivelt. He turned to go.

My cagey little traveler left by a different tunnel. No one voiced their curiosity. How was she not lost in the maze of tunnels?

We came to the exit, marking the path she took through the grasses. She was headed to her vehicle. I was about to say as much when Hivelt howled with laughter.

Our eyes shot to him.

"She stepped in a pile of kathe and immediately changed direction!"

"She must be from an intelligent race, then," I said. "She is headed for the water." The others chuckled, but I had an uneasy feeling in my gut once more. "Let us make haste," I said. "The lake is a gathering place for the grass-eaters and the rokhura."

Hivelt scowled at me but said nothing. My brethren owed no allegiance to the female. "I would see her alive again," I explained to them and ran toward the lake.

We felt the rumble in our boots as we drew near a hill. We crested the hill to a magnificent sight. Hundreds of grass-eaters huddled in a giant mass, more than half of them milling in the water while a frantic few brayed at the loss of their younglings. No less than fourteen rokhura snapped their jaws through the meat and bones of the fallen grass-eaters. But one.

He was charging a running grass-eater.

And standing on its back was my little traveler, a bunch of fur clutched in one hand while the other aimed forward. I used my sight-capture to zoom in on her expression. Her eyes were wide, her brow raised. I zoomed in one more veltik. Her mouth resembled a laugh, a smiling shout. My heart gave a single, powerful thud. She bore the face of terror *and* exhilaration. She was magnificent to behold.

"Raxkarax, take point!" I said as Hivelt and I took the rearward. "Natheka and Raxthezana, flank us!" We would funnel the galloping grass-eater into our group to protect the female, and then we would kill the rokhura. I trusted them to leave any punishment to me. *She was mine.* "Do not send the sight-capture of this fight!" I yelled to my brethren. Whether or not they agreed with me, they obeyed.

The charging grass-eater would spook upon seeing us rise from the grass, but the traveler had a tight hold upon its long ears. With surprising skill, she guided it into our funnel, then we closed ranks behind it, facing the lone rokhura.

With a primeval rumble we felt through our armor, it faced us as all rokhura do: with malice and war. Hivelt attacked first, sending a flying blade into the swollen orange sac at its throat. Natheka darted behind the crazed beast and severed the hamstrings of its back leg. Raxthezana and Raxkarax fought against its thrashing tail and clawing arms. Hivelt and I stabbed at its abdomen as it fell, ensuring it would never rise again. I threw a leery eye toward the hungry pack, but the rest were still devouring their prizes. We watched its black blood soak into the trampled ground.

"Natheka and Raxkarax," I called to them. "Butcher the meat we can carry." They nodded and began the foul job.

As the rest of the pack was still preoccupied with its meal, we trailed the grass-eater and its rider, a slower pace allowing us to keep a wary eye out for other predators. Down the hill, through the meadow, and then toward the traveler's vehicle.

None of us spoke. Natheka and Raxkarax joined us with their full packs of meat. We all glanced at one another, wondering what would be accomplished next.

A more awkward encounter with another race was never seen.

My brethren and I shared looks and watched the female stand and ride. We reached the clearing where her ship stood, tiny and proud. She pulled up on the beast's ears, and it stopped.

We approached the front of the beast. She gazed at us.

"Yubrotyurfrenz." Her voice pleased me. It was amplified from inside her helmet.

I did not know this greeting, but she addressed me. She recognized me. My heart thumped against its chamber with great force, bringing me great alarm and confusion. I did not speak.

"Du jax za talajofal," Hivelt said with surprise in his voice. *You ride the grass-eater.*

She stared at us a moment. Then, as if remembering where she stood, her face crumpled in horror. It was clear she did not know how to dismount the creature. We couldn't help her. The grass-eater stood still. She still had its ears grasped in the one hand.

Her brows lifted as she met my eyes.

I mimed she should let go of the ears.

I studied her eyes, so like a pale lake jewel. She nodded. Our first communication. My chest swelled as she stared at me and dropped the ears.

The *talajofal* didn't move. Her face relaxed.

Her mouth moved, but we heard nothing.

Then she gestured to her vehicle behind us. I noticed a panel open in its side and a long metallic pole extend. I walked to the pole and grasped it. It released from the vehicle and I approached the animal cautiously. I peered up at the female, and she held her hand out for the pole.

I leaned it toward her and she took it, shaking her head and moving her mouth.

I wanted her to remove the helmet. I wanted to hear her voice again, even though I didn't know her language. Or her race. Or her home world.

She grasped her hands around the pole about one-sixth of the way from the top, then jumped.

We stood astonished, as she vaulted off the grass-eater, using the pole for balance. She landed in a crouch, just south of us and nearer her vehicle.

My lips rose in a smile. Clever female. She now had a weapon and a bunker.

She stood, leaning as if to rest on her metal pole. I knew better.

"She's a clever one," Hivelt spoke my thought aloud. "She has a weapon now."

"And her ship. She could leave at any moment," Raxthezana said.

"No," I said quietly. She watched our mouths carefully, as if to decipher our language. "If she could have left, she would have already."

"Her little ship will not have enough fuel to break through the atmosphere," Natheka said. "She is stuck on Ikthe."

"Aren't we all?" Hivelt muttered. The others didn't hear him.

When we didn't make any move toward her, she relaxed her stance. She used one hand to reach behind her helmet.

She removed it, and my heart and heart-home sang together. She wore her braids. Too late, I saw my error. Hivelt leaped and grabbed her, holding her against him with one huge arm, and gesturing to me with his other. "What is the meaning of this?"

29

"VELMA," I croaked. "Do you have any idea what they're saying?"

The last time a man held me like this, it didn't end well for me.

The huge one almost had me by the throat, but he couldn't squeeze because of the inflexible axial ring that connected my helmet to my suit proper. My feet were dangling, and my ride had wandered away without so much as a by-your-leave. Thanks a lot, Snuffle-upa-gus. And I could feel the blood thumping across my chest and shoulders where the alien had me in a vice grip. *Breathe, Esra.* I took a deep breath, and the sweltering stinky air burned my throat. I had both hands gripping the huge metal-encased arm across me, and I flailed my legs, trying to reach the solid ground beneath. Images of Chris's bullying flitted across my mind.

"I cannot translate at this time," VELMA announced from my helmet that lay at the big alien's feet.

I let my eyes plead with the red-armored alien. The one who I guessed had braided my hair. I recognized his helmet and armor color. They all wore ferocious helmets, but they were all different. Customized. They were equal in their menacing construction, but that red armor? I'd remember it anywhere. I gasped when he lifted his arms to remove his helmet. Oh. Mica. Galvanite. I was going to see his face.

"VELMA, did you find out what race this is yet?" I squeaked. "Did you download the language? A little help here?"

The muffled voice said, "I do not have access to that information."

His entire armor was angular with sharp edges like the F-117 Stealth fighters of a few centuries ago. (Got an A in my Ancient Aerodynamic Mechanisms class.) His helmet came off, and I saw the most amazing and terrifying eyes of my life. They were black with a bright-golden ring around a blood-red iris. I saw no pupils, just the red. His skin possessed the texture of shark skin, but it was a sage green. He had no beard but a wide square jaw and at least two big incisors. Okay, fangs. He had fangs. His cheekbones were high and angular, just under his eyes, and his sleek brows slanted away from his eyes, almost like a bird of prey. His nose was humanoid, but sharp and hawkish with two nostrils. His ears were obscured by long, greenish-brown hair fronds— I didn't know what else to call them. It was like hair, but also like palm leaves. The fronds fluttered about his head when the wind blew. He had a thick neck, and I could just make out the musculature of his shoulders before his armor covered everything else. In a word, he was beautiful.

I blinked away some moisture gathering in my eyes as I regarded the alien. "Will you help me?"

The big guy holding me spoke first. "Du rax za Ikma yashezaza … bu za Yasheza Mahavelt?" He flipped my braids when he said it.

Oh snap. Was my potential ally in trouble for the hair? I had considered letting the big hairy beast carry me all the way into the forest and leaving my pod camouflaged. But I took a gamble these guys weren't going to kill first and ask questions later. Now I was sweating it. Even if the red one wasn't going to kill me, maybe the braids were a bad idea for some cultural reason I wasn't privy to. I needed to make them understand.

"He was being nice! I was almost dead!" I wished I could see the others' expressions, but … helmets. I had another idea. I snaked a hand under his arm and up my chest and unfastened the front of my suit.

Day three or four? My bruise was *hideous*. I bared my chest, where the black and blue had turned purplish and greenish and ... it was a mess. I had inspected it when I bathed earlier.

"See this? I almost died!" I pointed to the red-armored guy. "*He* saved me!"

I had no idea if they were understanding my message, but the big one loosened his hold.

My friend took a step toward me, holding out his hand. His deep frown spoke volumes. His eyes flashed. He said some harsh-sounding words, and then the big one let me down.

I stumbled to the red one's side, not wanting to give the big guy a second chance to put me in a chokehold. I didn't stand too close to the red one, but I gave him the side-eye. He spared me a short glance. I tried to gauge the mood. Were they going to fight? The assortment of weapons in just this circle of aliens could rival a platoon back home. I observed their hands, a couple of them poised near hilts. The blood drained from my face, and my extremities trembled. I needed an ally. The red one stared at his companions but laid a huge, steady hand on my shoulder. I could feel my pulse slow at the gesture.

To think just a few days ago he was going to put my head on a pike. I practiced a relaxation breathing technique, but couldn't help darting my gaze at all of them. Which one might snap? Who was most dangerous to me?

When I noticed a couple of the other guys were eyeballing my abdomen and gray sports bra, I zipped up my suit again.

The red one rumbled deep in his throat. Then he spoke some more harsh words. It sounded like they used the "ex" sound an awful lot. I wanted to know what they were saying to each other.

I watched the other ones. Their postures relaxed. The big one dropped his hands. Okay. My ally made some progress. I hesitated. Was it time for introductions?

I studied all of them, but I could only see Red's expressions. As long as no one was holding a weapon, I had to assume they weren't going to attack me.

"Hey, oh hey, hi, um." I waved my hands at them all when I started talking. They moved in closer. Sweat was pouring off me at this point. I was going to need *another* bath after this. "My name is Esra." I put my open hand on my chest and met their eyes in turn. I patted my chest for emphasis. "Esra."

Red put his hand on his chest. "Naraxthel Roika."

The others showed some surprise or disapproval. I couldn't begin to guess what kind of cultural nuances I was missing. I puzzled up my eyebrows at him. "Naraxthel?" I whispered. He gave a curt nod.

I turned to the next one in line expectantly. He shuffled his big boots. I raised my eyebrows.

He glanced at the others and spoke. "Iktheka."

"That wasn't so hard, was it?" I smiled at him and nodded. Turned to the next.

"Iktheka."

"Um," I turned to the first guy. "I thought you were Iktheka?" He scowled. The second one with the barrel chest scowled, too.

I pointed to the third.

"Iktheka."

"Oh, for Pete's sake," I said, throwing my hands in the air. "You guys are jerking me around, aren't you?" I shook my head and put my hands on my hips. "This is not the second grade, Mr. I P FREELY." I scrutinized the first guy, the one with the helmet that resembled a lion. I frowned right back at him and stared him down.

He stared right back.

Oh ho, I could do this all day. Jackass. I folded my arms. I heard Red chuckle behind me. I held a straight face.

Finally, the big one with the black lion helmet lifted it off his head.

I took a step back. He had the same features as Red, but different. Bigger. More fronds. Darker eyes. Longer lashes. And he showed *all* of his teeth. Uh. Fangs. Long fangs. I quivered.

"Hivelt," his deep voice growled. "*Iktheka* Hivelt."

He told me his name. And apparently it was a big deal, and apparently, I should address him as *Iktheka*. For the sake of interplanetary relations? I could do that.

"Thank you," I said, dipping my head. "Iktheka."

Then the next one did the same. He lifted his helmet that was reminiscent of that shark-thing in the lake, with lots of emblazoned teeth, a dark-gray color, and blunt snout. With his helmet off, I saw his skin was a darker green, and his eyes a less-intense red. He was burly and hard-edged. He spoke with a frown. "Raxthezana. Iktheka Raxthezana."

"Iktheka," I said, bowing my head a little.

The third guy lifted his helmet along with the fourth. I frowned at them. The third one was reminiscent of a dire wolf, which was terrifying. And the fourth one? An awful lot like that spider that about killed me. I took another tiny step back.

Wolf-armor spoke. "Natheka." He was leaner than the others. Like a runner-version of the alien race.

I raised an eyebrow when he didn't add the prefix. "Iktheka Natheka?" I pronounced, hoping I wasn't butchering it. He smiled. I exhaled.

And finally, Spider-armor. He was as tall as Red, but thicker around the middle and sported longer hair fronds.

"Raxkarax," he said, then turned to Red. "Yasheza Mahavelt hicon Ikthekal bu ropazathelvelt Shegoshel."

"VELMA, did you catch that?"

A muffled reply.

I held up a finger and retrieved my helmet. When I turned back around, I noticed everyone but Red had their hands on their hilts. Oh geez. Like I was any kind of a threat to them *at all*.

I held the opening toward my ear, so I could hear VELMA's response.

"Can you repeat that?"

"I am cataloguing the language. I should have a working translation in seventy-two hours. The more of their language I hear, the better I will be at translating."

"Thanks."

Red spoke in harsh tones and shook his head, no. I marveled that nodding and shaking were universal symbols. Yes and no. Life and death. Black and white. It gave me some hope we might be able to communicate. From what I could guess, Naraxthel didn't like Rax's suggestion. And he was very vocal about it. And gesturing with his clawed hands. Wait. Were those clawed gloves? Or actual clawed hands? I swallowed. The sweat continued to pour down the back of my neck. I kind of wanted to replace my helmet and escape the stifling heat and powerful odor of overripe vegetation, but I felt like every move I made would be scrutinized and suspect.

The one who smiled at me, what was his name? Nath—something. I'd call him Nathan. He sided with Red, judging by body language.

Hivelt, I could remember because he was so tall, you know, high in the air. Hivelt. He agreed with Rax.

So, shark-face with the long name I couldn't remember had the deciding vote. I tried to swallow but my mouth was too dry. I offered him a small smile and raised my brows. Tried to look as non-threatening as possible. But then I realized the combined weight of their helmets *alone* was heavy enough to crush me. Who was I kidding? I didn't even rate on the threat scale for them. I stepped closer to Red. I figured I would agree with Red if I knew what he was saying. Because we went way back. Like five days or more. We were tight. I hoped. I forced a swallow down.

Shark-face stepped near Rax and folded his arms.

Oh schist.

With three against two, I mean, I could stand next to Red all day, but I knew my vote didn't count, Red lost this one. I tossed him a hopeful smile and walked to my EEP.

A shout. I looked back and Hivelt was walking toward me.

I took another step toward my EEP.

He took a giant step and stood between the hatch and me.

I closed my eyes and took a deep breath through my nose. Opened my eyes. I pointed to my hatch. "Esra. Esra go inside." I motioned ducking and entering. Hivelt growled.

"Esra." Naraxthel's voice came in my ear because he stood right behind me. I didn't even hear him move. You would think someone his size would be louder. He touched my back with a claw. "Esra, hicon Naraxthel."

He patted my arm and then his own arm.

I stepped back. "No," I spoke firmly. "Esra ship." I indicated my pod. "Esra ship. Now." I took another step, even though it brought me closer to Hivelt.

"No," Naraxthel repeated. "Esra hicon do. Naraxthel." He didn't come after me. Just used his voice and his eyes. I was to stay with him.

I blinked away tears. I had things I had to do in my pod. Eat. Pee. Stuff. "No hi-cone-doe-Naraxthel!" I stepped right next to Hivelt and raised my eyes. "Esra. Ship." I frowned at him. A tear slipped out of the dock and I swept it away. Hivelt's brows wrinkled and his mouth grimaced. Turning away, he left an opening, and I took it. I leaped inside my EEP and shut the hatch.

I took deep gasping breaths.

I was alive. I felt like checking all my limbs. Oh my gosh, I was alive. That thing in the water. And the stampeding herd of shaggy huge grazers, and then the reptiles ... I let the horror wash over me with quivers and shudders that racked my whole body. I filled my lungs with air and blew out. I. Was. Alive.

I did my business, wiped down my face and peered out the port-hole to see the aliens. They stood watching the EEP, as if waiting for it to launch. I shook my head. Is that what they were worried about? I yearned for translation. I pressed my hands into the inside wall and put my head down. I needed to exit this planet and re-enter the human race. "VELMA, can't you run some kind of program that gives me the odds of being rescued?" She was silent for a full minute.

"There was not an appropriate time to inform you."

I tipped my head and let my vision of the inside of my ship go blurry. "Uh, since when does AI care about timing? What on Earth ... er ... this planet, are you saying, exactly?"

"The likelihood of anyone receiving your distress signal is one chance in a hundred quintillion."

"Wait, wait, wait. What?" My heart stopped for a second.

"You seem to be experiencing a mild arrhythmia. Do you require assistance?"

"Oh, don't you change the subject, you ephemeral piece of excrement!"

This was not happening. This could not be happening. I busted my back to finagle that beacon up and running. Hope was my only fuel at this point. Dinosaur-sized reptiles, deadly serpents, spiders the size of small cars, and an alien race big enough to make gorillas think twice...

not to mention I had a limited number of MREs and a finite supply of medicines in the EEP. Add to that I had to wear my suit everywhere I went if I wanted to live, and I was a walking-talking recipe for a nervous breakdown.

"You use excrement and euphemisms for excrement out of context," VELMA replied.

"How could you do this to me?" I asked. I started to hyperventilate. "How could you let me hope something and then dash it all to pieces! I don't even know what to say right now!" I clenched and unclenched my fists, removing my helmet and tossing it on the floor. I sat with a huff and rested my head between my knees.

VELMA spoke. "This planet is uncharted. The Interplanetary Unification of Races doesn't know about this planet or this people. But the race does have interplanetary travel. Perhaps you could convince them to help you."

Was there some possibility we could work together? To find a civilized intergalactic society? I grimaced. Maybe these aliens were civilized. I took a restorative breath and cracked my neck. Time for Interplanetary Peace Relations 201. I grabbed a few pouches of food, hesitated over the water pouches, but pulled my hand away, and egressed.

They regarded me with an eerie stillness.

I offered them each a pouch. The pouches resembled ramen noodle seasoning packets in their big hands. Oops.

I demonstrated opening one up and took the water canister I had filled at the lake out of my pack. I poured it in each of their pouches. Then I ate. They watched me and each other with raised brows and wide eyes.

Finally, Red slurped up his meal in one gulp. He cocked his head then licked his lips. He smiled and nodded. Beef stroganoff. Check.

The rest of them ate theirs in one bite as well. They nodded but withheld smiles. That was okay. I wasn't a fan of spaghetti and meatballs or beefy mac either. That's why I gave Red my favorite. I winked at him, but he just stared. Okay, winks weren't universal.

"Well, we should talk," I said, and sat on the ground with crossed legs. I patted the ground. "Actually, I need you guys to talk. So my computer can decipher your language. There's a lot of "ex" sounds and "kay" sounds and basically a lot of hard consonants." I smiled at them. They returned my gaze with blank looks.

I motioned to Red, then the others. "Talk, you know, blah blah blah?" I pointed to my mouth, and then Red's. He paused, but then sat beside me. I pointed to his mouth again. "Talk." I pointed to the others. "Blah blah blah."

Abject confusion.

I smacked my head. Ugh! I stood and walked up to the pod. I put my hand on it. "Ship." I repeated myself. Then I waited.

Naraxthel's eyes lit up. "Woashegoshenaiksheza."

"That's your word for ship? Holy crap." I slumped my shoulders. No way I was learning their language. They needed to learn mine.

Shark-face spoke up. "I, i, i. Yasheza Mahavelt pa *woahoza*."

Naraxthel stood and joined me at the pod. He put his hand lower, right by the engines and thrusters. "Woashegoshenaiksheza."

Shark-face stalked over. He put his hand on mine. "Woahoza."

"Okay, um," I stammered over the words. "Wo-uh-hoe …?"

Shark-face smiled at me. "Ik! Woahoza!" He slapped me on the shoulder so hard I spun. Red frowned and barked something at Shark-face. He called him Raxthezana. Um. I couldn't call him Rax, because the other one was Rax. Maybe Thezana? I rubbed my shoulder.

Naraxthel knelt by the engines. "Woashegoshenaiksheza," he said quietly. Oh crap. He wanted me to say the long word. It must mean engine.

"Okay, uh, wo-uh-sha-gosha-na-ick-sha-za?" I put my hand on the main thruster.

"Ik!" He beamed at me, those pearly fangs gleaming in the fading light. My heart did a flip-flop.

The afternoon suns cast a rosy glow upon our faces. Even so, it was a hundred degrees or more. I didn't have my helmet, so no more temperature control. It made me think of another word we could try. I pointed to the suns. "Suns." Then I thought better of it. I held up two fingers. "Sun," I said, and pointed to one. "Sun." Pointed to the other. "Suns."

"Ah." Hivelt nodded from his spot on the ground. The others had sat. "Shegoshe. Shegoshe. Shegoshel." He pointed with long claws to the suns.

Wow. We were talking. I stumbled a little and Red caught my elbow. He showed me to my spot. He raised his eyebrows and lifted the water canister from my tool belt. He offered me a drink and said, "Hohishe."

Water. I drank and sat, suddenly very weak. It had been a long day, after all.

"Hohishe. Water."

They all murmured "Water," tripping over the "er" pronunciation a little, but it made my heart swell. We were having a Helen Keller moment, and it was awesome.

30

NARAXTHEL

If another hunter laid a hand on my soft traveler, I would remove his head from his body. For the sake of peace and the Holy Sisters of Shegoshel, I remained calm. But I had seen the curiosity and wonder in the hunters' eyes when her suit was open. Esra was mine.

After some stumbling attempts at speech, we learned she wanted to sleep inside her ship. She also made a show of placing her helmet near all of us, and made an odd motion with her hands, bringing her thumb in contact with her four fingers in a repetitive movement. She pointed to all of us, at our mouths and ears, and patted her helmet. We did not know what she wanted, but we had no quarrel with tending her helmet, if that was what she wished. She also showed us the interior of her ship, though we were too large to fit in the doorway. It was as we suspected. Her ship was created to land, not to leave. She was trapped on Ikthe.

Our language was not developed enough to ask why she came to Ikthe in the first place. But with time, we would speak together.

My brethren and I created a perimeter around her small ship, rather than return to mine. I walked around her pod, inspecting the alien design. I noticed several scratches and the prints of the rokhura as if it had been stepped upon. One of the legs was propped up on a flat rock, but otherwise, there was no extensive damage. I wondered what material her ship was constructed with.

I joined my brethren in making a fire and cooking some of the butchered meat and smoking the rest for our cross-planet journey. I considered retrieving my ship, but our path to the mountains did not provide a convenient place to land. We would hike. I added a large piece of deadwood to one of the fires and glanced at the soft traveler's ship. I puzzled at her fragility and my own curiosity. I snorted. What of it? My brethren and I would take turns at watch this night.

I was satisfied she was well protected within the walls of her little ship. I sat against a tree, a few veltiks from her ship, facing the hatch.

"The soft traveler has a hardness about her," Natheka said. He sat down beside me. "I have never seen a female ride a grass-eater."

"Have you ever seen Theraxl ride a grass-eater?" I asked him.

"No." He stuck a long blade of jokal grass between his teeth. "I have also never seen a female cause Hivelt to turn away in shame."

"You know the songs," I said.

"Yes, yes, the songs of raxshe and raxma. *Should you make your female cry, the Sisters will bleed you dry*," he said. "It is an Elder Sister's tale to scare the younglings."

"And yet do you know of any hunter who will willingly cause a female to cry?" I stared at his calm face, the pale moonlight casting his red eyes into shadow.

He snuck a glance at me and grinned. "I am looking at one."

He referred to our Ikma. "She did not cry."

"Not with her eyes, fool," he said. He considered the small moon. "She cried with her anger. Commanding us to retrieve the Waters of Shegoshel and the cold lava."

I sneered. "If those are her tears, then I am truly afraid of her fury."

"You know Raxkarax is right," he said after a tik. "Yasheza Mahavelt comes with us to the mountains of Shegoshel."

"If the Ikthekal Raxthel die so easily in the mountains, what will the soft traveler do?" I asked quietly, staring at the ship limned by blue moonlight.

"Perhaps she will ride the agothe-faxl and lead us into battle."

I laughed. I had forgotten Natheka was a good friend with humor to lighten a dark day.

"I do not want to put her in further danger," I began. "But Ikthe *is* danger. She will be safer with me."

"With all of us," he parried.

"You, yes," I said and pulled my own shaft of jokal grass. Bit into the peppery blade. "But I do not trust Raxthezana."

"He doesn't trust you, either," he said. "You are the reason we are not enjoying the act of creating more mighty hunters of our own."

I pondered his accusation. I wondered if I should confide in my friend, the odd behaviors of my own heart. Perhaps it was the ingestion of too much fruited wine.

"How are your two offspring? You have two hunters, no?"

He shrugged. "They are two and four. Their mothers say they are mighty, mightier than their father."

Something in his tone was sad.

"Is it not the pinnacle of your life? Your lineage continues onward," I said. "You are a true Iktheka. Theraxl with posterity."

The nighttime insects sawed in our ears, escalating with the deepening gloom.

"Sometimes I wish for my adolescence again," he said quietly. "When my heart and heart-home were free of one another for three cycles. Do you ever wonder why …?"

"What are you two sods talking about?" Raxkarax lumbered over and sat with a huff. "These damned bugs are so loud. I miss my ship," he said. "Why are we not bedding down in your ship, Naraxthel?"

"We leave for the Great Mountain on the morrow," I said simply. "Good night."

I wondered what Natheka had been about to say. I suspected it was the same thing I had wondered for many cycles. Why would the Goddesses give adolescents the sensation of finding their Heart Mates, that fleeting liberation of hearts from heart homes for three cycles, only to reintroduce the heart to its cage, never to release again? The old tales made no sense of our physiology. But I did remember that exquisite torture of my youth, when my heart breathed free and optimism shone from every light in the sky.

31

"Would you like to hear what I have deduced from the language so far?" VELMA asked me just as the second sun came up.

"Um, how about in two hours? I'm exhausted." It didn't matter how much sleep I got, I always felt tired. Plus, I tossed and turned all night, knowing they were right outside my ship. I didn't know if I should feel safe or oppressed.

"You were snoring. I will run a diagnostic scan for sleep apnea and administer the necessary medicines as needed."

"No, VELMA, that won't be necessary. I think I just have some allergies." Allergies to nosy artificial intelligences. "I don't suppose you're going to let me go back to sleep, are you?"

"The hunters outside the EEP are eating a morning meal," she said. "They appear to be waiting for you."

I sighed and stood up, stretching. They were the reason I couldn't sleep. And now the reason I couldn't sleep in. Somebody was going to pay for this.

I took care of my morning ablutions and then mulled over the idea that kept me up half the night. VELMA reminded me they had interplanetary travel. There were no signs of dwellings on this planet. Presumably, these hulks came from somewhere. I slid open a drawer of pouches and counted them. Took a deep breath and closed my eyes. Was this fun? No. Could I live here for... a while? Yes. I shelved my idea for now.

I peeked out the window again to watch them mill around, scratch themselves and spit. They had constructed a rack over a smoking fire; it appeared they had been smoking meat all night. I raised a brow then turned away. I found the vial of water from yesterday's adventure and popped it into the analyzer. "VELMA, this sample is from the pool in the spider cave. Check it for precipitates such as calcite, or for bioluminescent bacteria."

The analysis wasn't necessary for my survival. Just my curiosity.

I reviewed my new to-do list. Reframe my life on a predator planet. Make friends with the warriors. Finagle another bath, although I'd probably have to go without soap. I wouldn't want to kill the harmless jam blobs.

I paced inside my pod. I needed to go out and face them. I needed to prove to them I was valuable. But how? I rapped the wall of my pod with my knuckle and took a deep breath. It was go-time.

"Naraxthel?"

He stepped from behind my pod, bigger than I remembered. More handsome than I remembered, and that was strange because, you know, different evolutionary path and all that.

"Esra?" He crooked his brows and cocked his head.

I offered him a pouch of hydrated scrambled eggs. I searched out the others and noted one stood aloof and three others stood together murmuring among themselves.

Naraxthel took my offering with a gracious nod. I strode to the group of three and offered them food as well. I watched the play of emotion on their faces, amused to recognize discomfort as they shuffled, frowned and avoided eye contact. They didn't like the food. I smiled and shrugged at them, retaining the eggs for my storage. In all honesty, I couldn't afford to share so generously. I spied the lone warrior, the one with the shark-like helmet of yesterday, though he didn't wear it at present. I racked my brain to recall his name. Rax something. Rax...the...Zana!

"Raxthezana," I said. His head shot up. He brushed his boot over several scratches in the ground. At a glance, it appeared to be a map. I offered him a pouch. He stared at it a long second. Then held out his hand.

My heart burst with a tiny joy bubble. "Eggs." I pointed to the food.

"Aygzz," he repeated. I smiled at him.

He took a bite and chewed, then swiped at his lips with a thick tongue. I glimpsed his fangs; one was broken. He nodded.

"Ik. Hirax," he said.

I felt my face grow warm when the others looked at me but remained silent. He stared at me while he chewed his bite, so I ate mine and stared back. When we both finished, I held my hand out for the pouch. He turned a quarter-turn away from me and inspected the pouch. His dour expression returned, and he brushed at me with his hand, as if to shoo me away. He kept the pouch.

"Um, okay then. Bye." I backed away, but let my gaze fall to his dirt sketch. What was left of it showed crude renderings of mountains and something resembling the spider-scorpion creature. My heart stuttered, and I swallowed. He grunted at me, seeing my face, and rubbed out the rest of the scratches with his big boot.

I walked past the three who stared. Naraxthel leaned against my pod, sharpening one of his knives with a whetstone. I watched his eyes as they traveled from my boots up to my braids. It quickened my breaths. I felt sweat bead at my hairline. I couldn't help the curiosity, wondering what it had felt like to have his fingers twist and pull my locks into braids. I wiped my eyes with a hand and shook my head.

"Are you finished?" I pointed to the pouch he'd stashed in a loop at his waist.

He sheathed his knife and pulled the pouch out, handing it to me with a small smile. He nodded at the group of males who now talked quietly, occasionally glancing at us.

"No pax," he said. I frowned and shook my head. I thought he learned "no" last night, but I didn't know what pax meant.

He pretended to eat. "Pax." He nodded to the others again. "No pax." He shrugged.

I laughed. "Oh. Right. No pax." I looked beyond the group to Raxthezana. "Uh, Raxthezana pax."

"Ik, ik." He pocketed his whetstone and stood to his full height, taking my breath away. He spoke loud enough for the others to hear, but he looked at me. "Shegoshel havelt."

The others, including Raxthezana, bent to retrieve their packs or weapons and helmets.

Taking my cue from the others, I grabbed my helmet and put it on.

"Woa is the word for sky," VELMA said. "Woahoza means ship. Woashegoshenaiksheza is the word for engine."

"Uh, VELMA, I already know all those. Add "Shegoshel" to your dictionary. It means "suns"."

She ignored me and kept speaking. "I have parsed out some of the phonemes and their morphology."

"Oh," I said. I watched the huge males methodically pace the perimeter of my landing site, gathering the dried meat, putting out the fire, sweeping away signs of their presence and going so far as to fluff up flattened grasses. They shouted and gestured at each other, distracting me, but I wanted to pay closer attention to VELMA. I glanced at Red and pointed to my ship, then entered it.

When I entered, VELMA picked up her lesson right away. "The following phonemes stand out. Woa, as you know, means sky. When placed next to the phoneme "ho", it seems to denote movement, such as come or go."

"Go on," I said, trying to remember everything.

"The phoneme "za" might be a particle denoting an object. For example, in the word for engine, "za" is found at the end of the collection of phonemes."

"Okay," I said and sniffed as I stared out the porthole. They tightened scabbards and adjusted their armor.

"Would you like me to administer an allergy shot?"

"Thank you, no. It's not a big deal," I said.

"Would you permit me to test your blood for mild dehydration? Or perhaps you would like to utilize my psychotherapy program?"

"No." Not what I needed. "Listen, VELMA, I wondered about

asking the aliens if they could take me off-planet and contact the *Lucidity* or the Unification somehow." I sniffed again. "But I'm not sure if I trust them just yet. So, I guess I'll bide my time."

Sniffing reminded me of when I cried in front of them yesterday. Why did they act strange every time I shed a couple tears? So many barriers. Language, cultural, physical ....

"Have you received any pings?" I asked.

"I have not received any pings. The beacon is functioning properly." She paused. "Your repair was adequate."

I laughed a little. "Thank you for the compliment."

A slap on the outside of the hatch startled me.

"VELMA, who's at the door?"

"The one called Naraxthel. I have deduced the phoneme "ell" signifies a plural. When I have the lexicon established, I will be able to translate the noun in Naraxthel's name."

"Okay," I said. "Thanks."

I opened the hatch but didn't go out. I stayed right inside.

"Ah, Esra?" He gestured "come here" with a clawed hand. "Esra hicon Naraxthel." His helmet was under his arm, so at least I could attempt to decipher his expressions.

I scowled but raised an eyebrow. "Esra hicon Naraxthel now?"

He growled. "Esra hicon Naraxthel." Again, he gestured. Impatiently.

"The phoneme "cone" seems to denote the word "with"," VELMA said in my ear.

"Thanks, VELMA. I got it."

He stood, sober and determined. But he didn't reach in and try to grab me. And he could, if he wanted to.

I peeked around the corner at the others. All of them were standing with packs and weapons and helmets on. Oh. They were going somewhere. Oh schist. Were they leaving me? Was Naraxthel saying goodbye? Were they flying off-world? Should I ask if I could come with them? My grip on the doorway tightened. Let's run through that scenario. What if they took me to their ship? Brought me closer to real civilization instead of this tooth and claw existence? But what if they had more sinister plans for me? Nausea gripped me for a moment. I felt blood drain from my face. I looked into Naraxthel's eyes, trying to find something, anything, a sign of goodwill.

His brows softened and he smiled. He waved his hands at the packs and weapons. Then tapped his own. Then he pointed to me. "Esra zal? Esra hicon Naraxthel?"

He reached out a single claw and caressed my chin. My heart flipped, and I gasped. His touch startled me with its tenderness. Why did I react this way to an alien? I shook my head from the fog of confusion.

"Um, okay, hang on," I said. What did he say? Zal. I knew this. VELMA just told me "za" was like an object. Like a thing, or something. And "ell" was plural. So, objects. Esra objects? He had indicated all the packs.

Oh.

Ohhhh. I was supposed to pack my things. Maybe? And go with them?

"Esra hicon Naraxthel. Esra *zal*," I said back to him. He nodded and bared all his fangs. All his lovely fangs. How did they keep them so white? My mouth dried up. Okay, things. My things. What things? How many days?

I had to think about this. They probably weren't planning on killing me. All of them, including Red, had had plenty of opportunity, and maybe even reasons to. But they hadn't. I could insist I was staying, but do what? Wait for the beacon to summon help? My one in a quintillion chance or whatever? And there was the possibility they wouldn't even let me stay. I couldn't really fight against them, shedding a few tears notwithstanding. I may as well go and see what happens. And again, try to show them I was worth keeping around. Naraxthel watched me bite my lip and look at all the others.

I found my biggest satchel and stowed MREs and water pouches. I already had some sample vials, my multi-tool, and assorted other gadgets, as well as my mineral test kit. A last look. Anything sentimental was left on Earth a *very* long time ago.

I activated my mic. "Okay, I'm ready."

"Esra zal?" he asked me again and touched my pouch.

I slung it over my shoulders and fastened it everywhere, so it became seamless with my suit.

"Esra zal," I confirmed.

Wow. I followed their single file line as we headed into the woods. I spared a single glance to my lonely ship, its gleaming metal harsh in the wild landscape. "VELMA, activate hDEDs."

"Confirmed. Pod camouflaged."

32

NARAXTHEL

I brought up the rear of our line, watching Esra step carefully through the woods. And yet she was as loud as a rokhura breaking through the tree line. How was it possible one so small could make so much noise? Perhaps her helmet prevented her from hearing her own noise?

"Esra," I spoke softly. She turned to me, a question on her face. Hm. She could hear. But what would I say now I had her attention? "Ah, hohishe?" I offered her my water flask.

Her lips turned up in a slight smile and she struck her helmet with her knuckle. Of course. So foolish of me. I nodded, realizing I also wore my helmet.

She spoke in her soft language. "Thenquewwaneewaaa."

She turned to face the front and continued on, stepping on every single stick, rock, dried leaf, poisonous fungus and one stupid jokal that didn't move fast enough. Its squeal alone could awaken a sleeping mud-beast. Perhaps she had survived as long as she had because she made the sounds of a giant predator when she traveled on foot. I scowled. At any tik, one of my brethren was going to …

"Will you tell your traveler to stop making so much noise?" complained Raxkarax. "I can't even hear my own breaths over the quaking noise erupting from her footsteps."

"Yes," I said. I put a hand on her shoulder. She stopped.

I tapped her helmet with a claw and then used two fingers to indicate eyes. Watch me. "A-do."

I put my boot on a stick and pressed. I clapped my hands together by her helmet. "Krak!" I mimicked the sound. She flinched. Then I showed her how to slide a stick aside or step over it. I made the sound of the wind on a hot day. "Shhhh."

Her brows pinched in understanding.

She said words I didn't understand, but she managed to walk more quietly after that.

Raxthezana spoke from the front. "I smell the rains. Is it not too soon for the rains?"

Hivelt replied, "It is the wet air season. The rains are not to come until another moon cycle."

"We must find shelter," I said from the back. "I do not want the soft traveler to suffer."

"Yasheza Mahavelt can walk in a little rain," Hivelt said. "You cannot coddle her. From my view, we are here, and she is here, all because of you."

I grumbled but said nothing. I knew I walked along a precipice with Yasheza and my brethren. I must not show her too much preference. Yet without her suit, she was as vulnerable as a jodax egg.

She peeked back at me with raised brows, no doubt wondering what we discussed.

I pointed to the sky. "Woa hohishe." It was not our word for rain, yet she should understand. Within tiks, the rains descended with a vengeance.

She screamed.

"Woawa," I said over the pounding of rain.

"Woawa?"

Her voice had a tremor. She bowed beneath the powerful slashing rain, stumbling.

As the rain fell, our hike became more strenuous. Mud filled up each boot print as we walked. Yasheza had to take thrice as many steps to each of our strides. She would tire soon.

Thunder rumbled overhead, and she jumped. She said something indecipherable and questioned me. "Woahoza?"

Ship? Did she think we were taking her to our ship?

If I told her the truth, would she run? Swallowing acid that rose from my throat, I pointed forward. She would find out the truth soon enough.

#

33

The thunder shook the ground we walked on, and I longed for the safety of my pod. My suit shed the rain, obviously, but being out in the open during thunder and lightning seemed like a horrible idea. At least, that's what I thought before the rain became torrential.

As if giant wasps and spiders wasn't bad enough, apparently, the raindrops were in competition for Most Freakishly Large Thing on Death Planet. I held my arms above my head and screamed. The rain felt like actual buckets. Not buckets full of water. Actual buckets. The force of their drops brought me to my knees, but I was not about to show weakness in front of these massive hunters. I strove to climb back up, slipping repeatedly.

I was grabbed from behind and then sheltered in Red's arms. He hunched slightly, offering me some protection from the drops.

"Hicondo, Yasheza Mahavelt," he said. Then he snatched me up and picked up his pace to run ahead of the warriors. He shouted something to them, but I didn't catch it. I couldn't see our destination due to the downpour.

The first thunderclap had been loud, but a second one ripped the clouds above with its ferocity. Its mother bolt streaked across the entire horizon, lighting up the surrounding area like the light from two suns.

My heart raced with each step Red took. It was at once exhilarating and frightening. For the first time in what felt like an eternity, I felt safe wrapped in a male's arms, despite the deluge around us.

We reached a cave opening and once inside, I could see it was the other entrance to my cave. Er, his cave? I recognized the grainy salt walls and floor. I could even see boot prints. I frowned. Several huge boot prints. They had all been in here. I swallowed. They had tracked me. That's how they found me running away from the alien dinosaur from hell. I closed my eyes briefly. I was still alive.

I waited for Naraxthel to put me down, but he didn't.

I marveled at his red battle-slashed helmet, and angular, sharp-edged armor. It wasn't fair. My helmet was made of a glass and Galvanite alloy. He could see my face. I could only guess at his expression through the black visor. The faint image of glowing eyes revealed nothing about his emotional state.

"You can put me down now," I said.

His helmet eyes were turned to me. I assumed he was looking at me. My lips wobbled in a hesitant smile, and I pointed down. "Down. Esra down."

He held me a second longer, and then lowered me to standing.

"Thank you, Naraxthel," I said. Nervous perspiration coated my skin inside my suit. I was alone with him. "Uh, woawa! Wow!" I wished for the hundredth time I had more of his words. "So, are we going to wait for the others? Rax and Hivelt and them?" I waved my hand toward the cave opening, hoping to indicate his companions.

He cocked his head, then nodded, turning to face the entrance. He put his glove to the side of his helmet and pressed an inconspicuous button. Ah, communication devices.

I stepped further into the cave, appreciating not being stoned to death by rain, but turned to observe my rescuer.

His armor gleamed, having been washed in the downpour. I inspected it, noticing seams for panels. His armor was tricked out with all sorts of interesting devices, in a way like mine. Though mine was exclusively for geological expeditions and survival scenarios. He had weapons strapped to his back, and I wouldn't be surprised if many of his "extras" were used for the work of death. He had a tool belt, too, from which hung a variety of implements. Knives, vials and pouches, as well as something that could be a stylus or a pen. These guys didn't strike me as the writing type, though.

He said words I didn't understand, his back to me, as he stared out into the rain.

I stared at his perfect posture and the width of his shoulders in awe. The alien was massive. As long as he remained on my side, I should be safe. I couldn't be sure where his allegiance lay, without communication. I supposed he couldn't trust me, either. It was a sobering thought and dampened the momentary thrill of having been secure in his arms just moments ago.

And then I realized we weren't just anywhere. We had traveled in the opposite direction of their ship.

"VELMA, show the video feed of the alien ship." My little bug camera was still active, right where the drone installed it.

"The rain is obscuring the video. Activating thermal and mineral imaging."

A faded heat signature showed where the ship's engines were, and the wavy violet lines created a vague outline of the entire ship, picking up compounds in the ship's metal. Yep. There it sat. Miles away from us.

They were never taking me to their ship. What I didn't know was if they weren't going to their ship, and I wasn't going to their ship, then where the hell were we going?

I felt sick to my stomach. I didn't know where he was taking me. I didn't know when I'd be back to my pod. I didn't know anything.

Maybe he felt the weight of my stare, because he turned around, removing his helmet as he did so.

When his eyes met mine, I blinked away tears. I was afraid, and I hated feeling afraid.

34

NARAXTHEL

For a blissful moment, my heart-chamber's barrier began to open, and my heart started to slip out. I was grateful my helmet obscured my face, as my brows rose, and my jaw clenched. I was many cycles removed from my adolescence, when the heart leaves its heart-home for a short period. The myths explain the phenomenon as a preparation for finding one's life mate. But the Theraxl people hadn't had true life mates, *Heart Mates*, for centuries. My heart should not be behaving in this manner.

I blinked commands to run a scan on my life systems. All appeared normal, save my rapid breathing. I held Esra close to my chest, and everything felt as it should. The shegoshel aligned with the sister planets and our single moon, and the songs of the jodaxl rang through the ikfal.

And then she pointed down, and I realized I was overcome with foolishness.

My heart was over-exerted from running in the rains.

I cracked my neck. Even if it wasn't frowned upon, even if mating with her wouldn't forfeit my standing in the clan and all my possessions, even if my own family wouldn't disown me for such a pairing, how could we be one? She was small and fragile. Compared to her, I was as monstrous as a rokhura. And yet, it had been sung the heart-home never lies …

Natheka's voice came through my comm. "The Royal Court wishes to be given sight-captures of our expedition."

"Kathe," I spat out. "We must keep knowledge of Yasheza away from the Ikma."

"I agree. Hivelt and the others suggested we separate for now," he said. "We will tell them you are reconnoitering, and we will send a variety of sight-captures to satisfy their curiosity." He paused. "As you know, the *pazathel-nax* will come out after the rains."

"Yes. May the life of Shegoshel shine upon you and your offspring."

"May the death of your enemies bring peaceful slumber."

I ground my teeth together. I should be with my brethren as they faced those toothy beasts. They had many names: teeth-dividers, devil dogs, dogs of the night. They were ferocious and large, hunting in packs after the rains came. The floods purged the dens and delves of the smaller animals, and flesh was plentiful for every predator on the planet.

I considered the cavern we were in; it adjoined a smaller mountain range, the younger sister mountain range to the Elder Sister Mountain of Shegoshel. It would remain dry for now.

We must make our way further inside and begin our trek to the under-mountain passageways.

I removed my helmet and turned to try to signal to Esra our next walk when I saw her expression.

Her lips drew together in a thin line. She blinked.

She looked at me through the glass, her eyes lowering by the tik. With lethargic movements, she released the pressure valve in the back of her helmet, and then pulled it off. Her chest rose and fell in sluggish breaths. Her cheeks paled, and she avoided my gaze.

I smelled despair. And fear.

She stood as still as stone. I watched her jaw work and muscles feather across her cheek. What we lacked in speech, she made up for in her expressive face.

We couldn't converse, but perhaps she would see the regret and apology in my face. Until we could understand each other, she had no way of knowing my plans. I frowned. There must be something I could do to show her. Or some combination of words that would make her see.

"Hicondo," I told her, and walked deeper into the tunnel, headed toward the spot where the agothe-fax still lay.

I placed a small illuminating bead on the wall of the cave. It grew in light until every corner was revealed. I placed a hand on the dead beast and met her searching gaze. She paled but said nothing.

"Agothe-fax," I said. I nodded my head to the animal. "Agothe-fax."

She frowned. I watched her eyes trace the lines of the night-walker. "Ah-go-the-fax."

Yes. I smiled at her. Then I arced my arm under the cavern ceiling, indicating the entire cave. "Agothe-fax *shevelt.*" I emphasized the word I wanted her to learn.

"Kayv?" she asked me. I did not know what she tried to say.

"No. Shevelt—" I jabbed toward the night-walker again. "Agothe-fax shevelt."

Her brows met, and her mouth turned down.

I scratched my chin. "Esra woahoza?" I asked her.

She nodded.

"Esra woahoza—shevelt."

I watched her face for signs of understanding. She mouthed the words I gave her. She nodded.

"Esra woahoza, my shevelt," she said, and patted her chest. Ah, she understood.

"Ik." I took a step closer to her. What was that word she used for immediacy? "N-oww," I attempted it. "Esra Hicondo, Naraxthel. Esra shevelt—Naraxthel."

How could I make her understand that for now, her home was with me? At least until we figured out what to do with her. I pointed to her and shrugged. "Esra hi con Naraxthel," I said, patting myself. My heart hurt with the desire to communicate with Esra. I watched her teeth clamp on her lower lip. How strange, they were flat and ineffective as weapons. Yet they were white and appealing. I shook myself. She cocked her head and mouthed the words.

I waited, all the while my heart stretching and yearning toward something it could not grasp.

Her eyes squinted, and she spoke. "Esra hi con Naraxthel," she said and nodded, her shoulders slumping. I sighed.

"Ik." My heart swelled within its confines, aching to break free. We had crossed a hurdle. But there were so many more to clamber over. And the drumbeats of my Ikma's anger pounded at my flank. I didn't know how long she would tolerate silence from my sight-capture.

35

"VELMA, does "doe" mean "me" in their language?" I had replaced my helmet, wanting to pull the AI in on the conversation. The stunted talk Naraxthel and I shared was difficult and slow. Not to mention, I was unnerved. I think he just told me my home was with him. Not in a lovey dovey way, or even a rapey way. More of a, "You don't have a better option." Which was very true. But I didn't have to like it.

I observed him through the barrier of my visor. He stood so straight and tall. Proud. His helmet rested under an arm, and he watched me with his blood-red eyes. I sweated under his scrutiny.

"It appears to, yes," she replied. "The one called Naraxthel has used it in conjunction with the phoneme "high cone," suggesting the phrase, "Come with me.""

"I think I learned the word for shelter or home," I told her. "Run *shevelt* through your language program or, whatever." Despite every-thing, his smile did a number on my respiratory system. I was surprised VELMA didn't call me out on it. I studied the cave wall rather than be caught memorizing the lines of his jaw or the shape of his nose. He was an alien, and furthermore, I had little choice but to stay with him. I stoked the roiling heat in my heart a little. "Do you think you could translate "Screw You" into their language?"

"It is inadvisable to provoke your only means of escape from this planet."

"I wasn't really going to say that to him," I said, rolling my eyes. I didn't want to consider the thrills that jittered up my spine when he had smiled a couple minutes ago. That didn't make any sense to me. Fear paralyzed me, but I could work with anger. I quirked my mouth, disengaged my helmet and tossed it aside, sitting with a huff and resting my head between my knees.

I heard Naraxthel approach. He squatted down.

I raised my eyes to his.

He must have deduced I was talking to my computer. Either that, or he thought I was a complete nutcase. His eyes squinted with concern or curiosity. He flicked a finger toward my helmet and raised his eyebrows.

I shook my head. "I have no way to tell you what's going on," I said, dismal thoughts dragging my head and voice lower. "I'm stuck on this." I slapped the cave floor. "Damn planet for the rest of my natural life." I returned his gaze. With brows drawn together, he did kind of look like he cared. I continued. "Esra? No *shevelt*." And that did it. Tears brimmed until he was a blurred green shape in front of me. I frowned and swiped the tears away with my other hand. My gut roiled in a soup of anger and hopelessness.

Naraxthel reached out a finger and touched the wetness on my cheek.

"Maikquo," he said so softly I wasn't sure if he intended me to hear it. I guessed it meant tears, but until VELMA had the language decrypted, we were at an impasse. Just like me on this god-forsaken predator planet.

36

NARAXTHEL

I watched her move her mouth animatedly within her helmet. Her brows formed an angry arrow. She yanked off her helmet. Esra was a fiery little female. But when she threw her helmet aside, I could see her fire was reduced to ash. She sank to her knees, her face crumpling in defeat. I recognized the salty and crushed herb scent of homesickness drifting from her skin. I did not understand her words until she used the one I had just taught her. Her simple statement caused an ache inside my chest. I rubbed my armor over my heart-home, as if I could alleviate the pulse there. No, Esra did not have a home here. Her desire to leave the planet tapped at my conscience. No enemy of Theraxl could leave Ikthe. Her tears—I understood the songs then. Tears were the blood of a wound you could not see. I wanted to touch this clear blood.

Holy Goddesses. Is this why you brought me a female from another world? That I would try to heal a wound without words? Even if words could bandage Esra's sadness, I could not speak them.

I hefted my pack to the floor beside her and sat, my ankles crossed in front of me. I pulled food out, hoping to entice Esra's smile out from its hiding place. I smelled sadness, but also hunger.

I placed my seasoned and dried rokhura meat on the cave floor between us and unwrapped the sister bread. I put my drink canister beside it.

I drew her attention, and she tilted her head with an arched brow.

"Wa," I said, pointing to the canister. "Kafa." I held the food in both hands, offering it to her.

She sniffed and blinked her tears. "Water? Nowayt. Hoe-high-shuh wuzwater. Drink?" She took my canister and opened the lid. Sniffed it with her tiny nose, then placed her pink mouth upon the rim and drank deeply. My eyes caressed her throat before I forced them to blink. Still, I held the food out to her. She took it. "Kafa? Food."

I nodded. The soft lilts of her language appealed to my ears, as did the foreign yet fragrant smells that wafted from her hair and skin. Ever it reminded me of the flowers on Ikshe. I crooked a brow, studying the unexpected fluttering in my chest and shallow breaths. I swallowed, yet no food was in my mouth.

I watched her take small bites of the meat, and then her face broke into a smile, showing the flatness of her teeth. I cocked my head and peered closer. Where her fangs should be were tiny fangs, just the smallest point on each. She caught me staring and covered her mouth. She mumbled something. I dipped my head in apology.

"Wa," she said, shaking her head and recovering from embarrassment. She pushed the canister toward me. She smelled the bread, closing her eyes and inhaling its fragrance. Sister bread was made from the grains on Ikshe. I wanted to tell her such trivial things. I clenched a fist briefly. There would be time. She tore a chunk off the bread and ate of it, moaning in delight. She swallowed the bite and a stream of words flowed from her mouth. She unfastened her own pack and pulled out the strange soft metal pouches. "Esra kafa." She gave me a pouch and pointed to it. "No bred." She pointed to the sister bread. "Bred. Soooguuud. Thenkyew." She smiled a little, her eyes still touched by sadness and nodded, eating more sister bread.

"Kama favelt-rax," I told her, pressing a claw into the soft salt-encrusted dough. She cocked her head and attempted the sounds. Poorly. My mouth curved up on one side, but I said nothing.

I held the tiny pouch in my hand. I recalled the strange mixture of flavors from yesterday. It was not unpleasant. However, I needed more to satiate my hunger. I tore the flimsy material and poured some water in it. I saw her from the corner of my eye, watching my every movement. I stirred the food inside with a claw, then poured the mash into my mouth. I drank from the canister and replaced it on the floor between us. A light aroma, something akin to morning dew, teased my nose. I glanced at Esra to see her skin change from its pale cream color to a rosy sunrise. She averted her eyes and cast them down. My eyes widened in surprise. My heart strained against its encasement, accompanying the fragrance in its common desire. I stood abruptly and walked away, a crease deepening between my brows with every step.

Holy Goddesses of Shegoshel. What would you have me do with these sensations? There is no ... pattern to follow.

I took a deep breath, allowing the smells of the cave to flood my senses. I needed to dilute the fragrance of the naïve female. Too late, I caught the scent of a new agothe-fax—on the hunt.

I spun on my heel to see the Elder sister agothe-fax stalking Esra from behind. A muffled voice sprang from the helmet still on the ground, and Esra's eyes grew large. She stared at me and stilled. Did she sense the danger? Did her helmet technology warn her?

She made the tiniest whimper, her eyes beseeching me.

I watched the agothe-fax's spike rise in position to strike. I drew the raxtheza's singing blade from its sheath with my right hand, holding my left out, palm down.

Do not move, Yasheza Mahavelt.

Every sense hummed in tandem as I prepared to kill. The acrid stench of the agothe-fax's hunger competed with the snick of one of its feet scratching against the grainy cave floor. I saw a bead of sweat form at Esra's brow, and a droplet of agothe-fax venom shimmer poised at the tip of its striker.

With a sudden lunge, I flung my blade at its head and leaped upon Esra to shield her from the glancing blow of its striker. I knocked her to the ground and felt the merciless hammer upon my back, but my armor shielded me from its venomous limb. I turned my head to see the beast collapse, but there was no time to celebrate my victory. Soon, the younger sister would seek vengeance. I grabbed my second blade from my back and rolled off of Esra, sparing her a quick look, to see she was shaken but unharmed. The second agothe-fax was not far behind, and I heard its clicks and whistles of dismay.

With my double-blade poised to defend, I crouched. The agothe-fax clambered atop the mound of her dead sister and leapt at me. I grasped its foreleg with my free hand and gutted it with my double-blade, its blood drenching my arm up to the elbow.

Its gore dripped from my armor, and I turned to see Esra backing away from me, her face ashen and her eyes wide and unblinking. I huffed a grim laugh. I no longer smelled the morning dew from her skin. It was just as well. I did not know what to do with the aberrant behavior of my heart.

I investigated the corpses, puzzling out their appearance. It should have taken them many days to occupy this territory only recently disposed of its owners. The Elder and younger sister agothe-faxl were looking for new nesting grounds. I gave pause.

The mating season was starting a full moon-cycle early.

My heart drummed a beat against the walls of its heart-home. Esra was in more danger. The roaming packs of male agothe-faxl would not be far behind. I cursed.

Thrusting my filthy blades into the ground to clean them, I sheathed them and stuffed our meal back into my pack. I looked to Esra, wishing I could instruct her. Instead, I pointed to her helmet. "E du zaza!" I replaced my own with a quiet snap and held her pouch out to her, shaking it as I did so. She sensed my hurry and slung it over her shoulder and then put on her own helmet, all the while staring at me with those round blue-green eyes. She noted the place where I had dug my blades into the ground, a question forming on her lips. I shrugged.

I dialed up my air flow, bidding the smells of the cave to assault me. There were three tunnels to this vast room. The males could arrive from any or all of them.

Esra spoke, but I could not decipher her question.

"Agothe-faxl hi!" I answered her. I saw her throat bob in a swallow.

Ah, she understood. Good. I reached down to my calf and unsnapped my smallest blade. I handed it to her, hilt out, and she took it without hesitation. I smiled, my fangs clipping my lip. "Joiktheka." *Little hunter.* I crouched and beckoned for her to stand at my back. We would fight the pack together.

#

37

I felt a rumble through my boots while VELMA said, "Subsonic scanning indicates the approach of five separate creatures called Agothefaxl." With Red at my back, we held our weapons poised for battle. I thought two spiders was bad?

I wielded my multi-tool in one hand, and the borrowed knife from Red in the other. My machete swatter was back at the EEP. I didn't think I would need it surrounded by the hulking aliens and their weapons. Although, after witnessing the spider blood-bath up close and personal, I wasn't as worried as I would have been if I were alone. I glanced at the borrowed blade for a second. Red's knives could pierce the very ground, as well as the spiders' exoskeletons. Good to know.

My blood pounded in my ears; my breath rushed out in gasps. I stared at the single opening I faced. Red had positioned himself between the other two tunnels. The little light he'd stuck to the wall cast our bodies in long shadows, disfiguring our shapes into such distorted monstrosities we resembled an arachnid ourselves.

I gulped, wishing I'd had more than just the one drink from Red's canister. Any second now—I felt more than heard a shift and tumble of heavy bodies advance from the tunnel in front of me. My hands were slick inside my gloves. I lost sensation in my toes, feeling a chill from my bones. My vision narrowed on the opening, and then the dark hairy legs entered the room first, tapping the ground and walls with their sticky pads. Their heads cleared the tunnel. They saw me and rushed. My heart in my throat, I squeezed my weapons so tight my hands hurt, and swung them without strategy toward the dark-brown furry bodies. With my heart in a full gallop and my breaths rasping in my dry throat, I slashed wildly. I screamed and hacked, one of them seizing my left arm with its many legs and hanging on. Revulsion crested over my body. I hacked downward at the agothe-fax attacking my feet while thrashing my other arm up and down, trying to shake the other one off. I felt a tight pinch at my wrist, but ignored it in favor of driving Red's dagger down into the agothe-fax's head. A flashing red light appeared in my visor, but I didn't stop to read the notification. The agothe-fax collapsed, and I turned my attention to the one on my arm. I watched in horror as its mandibles chewed away at the cuff of my suit. I could see my skin.

I roared and swung the knife at its head. The knife sliced through the hairy exoskeleton. It went limp, lost its grip and fell. I panted and narrowed my eyes at the ugly, creepy things that made my skin crawl. I'd been so busy fighting for my own life, I forgot Naraxthel was at my back. I dragged myself around, gasping for breath. Naraxthel sat against a cave wall, polishing his weapons with an oily cloth. Three agothe-faxl lay in crimped pieces, bleeding out onto the crusty ground.

How long had he been sitting there? I stomped over to him and opened my mouth to yell, but nothing came out. He placed his weapons on the ground. He removed his helmet and shook out his hair fronds. His swirling blood-red eyes penetrated my gaze. His fangs peeked out as his mouth turned up in a smooth smile. He looked beyond me at the two dead ones then back at me and nodded once.

I felt a flush of blood to my face. My chest puffed out, and I couldn't help the smile that snuck up on me. I had killed *two* of those nasty things. Alone. I took a deep breath and nodded back.

He gestured to the borrowed knife that dripped with goop. Recalling how he'd driven his weapons straight into the cave ground to remove the mess, I dropped to one knee and did the same.

The dagger entered the stone floor as easily as if it were butter.

What was this material? I removed it and inspected the metal. It gleamed with a faint purple light, but not in a glow-in-the-dark way. It was more the color of the metal, like the purple was infused into it. I twisted it this way and that, watching the light play off its beveled edges. I'd bet if I dropped one of my long hairs onto the blade it would fall away in two pieces. It was an enviable piece of work. I didn't know metallurgy, but I was familiar with an alloy or two. This blend of metals was like nothing I'd seen before. Its heft was substantial, however. I doubted I could handle one of his bigger swords.

I returned my gaze to him and discovered he'd been watching me inspect his blade. I sensed approval in his calm stare. I returned the dagger to him, hilt first, and he nodded once again. The flashing red lights returned, along with VELMA's voice.

"Your suit's integrity has been breached. Please return to the EEP for possible medical treatment."

Schist, I was so jacked up with adrenaline I had forgotten the tingling burn in my wrist. I wrestled off my helmet and pulled at the material of my suit. After peeling it back I saw a scratch on my skin. That hairy bastard. I must have made a noise because Naraxthel stood and came to my side. He then tugged my left hand closer to him. I found his eyes. His brows furrowed deeply, and his mouth turned down. He spun me to face him with his huge hands on my shoulders and searched my eyes.

"La du paza!" He said.

I shook my head. My heart was racing, and I was breaking out into a cold sweat. He was still frowning, and his eyes peeled me layer by layer. Did the agothe-fax poison me? Was I about to die?

He cradled my jaw with his hand and opened his own mouth, nodding at me. I opened my mouth.

He tilted my head up, peering inside. He dropped his hands to my shoulders and patted them twice, nodding again. "Zaikshe," he said, releasing my shoulder with a squeeze. "Esra la ikshemaza."

"Please return to the EEP for possible medical treatment," VELMA intoned from my helmet.

"It's okay," I said loud enough for my voice to register. "I think Naraxthel checked me out. He seems to think I'm okay."

That's not to say my wrist was feeling better. It burned. I removed my gloves and unzipped the MDpak from its pocket below my breast. I snatched the anesthetic spray and zapped the shallow, inch-long scratch. I hissed through my teeth at the cold, prickling feeling, then it went numb. I returned the spray to its pocket and pulled out an antibacterial wipe. I hoped the agothe-fax's mouth wasn't venomous like the Komodo dragons' back on Earth. I shivered. I stashed everything away and saw Naraxthel grimacing.

"What?" I said.

He poked my MDpak then touched his nose and made a face.

I shrugged. "Sorry, I don't know what you're trying to say."

Maybe my medicine stank. I was quite certain I stank. I sniffed, noting the tang of the antiseptic odor. It tickled my nose, and I sneezed. "I swear I'm allergic to something on this planet." I shook my head and put my helmet back on, watching Red watching me. His expression softened, his fangs disappearing inside his mouth for a second and the crease between his brows fading.

"Please return to the EEP for possible medical treatment," VELMA repeated.

I turned away from Red to talk to VELMA. "I know my suit's been breached, but I feel fine," I said. "Have you made any progress with the language? I know a few words, and something tells me I need to know a lot more than how to say giant freaking spider."

"I have a growing database of words," VELMA said. "However, I would like to try something different."

"What's that?" I said, suspicious.

"I can wirelessly access Naraxthel's helmet technology," she said. "If I hack into it, I could learn the language and facilitate your communication at a faster rate. However, that could impact interplanetary relations in an unpredictable way."

I sucked my bottom lip. "Interplanetary relations. That would involve actually communicating with these guys, an impossibility at this point."

There was an old maxim on Earth: Better to ask forgiveness than permission, and this was the edge we needed. I watched Naraxthel pressing buttons on an open wrist panel. VELMA could have access to a lot more than just the Theraxl language. I frowned. I didn't want to cause an intergalactic incident. And I sure didn't want to damage the very fragile trust developing between the alien and myself.

I blew out a sigh. "I'm going to say yes with reservations, VELMA. Use your access to help us with translation. I know you could start dinking around in galactic cyberspace, but I'm going to ask you to refrain."

"Very well, Esra. Proceeding."

I exhaled and shook my hands out. Naraxthel closed his panel and raised his eyes to me.

"Hicondo," he said, and started walking through a tunnel. He secured his helmet as he walked.

I caught myself admiring his posture. I smirked, remembering my track-and-field hijinks in college. The tall lithe athletes always did catch my eye. I tried to imagine any of my old boyfriends facing that pack of slavering reptiles and couldn't. My alien was one of a kind. I shook my head and patted my pockets, assuring myself I had collected my things. I studied his broad shoulders a couple seconds. This was ridiculous, I was not walking behind him. I jogged to catch up.

"Hey," I said and cleared my throat.

He glanced at me.

"Uh." Crap, what was the word for water? "Hohishe?"

His stride faltered. He stopped and turned, looking down at me.

I wished I could see his eyes; the glowing red ones unnerved the hell out of me.

With deliberate motions, he removed his pouch and released the cap with a pinch. He offered it to me.

My fingers trembled for some reason as I unfastened my helmet.

The breach in my suit had my IntraVisor blinking alarms all over the place, but there was nothing for it now. I'd already removed my helmet and I hadn't died yet. The tear in my sleeve might be fixable with some of the carbon-polymer tape back at the EEP, but who knew when I would get there again.

We stood in the tunnel, our helmet lights outlining each of our shadows in grotesque display. Red's shadow was enormous, since my light was at my waist.

I took the offered pouch and drank, my throat working to swallow as much as I could and my eyes closing in rapture. The water was sweet compared to the recycled swamp muck in my EEP. I pulled the nozzle away from my lips and opened my eyes.

Red's helmet was off. His stare brought heat from my neck up to my hairline.

I wiped my mouth with the back of my glove and handed the pouch back to him. "Thanks." My voice was raspy.

Without breaking his gaze, he lifted the pouch and drank from it, his wide mouth enclosing the nozzle where my lips had been. I couldn't pull my eyes away from the bobbing of his throat as he drank. He withdrew the nozzle and licked his lips with a deep-pink tongue.

I felt my eyes grow wide. I looked away and down, blinking fast. I stole another peek at him.

He pinched the cap back on the pouch and stowed it at his side amongst the other items in his harness.

My heart picked up its pace, but I ignored any significance from it.

We replaced our helmets, and he gestured to the trail we followed. Before I took my first step, he placed his hand upon the bulb of my helmet. "Zagoshe." Then he pointed to his own light. "Zagoshe."

"Light," I said, pointing to my own.

His lips pulled into a smile, revealing his white fangs. "Lll-eye-t," he repeated.

"Yes!"

We smiled and began walking side by side.

When the tunnel narrowed, he patted the wall and said, "Naxaxza."

I patted the wall on my side. "Naxaxza?"

"Ik." He rapped it with his knuckle as we walked on. "Naxaxza."

I thought he was saying wall, but I couldn't be sure. Maybe he was saying tunnel. Or rock. Hell, maybe he was saying, "Having some little girl tag along sucks." I wondered how VELMA was doing with her covert mission, but I knew she would tell me when she succeeded.

I tripped over a rock and stumbled. Red caught my arm but released it as soon as I stood. "Thanks." I bent to retrieve it and hefted it in my hand. A cursory study showed it to be limestone. "Rock," I told him.

"Ah. Laveltrax."

"Laveltrax." I remembered how smooth his blade drove into the rocks. Limestone was soft, but not butter-soft. "Um, can I see your blade again?" I reached out and patted the dagger he sheathed in a thigh harness.

He pulled it out and handed it to me hilt first.

I smiled and took it, then held the rock against the wall. I positioned the blade as if to cut an apple and clove the limestone in two. "Wow."

"Heh. Do raxtheza nax laveltrax."

I returned his knife to him and unsnapped my multitool. "Watch my blade," I said. "It should scratch it." Carboniferous limestone, especially Tula, could be a five on Moh's scale, but not any higher. My tool should be able to do a bit of damage to it. I sawed at the rock, and dust fell away. I shrugged and offered him my tool, so he could see the metal.

He took it and inspected it under his light. "Ah. Rax bi ropazathelvelt." He compared the metal of my tool and then the metal of his purple dagger. "Woaiquovelt."

I touched the flat of his blade with my glove. If I was understanding correctly, he was comparing the two metals. I grasped the tool. "Multitool." I showed him the pliers, the screwdriver, the utility blade, the soldering tip and the Galvanite awl.

"Ik. Naxl." He flipped a pocket open on one of his many packs and pulled out something similar but obviously made for his much larger hands. He offered it to me.

I held it, delighted at how light it was. It didn't gleam purple like his dagger. I raised my brows and asked him. "It's not the same metal?"

"I." He jabbed at his multi-tool. "Rax bi ropazathelvelt." Then he ran a finger along his blade. His voice softened. "Woaiquovelt."

"Wow." I felt my face grow warm. I didn't know why I couldn't think of anything else to say. It's not like it mattered. He wouldn't know. And yet my profundity knew no bounds. "Cool."

We stashed our tools once again, and I let the rock tumble to the ground.

My mind raced as we walked along. The cave left little to talk about. Rocks, walls. Light. We'd compared tools. And some food earlier. My ears burned and my face flushed as we walked side by side in a wide tunnel; there were always body parts.

I swallowed and kept my mouth shut.

And sneezed.

38

NARAXTHEL

Yasheza Mahavelt puzzled me. She had ceased speaking with the technology in her helmet. I longed to ask her why. I longed for many things. I searched my mind for words we might share. An empty cave in the belly of a mountain did not lead to stimulating conversation.

When my tracker indicated we had traveled three hundred veltiks, I deemed it necessary to make camp. I knew this place and felt chills along my arms when I anticipated Esra's reaction to it.

"Here." I pulled the latch that adhered my packs to my suit, and everything dropped to the floor. I had scanned repeatedly for agothe-faxl. It was clear for now, but the roaming band of agothe-faxl in rut had thrown me off guard. They should not be rutting for another moon at least.

I swept pebbles from an area by the alcove with my boot. Some splashed in the pool, and I watched Esra. She heard the splashes and looked to the pool. The rocks disturbed the little water Suns, so they glowed. I waited until she approached the pool to stick the bead light upon the cave wall.

I watched her mouth break into a wide smile and her eyes light from within. I felt a stuttering within my heart-home and grasped my chest in surprise. It abated, and my breaths returned to normal.

Words spilled from Esra's mouth, among them, hohishe. I smiled.

She didn't wait to pull off her helmet and removed her gloves next. She strode to the edge and looked up at me as if to request permission.

"Yes. The water is safe." I gestured she could touch it. I pulled off my own gloves and helmet, placing them alongside the alcove wall. When I turned, I caught her staring at my hands. I looked down and examined them as if through her eyes.

Scarring marred the green skin, great gashes and crosshatching revealed many cycles of hunting, sparring and fighting. My dull black claws jutted mercilessly from my fingertips. I couldn't remember what her hands looked like, so when I knelt beside the pool to run my fingers through the glowing water, I studied hers with a frank gaze.

The pale skin appeared lighter in the glow of the little water suns. Her nails were colorless and short. Ineffective. I swallowed and looked down at my own again. Hers were ineffective against the beasts of my planet, yes. But I considered the little tool she'd shown me and how she manipulated the moving parts with her small fingers. The Goddesses formed her as she should be for her purpose. Ever had I known my purpose was to kill and serve the Ikma of my people. I had yet to learn the Goddesses' purpose for Esra. It must be different, and I would be a wise disciple of the Goddesses to remember that.

A splash of water jolted me from my thoughts. Esra wore an impish grin as she squatted by the pool. My eyes traced the line of her curved back and hind end. She was even more small in the pose. Her smile wavered then disappeared. I had waited too long. She worried she offended me.

What could I do? I used my large hand to splash a wave into her face. She fell back, spluttering and gasping.

"Naraxthel!" Her shout amused me, but I couldn't resist the urge to peer into the depths of the tunnel beyond for interlopers.

I heard her gasp. When I looked, her hand covered her mouth and water dripped from her lashes. I gestured for her to calm. "It is safe." I cocked my head. "Ahh. No agothe-faxl. Safe."

She let her hand drop, and a small smile appeared. I smiled at her and reached for the water.

"No! No hohishe!"

I laughed at her round eyes and leaned to drink from the pool. Its flavor on my tongue brought happy memories. I slurped greedily, then let my gaze drift to the soft traveler.

She looked on with mouth agape and large eyes. I recalled she had bathed in a similar pool. She must not have drunk the water. I made my hands into a bowl shape, scooped some water and offered it to her to drink.

Her brows rose and her eyes darted between my own, doubting. She leaned toward my hands and used her small ones to hold mine and lift them gently to her lips. She took a small sip. I held my breath. My skin seemed to tingle where her lips touched my fingers. The only sounds in the cave were gentle drips from the water and my armor creaking as I moved. I could hear Esra's breaths. They were shallow and erratic. I did not mistake the fragrance wafting from her skin, but I ignored it. For now.

She puzzled her brows and pursed her lips, then licked them. I mirrored her actions before I realized it. She cocked her head and grimaced. "Tooosalltee."

I shrugged and quaffed the rest of the liquid in my hands, never letting my eyes leave her face. She watched me as well, and I felt my skin heat under her scrutiny. My heart hammered as if I were battling the rokhura, yet I squatted here beside the johohishe Shegoshel pool in complete safety. Perhaps my heart was not safe from the Soft Traveler. The myths ... but that was nonsense.

I sat in the pose of the young student and unpacked more food and my fire kit. Out of the corner of my eye, I noticed her watching me. I frowned, realizing I took more care with each motion, the unwrapping of the bread, the stacking of the slender fire sticks. I was a Mighty Hunter. It did not matter what this little female thought of me. I growled at myself. I heard her chuckle, so I shot her a glare.

She coughed into her hand and sat across from me, unpacking her own bag. Redness bloomed on her neck and cheeks when she pulled out a pouch and spilled dark-green seed pods upon the rock floor. She offered me the pods. I smiled.

"Ah! Talafa! Food from the black tree. It tastes good with rokhura meat." Her brows pulled together, so I held up a finger. I pulled a rasher of dried meat from a pack and placed it beside the pods. "It's good. Very good together." I grabbed a slice of meat and a small handful of pods and ate them, watching her reaction.

She nodded and ate some talafa, then held the meat up to her nose and inhaled. She would smell the ground kernels of the ikquo plant from my home world. She closed her eyes, breathing deep of the aroma, then took a bite. She chewed with her eyes closed, and I allowed my gaze to drift over the skin of her face. So many soft features. Translucent skin I might tear with a single claw if I weren't careful. The small nose, the pink lips…her tongue darted out to lick a fleck of pepper and her eyes opened to see me focused intently on her mouth. I had leaned forward with nostrils flaring to smell the fragrance of her.

I sat back and grunted, tearing off a huge bite and chewing.

"Thississgud." She gestured to the meat and nodded, then took another bite. She liked it. I mimicked her nod.

What else could I teach her of my language? In the absence of trees, flowers, animals and weather, not much was available or interesting. We had a few different names for the rocks and gifts of the mountains, but the subtleties would be lost on her until she had a better grasp of my language. I watched her lick seasoning off her delicate fingers. Ahh.

I swallowed my bite and stroked her hand briefly. "Yaza."

Her eyes lit up. "Yaza. Hand!"

I smiled and pointed to my eyes. "Azal."

She pointed to her eye and said, "Aza?" Then pointed to the other. "Aza? Azal?"

"Yes!" I shouted. She understood the multiple.

She laughed, and my heart thudded painfully against its cage. I coughed and pounded my chest as if to force it into submission.

Her brow creased and her mouth turned down.

I brushed my hand down my chest. "Ah, it is nothing." I pointed to my nose. "Saza."

"Saza," she said with a small smile.

I swallowed. Pointed to my mouth. "Paza."

Her voice lowered a notch. "Paza."

My gaze drifted to her lips the same time my heart began a faster march. I resisted the urge to press my hand against my chest once more. It would stop. I hoped.

I jerked my eyes away from her lips. "I will teach you the children's song of the body." She blinked but said nothing.

I began the song and the hand motions to go along with it.

"My body is big, my body is weapon!
My eyes and hands, hunt! Hunt!
My ears and legs, hunt! Hunt!
See the animal! Touch the animal!
Hear the animal! Hunt the animal!
Drink the animal's life! I hunt!

My song ended with the dagger angled at Esra's throat. Her face had drained of color. I panted and sheathed my knife with a chuckle. "It is a child's song. Just a play song."

Her halting laugh and uncertain smile revealed she did not understand at all. "Ah," I said. I looked around the ground near us and found a powdery spot. I withdrew my stylus and drew a crude drawing of the pazathel-nax. I made sure to include the sharp teeth and claws. I sang the song again, more slowly, and pointed to the animal when called to do so. The gestures used many body parts, and it wasn't long before Esra sang with me.

We ended the song a fourth time with our daggers aimed at each other's throats. Her laughter unleashed my tethered heart, and its trembling concerned me. I stood. "I go to give water."

She seemed to understand and looked around as if to choose a spot for herself. I pushed on her shoulders that she would stay. "Do not move."

I retreated a veltik into the tunnel and ran a scan of my vital signs yet again. Nothing was amiss. I breathed deep of the tunnel air, scenting for agothe-faxl. All clear. I finished my business and returned to Esra. I gestured she could squat down the same tunnel. Her skin flooded with her red blood, changing the white to pink. Its aroma filled my nose.

She walked into the tunnel, and I frowned, grasping my chest. What was this betrayal of my big, strong body? And for how many tiks had I forgotten my brethren, the quest, the Ikma? I only had eyes and attention for the Soft Traveler. I sat with a huff and gnawed further on my meat. My simple life had become a puzzle.

39

I couldn't help but chuckle. We danced and parried like a couple of kids. I couldn't remember the last time I had laughed so hard. Furthermore, Red had armed me with a few more words. I knew some of the body parts and the word for fight, kill or hunt. I wasn't quite sure which one it was, but with a knife aimed at an animal's neck, I had the gist of it.

I murmured the words as I reattached my many zippers and fasteners.

"Do azal, do yazal, theka! Theka!"

Still smiling, I reentered the alcove Red's bead light set aglow. Between its brightness and the glowing pool of blue jellyfish, it was cheerful. I should be tired but talking to Red enlivened me. There was so much more I wanted to know. I paused mid-step and considered my crushing depression at being stranded alone was gone. I watched him for a moment. He bowed over something. His immense shoulders rivaled a barrel of propulsion fuel on IGMC's mothership. While his hands were clawed, his fingers moved deftly to open the ties of his assorted packs.

The scars shocked me when I first spied them. But they resembled the scars on his neck too. His skin, textured like that of a manta ray or shark, fascinated me. I had touched his hands briefly; what would it be like to caress them? I shook my head and pinched the bridge of my nose. Enough of *that*. I sat in my place again and watched him clean up his food. He offered me the last bite of jerked meat. I held my hand out, but instead, he placed it at my lips.

The pulse in my throat throbbed. Searching his eyes, I opened my mouth, and he placed the morsel between my teeth. His claw clicked against my teeth. He whispered, "Pazathel," and ran his tongue over his fangs. I blinked several times and bit down on the food. Hopefully we didn't just complete some sort of mating ritual, but the cave suddenly felt a thousand degrees and my mind wandered to rabid curiosity about his body beneath his armor. Chills raced up my spine, and I swallowed my bite.

"Thank you," I said and cleared my throat. I felt blood rushing to my face. I avoided his eyes and tidied up with haste. The meat and talafa filled me, so my foil packet returned to my bag. Flashing orange drew my attention. My helmet blinked erratically.

I grabbed it, fumbled to put it on, and searched the IntraVisor's messages. "Suit integrity breached. Please return to EEP for possible medical treatment."

"I'm fine."

"Solar panels at thirteen percent. Please return to sunlight to charge cells."

"VELMA, calm down," I said. "Geez."

"Rebooting."

I rolled my eyes and took off my helmet again. Red raised his brows at me. I turned the helmet's cells toward him and pointed. "Uh, zah-go-sha?" I said the word for light. I hoped he would understand I was losing power.

"Ah," he said and took my helmet from me. He examined the panels, running a claw down the smooth black surface. He held up a finger and gently placed my helmet beside his own. He opened a panel below his pectoral armor and fished out a slender red box. He placed my helmet solar cell down on top of the box. Then he grinned at me.

"Is that a charger?" I said. He just smiled.

I stood and walked to his helmet. "May I?"

"Ik, ik," he said and nudged it toward me. I bent to lift it and grunted. It weighed at least thirty pounds! I turned it to see the dark-gray circles at the back. They must function the same. I slid my fingers across them. I remembered them from when he was buried beneath the dead reptiles.

"Are these solar cells?" Er, star cells, I corrected myself. Sol belonged to Earth.

"Ah," he said. Then he spilled out a great jumble of words I couldn't even begin to make sense of. I handed him his helmet, and he took it with a couple fingers and placed it next to mine.

I saw more lights blink on each of our helmets. "Look!" He followed my finger to the flashing lights. Our helmet lights blinked sporadically for a few seconds, then began syncing up. Within a minute they were blinking together.

Red looked at me askance, then picked up his monstrous helmet and put it on. I did the same.

"I have decrypted Theraxl language," VELMA said. "Would you like me to translate?"

I jumped up and down. "Yes!" I looked to Red, and his fangs gleamed in a pleased smile. She must have introduced herself to him.

We stood facing each other. Where to begin?

He spoke first.

"Why are you here? How did you find this planet?"

Adrenaline branched throughout my chest. I could answer all of his questions! Feeling breathless, I spoke in a rush.

"My ship was damaged, and the emergency pod shot me out into space. It was programmed to find somewhere compatible with my physiology. I woke up when it was landing."

"Your technology found this planet?" He looked stern.

I nodded. "Yeah. I didn't know anything. I was," I took a breath, remembering. "I was asleep for a long time."

"Are there others?" His brows seemed to draw even closer together, and his mouth turned down. I took a small step back.

"I don't know. VELMA hasn't said," I answered. "VELMA is the technology."

"Ah. But your ship was large? There were many of your kind?"

I bit my lip. "Well, yes. But—"

He began pacing. "I need to reconnect with my brethren. If more of you land here, the Ikma Scabmal Kama may descend with her army and destroy us all. She may destroy Ikthe in her wrath." His stride allowed him only a few steps before he pivoted and returned. "I cannot reach them from the caves. We will leave in a zatik."

My adrenalin rush faded as quickly as it came. "You don't understand," I said. He stopped pacing and looked at me. "I jettisoned through space for *years*. The odds of others landing here are very small. My technology wasn't even familiar with your race. Your people haven't been catalogued by the Interplanetary Unification of Races, and your planet isn't charted." The words I spoke choked me. I would never reunite with the human race.

He stood with his fists at his hips. He stared at me.

"Your technology assures me what you say is true," he said, then cocked his head. "She stated a statistical probability of a handful of survivors reaching this planet but has not received any pings."

"Right," I said. I swallowed a painful lump. I watched his body, since his expressions were obscured by the helmet. His shoulders dropped a fraction, and he released his hands from fists.

"I am sorry. There is much to explain," he said. He opened his palm to the ground. "Sit. We will converse."

My heart rate picked up a little at his command. I sat in a crisscross fashion and rested my elbows on my knees. He continued to pace.

"My queen sent us on a death march. She does not know of your existence, yet, and I would keep it that way."

"Okay," I said. I wasn't sure what to say, or if I should just listen.

"The Ikma Scabmal Kama," he paused. "My queen. She knew we would all likely perish on this errand to retrieve woaiquovelt and Waters of Shegoshel. The planet is not kind."

I cleared my throat. "Yeah, I noticed."

He finished pacing and sat across from me. "You are brave for one so small."

I huffed. "Not so brave. I have cried a lot since landing here. Your planet tries to kill me several times a day."

He nodded. "Bravery and tears are sister companions. It is the way of the Goddesses. What you say about our planet is true. We call it Certain Death. It is the Sister Planet to my home world."

"The green planet I see in the sky?"

"Yes," he said. "It is my home." His armor creaked as he settled into a comfortable pose. "I apologize for hunting you like prey."

"Heh." I laughed. "I can't blame you." I sat in silence and reached my hand up as if to play with my braids. "Why did you...?" I couldn't finish. A rush of emotion flooded my throat and eyes. Somehow, I had landed in the middle of a political intrigue on a predator planet. Just because I had an alien friend did not mean my troubles were over. Far from it.

He reached for me and took my hand. We wore our helmets for communication, but neither of us had replaced our gloves. His hand felt cool and strong.

"You battled death. It is a victory ritual for the royal Sisters. I hope I did not offend."

I shook my head and blinked away some moisture. "No, I wasn't offended. I haven't been," I swallowed again. "I haven't been touched with gentleness in a long time."

"Ah," was his only response.

I rotated my shoulders and popped my neck. "Ahem. Well, wow!" I pulled my hand out of his grip. "What do we do? What is the plan?"

He didn't answer right away, but let the glowing eyes of his helmet stare into my soul.

I tried not to fidget, but I couldn't help squirming a little under his scrutiny.

"We will rest, rejoin the others, and we will complete the quest. You are coming with me."

My mouth dried up. I tried to work up some spit to swallow. "A quest?"

"Woaiquovelt is the prized metal of this planet. You have seen its power and beauty."

"Yes."

He touched the hilt of his blade. "Missions to collect it are rare. Few Theraxl return from them."

I opened my mouth, but nothing came out. I couldn't imagine anything so perilous that these monstrous beings couldn't survive. And I was coming with them on this journey? He must have seen my eyes grow wide, or maybe the fluttering pulse in my neck.

He grasped my hand once more; I wondered what PSI his grip had, but he held my hand as if it were made of glass. "I will protect you, Yasheza Mahavelt."

I clenched my jaw and formed fists while my gaze drifted to his dagger.

Red began to chuckle. "Or perhaps you will protect me, instead." He released my fist.

"Suit integrity breached. Please return to the EEP for possible medical treatment."

VELMA's announcement startled me. "Oh. Hang on," I said and muted the mic. "VELMA, I'm fine. Can't you cancel the warning or something?"

"The suit utilizes a separate OS. I will reroute it."

"Thanks."

"However, you will need to repair the breach otherwise I cannot guarantee your safety."

My mind cast over Red's promise of danger, and I fingered the torn sleeve on my suit. I toggled my mic. "How far are we from my pod?"

Red's glance skimmed my sleeve. "Many zatik's walk from here."

I frowned. "VELMA, what is a zatik?"

"My calculations define a zatik as 2.7 Standard Earth hours," VELMA answered. She displayed a modified clock on my IntraVisor. It appeared Theraxl used a metric system to measure time, units of tens comprising the clock.

I cocked a brow. "I have material at my pod that would allow me to repair the tear in my sleeve," I told Red. "Can we go back?"

His posture stiffened. He looked toward one of the tunnels,

presumably the one leading back. "I wish to rejoin my brethren. I will let no harm come to you."

I pursed my lips. "Of course you wouldn't. On purpose. But my suit is the only thing between me and death." I frowned and pinched the tough fabric together. "What about this? How about if I go back, and then I'll catch up to you and your brothers?" I looked up at him to see him removing his helmet.

He frowned at me, his black and red eyes searching my face. "No."

Taken aback, I scrambled to my feet so I could speak to him face to face as he sat. I pointed to his helmet. "Put that back on." My heartbeat raced. He replaced his helmet. "I *need* to repair my suit. You said yourself we would sleep and leave in the morning." I folded my arms. "I'll just go tonight while you sleep."

His helmet tilted to the side. "No. You yourself are aware of the many dangers on this planet. It is night above ground. You would not survive the terrors of the night alone."

"I may not survive the terrors of the *day* with a torn suit." I stood firm, my hand on my hip and my other one clenching repeatedly. I felt tight tendons in my neck and my eyes stung. I blinked a couple times and forced calm breaths through my nose.

Red leaned back with his huge hands poised on his knees.

Part of me wanted to rail at him, but as long as I'd "known" him, he had been unruffled. I hoped he would be reasonable.

"I long to return to my brethren. But I can see the urgency of your request as well." His helmet dipped forward. It rose again, its visor panel directed at my face. "Let us rest now. Perhaps the Holy Goddesses of Shegoshel will guide us to our next action."

I took a deep breath and exhaled with pursed lips. Okay. We could sleep on it. I nodded. "Alright," I said. I studied his calm pose.

Red cleared his throat. "Let us prepare pallets upon which to sleep."

I looked around inside the cave, trying to find a good spot. I didn't have blankets or a pillow. My suit would normally regulate the temperature, but compensating for the breach would use too much energy. I had disabled that feature.

A flat spot about a yard from the pool seemed like a good place. I walked to it, brushed some loose stone aside and sat down, settling my pack to use it as a headrest.

I looked over to see Red had unrolled a thick blanket. It seemed his armor and pack had many hidden pockets and stashes. I never guessed he carried such a luxurious comfort. I watched him move. For someone so large, he was graceful. He lay the huge sword by his side, but his other weapons remained strapped to his armor. He lay his pack at one end of his pallet as well, then sat.

"You have no pallet?"

For some dumb reason, I felt blood rush to my face. "No. My suit is supposed to make me comfortable."

"Ah." He continued to face me. "And you are comfortable?"

He sat so still with his hands once more placed upon his knees like a yogi.

I averted my eyes from his helmet for a moment. "Yes, yes I'm fine. Thank you." I noticed my nose running and sniffed.

"Very well," he said. Then he removed his helmet and placed it on his charger again. He pointed at me with a dark claw. Then tapped the charging station and pointed once more. "Oh, right. Okay." I stood up and took off my helmet, bringing it to him.

He took it, hefting its slight weight, and said some words with a half-smile. He placed it cell-side down and resumed his position.

I was close enough to smell pepper. My face felt hot and flushed. I skimmed his face once more, appreciating his striking features. I looked a little too long at his full lips and pulled my gaze away. Unfortunately, it fell on his broad shoulders and barrel chest. Everywhere I looked, his indomitable presence filled my vision. I swallowed and reached toward his hand. "Yaza?"

He startled at my touch, and I watched him raise his other hand toward his chest but then stop. "Ik."

I took a breath. I touched his armor at his shoulder. "Maza?" It was the word for body.

"Ik."

With heart racing, I reached to his ear. "Quaza." My pulse fluttered in my neck. My fingers brushed past his hair. It was silky, but I didn't let my fingers drift through it.

"Ik."

My chest rose. A bead of sweat trickled down the back of my neck. My trembling hand hovered near his face, but I drew it back to my own nose. "Saza."

"Ik." He stared at me, motionless.

I had run out of words.

He took up the torch instead and reached a huge hand toward my face. "Ikdu?" he whispered. He said it as his hand paused before my mouth. Was he asking permission?

"Uh, ik?" I croaked.

His clawed finger touched my lower lip. "Waza." He traced it, then circled up to my top lip. "Waza. Wazal."

"Ik," I said in a whisper.

Feeling brave, I reached for his face again, and touched his bottom lip. "Waza." I drew on his top lip with invisible paint, pausing at a scabbed over cut. "Waza. Wazal."

This time, he whispered. "Ik." His face contorted, and he once again reached to brush the armor at his chest.

What happened? One second he was fine, and the next he looked to be in pain. I blinked fast and stepped away, avoiding his face. My breaths came in short gasps. I hadn't touched another male since Chris. I clapped a hand to my own chest and concentrated on my breathing. I had no business playing kid games. I inhaled then met his eyes. "I'm sorry. We better get some rest."

He didn't know what I was saying, but he pressed his thumb between his brows and rubbed. He shook himself, then peered past me at my space. He looked at my face and cocked his head. With a grunt, he patted the pallet beside him. He scooted back to make room then lay down to face the wall.

I stood, uncertain. It was clear he welcomed me to share the soft blanket. But ... I swallowed and looked at his massive solid form. He still wore his armor, and I still had my flight suit. I rolled my eyes at myself. I sat down, and his spicy aroma enveloped me.

He didn't move or make a sound, so I lay down and used the crook of my arm as a pillow. The bead light grew dim, as did the pool of glowing creatures. I listened to the sound of trickling water. "Um, Naraxthel?"

A grunt.

"Agothe-fax?"

"I, i. Esra la ikshemaza."

I didn't know what he said, but he seemed unconcerned. I took comfort in his slow breathing and the warmth at my back. My lids drifted closed and I considered I was indeed very comfortable, if excessively hot for being in a cave.

40

NARAXTHEL

I dreamed of the Holy Goddesses of Shegoshel. Their beauty took my breath away, but they pinned me with stern expressions. I did not know what I did to earn their ire. When I tried to explain, they pushed me through panels of sheer fabric. I awoke in the pitch-black cave, blinking a few times. I sniffed for traces of agothe-faxl, but all was clear. Then the subtle fragrance of lilies wafted over me, and I realized Esra lay at my back. I felt heat radiating from her. A sour odor pinched my nose. "Light," I said, and my bead light glowed.

Frowning, I rolled toward her, careful not to bump her. Her entire body trembled. "Esra," I said her name and willed her eyes to blink open. "Soft traveler, wake to me."

My breaths quickened, and my heart stuttered in its chamber. She was barely breathing; the stench of sour water grew strong in my nostrils. I fumbled for a pouch with my free hand. Curse my family lineage for all time. I was going to use the vial. I flipped the lid open with my thumb claw and lowered her head. I needed my other hand. My claw clicked against her teeth as I held open her lips with my forefinger. I poured the sacred drops into her mouth. First the Elder Sister drop from the top, then the younger sister from the spout at the side of the vial. I stopped the holes and stuffed the vial in its pouch. I supported her head with my hands and watched for any sign of revival. The memory of pressing my lips against hers to give life surfaced. I could do so again.

"Esra," I whispered. I lifted my head and listened for the rumblings of any other night-walkers, then returned my attention to the little hunter. "Esra." My heart beat its way against the opening in the heart-home. "Holy Goddesses, what would you have me do?"

I lay her back down and retrieved her helmet, replacing it on her suit. Perhaps its self-sustaining system would freshen her air. I cuffed my hand around her slender wrist where the tear in the fabric revealed her pale skin. I watched her face through the helmet, my breaths coming in rapid gusts and my heart wrestling within its armored cage. The battle within my chest contorted my face as my blood pulsed and throbbed in my ears and my neck. My tongue felt thick in my mouth.

My helmet chirped. Startled, I returned it to my head, but I remained on my knees near Esra.

The female voice spoke in my ear. "Naraxthel," it said.

"Yes, translator?" I whispered.

"I am Esra's assistant. I am called VELMA. I am the Vector Egress Liaison Machine AI K90"

"Vel-ma?" I was familiar with the sounds as Esra had told me the name, but they made up a word that did not exist.

"Esra is experiencing a medical emergency and requires immediate attention," the voice said. "Please move Esra to the Emergency Egress Pod."

"Do you mean her ship?"

"Yes."

I gathered our possessions in a hasty bundle and secured them upon my back.

Careful of her fragile body, I lifted her, maintaining a grip around her wrist, hoping to prevent most of her good air from escaping.

"Will Esra live?"

"Her suit has switched to auxiliary power," VELMA said. "I am diverting all resources to her oxygen. Until the suit's light cells have been charged to one hundred percent, my ability to provide an oxygen-rich environment will be limited. Please return her to her ship."

I raced through the tunnels. Would the drops I gave her help or harm her? Every pounding step of my heavy boots echoed with the beat of my heart. I felt my heart-home shift; it reminded me of my adolescence on Ikshe, when my heart was free of its chamber and beat with unrestrained joy. Now questions hammered at my mind. I felt no joy at the thought of Esra's spirit leaving her frail body and joining the spirits in the Land of Shegoshel.

Esra and I had cleared the caves, thus my way was unhampered by agothe-faxl. My heaving breaths echoed within my helmet. I breached the meadow entrance of the cave and ran through the tall grasses.

"Natheka!" I signaled him with my comm. "The soft traveler has succumbed to an illness," I said. "She dies in my arms!"

Static rustled in my ears. "What will you do?"

"I am taking her to her ship," I said. "It has healing capability. We will ..." I studied her ashen face. "I—will join you when it is over." My voice cracked. He told me their coordinates.

"And Naraxthel," he said. "Hivelt has gone missing. We lost him when we battled *pazathel-nax*."

I cursed and closed the comm. Could the Goddesses rain further torment upon this hunter?

I carried Esra to her landing site, glancing at her pale face through the helmet glass. Her lips lost more color with every footstep. At last I reached her small ship; VELMA de-cloaked it.

A door at the rear of the ship slid open. I could maneuver Esra's body into the ship, but I could not fit through the door.

"Esra, wake to me," I said, squeezing her gloved hands. No response. "VELMA, what do you require of me?"

"You must place Esra on the table."

I inspected the doorway. If I removed my armor, I could squeeze my bulk inside.

I removed my helmet and entered the commands in my wrist panel to disengage the tendrils that connected my blood and my armor. I endured the sensations of a thousand barbed worms crawling out of my skin, willing the process to move faster.

At last, my armor detached piece by piece, leaving me with nothing but my simple undergarment. I collected my kit, and I slid Esra to the side as I contorted my body into her ship. The metal doorway abraded my skin, but I ignored it. I gathered Esra into my naked arms and watched as a chair unfolded into a flat slab.

"Place Esra on the exam table," VELMA said. "Remove her helmet, and I will do the rest."

I placed my soft traveler's body where VELMA directed and unlatched her helmet. A blinking red light on the wall showed a simple replica of her head gear. I secured it there, all the while watching metallic threads and cables unravelling from Esra's suit and plugging into holes all along the table. Restraints slipped up around her limbs save for one arm, securing her body to the surface.

"I am administering intravenous fluid and bio-autolyzed liquid oxygen. I will restore her organ function and oxygen saturation."

My eyes narrowed at the wires. They reminded me of the skin probes in my own suit. With my heart beating a frantic rhythm, I watched Esra's pale face and blue lips. Her chest did not rise and fall with breath. Her eyes showed no movement beneath the lids. With mounting anxiety, I stood as close as I dared to the table where a robotic arm, held together by cables and wires, manipulated a slender metallic implement above Esra's body. With a whirring noise, the implement drove into several ports on Esra's suit.

"I have detected an unidentified bacterium in Esra's system," VELMA's voice announced. "I suspect the substance I classified as chemically similar to Salvinorin A may have been the initial infection. I will attempt to manufacture a bacteriophage from soil samples she obtained, but I do not know if it will work before she loses organ function."

I swallowed a lump in my throat. Were the Waters of Shegoshel acting as the infection in Esra's blood?

"I gave Esra two drops of our sacred healing Waters," I told VELMA. "Could that have caused Esra's illness?" Heat flared in my face and my mouth dried up.

"Will you allow me to scan a drop of your healing Waters?"

I grimaced and clenched my fists. The Waters of Shegoshel were obtained at great cost to my people. "Will you transmit your findings to Esra's people or others?"

"I am unable to contact anyone from the planet's surface," VELMA said. "Esra's mothership is light-years out of range, and I have had no pings from other humans or any other races since Esra landed on this planet."

I inhaled through my flaring nostrils and closed my eyes. Unclenched my fists.

"Where do I place the drop?"

A lighted clear box slid out from a wall panel. A tiny clear plate ejected.

"Place the drop in the center of the glass plate. Do not touch it."

I retrieved the vial from the kit around my waist, opened and tilted it. A single drop of the milky liquid fell onto the glass. The plate withdrew, and a series of colored lights scanned the sample. A steady beeping noise sounded from Esra's table. I turned to watch her.

VELMA spoke. "When did you administer the Waters?"

"Just before you alerted me to her health emergency. In the caves."

"I am reviewing her health logs over the past several days. I failed to connect the micro-indicators of the bacterial strain. Your Waters did not introduce the bacteria into Esra's bloodstream."

I sagged against a wall inside her ship. Still my eyes were drawn to Esra.

Her eyes moved beneath her eyelids. My gaze jumped to her chest that rose a fraction of a tik.

"Esra?" I stepped closer, avoiding the bent metal arm. "Can you hear me?"

A low moan vibrated in her throat. My heart-home wrenched itself open, and my heart attempted to squeeze out into the empty chamber beside the heart-home. I felt its strain to release into its new dwelling place. I gasped and clutched at my bare chest. With eyes watering, I doubled over. If my heart-home had decided Esra was to be my mate, everything would change. With weak knees, I sank to the floor and watched her sleep, my brows arched and my throat spasming in disbelief. I reviewed the evening's events as I roved my gaze over her small body, searching for any sign of her previous vitality—her bravery.

I had stopped myself tiks before intervening in Esra's battle. I watched her form, the clumsy way she swung her weapons, the awkward stance of her legs as she tried to fight with her center of gravity too high. With training, she could learn to hold her weight on the balls of her feet, to bend her legs, to keep her arms closer to her body. She would be my little hunter indeed. If she lived.

I drew a shaky breath and reached a hand to grasp her boot.

She had walked to me, her brows raised, after her kills. I looked past her to the ravaged night-walker bodies and then gave her a smile. Her face flooded to a dark-pink. For a tik I wished to smell her, but instead I pointed to her filthy weapon. She colored again but drove the blade into the ground. After, she held it close to her visor, staring at the metal. Her eyes grew larger as she inspected the metal, turning the blade in the light. Her interest revealed a keen mind that appreciated a valuable weapon.

I observed the screen inside Esra's pod that flashed with lights and unfamiliar symbols. How had she fallen ill? I remembered yanking her wrist closer to see the wound. If the night-walker had injected its venom, her mouth would have turned black and I would have had seconds to give her the Waters of Shegoshel. But her mouth had appeared healthy to my view.

I had to move away from her. The halted ceremony of raxshe and raxma had my heart confused and yearning for something that was impossible.

My thoughts turned to my brethren. Had their sight-captures appeased the Ikma? Did they slay the pazathel-nax with ease? Had Raxthezana chosen an underground pathway through the mountains, or were they waiting at the Little Sister Pass? How would we find Hivelt? My heartbeat accelerated, and I felt my hands grow warm. I stood over the soft traveler and let my fingers splay through her braids. It was the only comfort available.

41

I heard the familiar beeping of my EEP, but I couldn't open my eyes. My mouth tasted like the water-recycler stopped working, I felt aches throughout my body and my *toes itched*. I wiggled them inside my boots and realized I would have to sit up if I wanted to yank off my boots and scratch my toes. Why were they tingling? Did I contract trench-foot? I wouldn't be surprised on this hell-hot planet.

I groaned and rotated my head, trying to work the kink out of my neck. I grimaced but couldn't swallow. Then I smelled pepper. I inhaled deeply, feeling my breaths slow and my muscles relax.

I had enough strength to push out a single word. "Red?"

A heavy hand rested on my bicep. "Esra."

"I can't open my eyes." Also, I couldn't vocalize, other than to whisper. My words would have been inaudible to anyone but Naraxthel.

VELMA said words in Naraxthel's language. Memories of the fight with the agothe-faxl sprung to mind, and I felt my heart race. Wait. We killed them. And then VELMA had suggested she could hack into Naraxthel's helmet. That's why she was using his language. It worked!

"VELMA," I squeaked out. "Why can't I open my eyes?"

"A side effect of the Pulmocet Mecaprotin is temporary ptosis. The oculopharyngeal muscle system will be compromised for a short time. You may also experience difficulty swallowing."

I moaned while VELMA spoke in Naraxthel's language.

I heard skin brush against skin, and then felt Naraxthel's large hand clasp my own. "What happened?" I asked.

Naraxthel spoke a few words in his language. The low rumble of his voice soothed me, even though I couldn't understand him.

"Naraxthel has asked I translate for him," VELMA said. "He wants to explain."

"Thank you," I said.

"VELMA discovered a bacterium in your blood," he said. "It is attacking your organs."

I moaned again, hating the invasion of something I couldn't see. But Red had a nice bedside manner.

"Am I going to die?"

Silence for a moment.

"You are a mighty little hunter," VELMA translated. "A jo-ik-the-ka."

I felt so tired. So ready to leave this place.

VELMA's voice sounded in the small chamber. "I am manufacturing a bacteriophage to battle the bacterial infection. Do not lose hope."

"What did I miss?" I said in a weak voice.

Red explained how I did not awaken and burned with a fever and that he had administered what he hoped were healing drops from a stash of prized medicine.

I nodded and inhaled again, letting the peppery aroma flood my nose and lungs.

"We can speak now," I rasped. "Talk to me."

I heard Naraxthel's soft laugh and he squeezed my hand.

"I have much to tell you, Esra."

"Please go on."

"I will start at the beginning."

I felt the scrape of a claw brush across my thumb through my gloves. I wished I could see his face, and I tried once more to open my eyes.

"I am from a poor province on my home-world, the Deadlands. It is isolated. Untouched by the intrigues of the Royal Court. But it is a very beautiful place, full of meadows and lakes. My mother foraged from the meadows and fished in the lakes for our meals. I learned to hunt the small animals in the Deadlands and, when I was old enough, I became an Iktheka."

Hunter. That explained why his companions had been so obtuse. Where were they?

"Theraxl hunters are given a simple ship to travel here where we must test ourselves. I was young and reckless."

"We all are at some point," I whispered, thinking of my bad judgment concerning Chris.

"The Goddesses of Shegoshel shined down upon me, and my hunt was very lucky. I was able to save a fellow hunter from an early death. Natheka. I hoped my luck would be enough for the Goddesses to bless me with a Lottery Draw."

I raised a brow.

"Theraxl hunters are only allowed to mate if they are selected from the Lottery Draw. Five are chosen at each Draw. To have offspring is the highest honor an Iktheka can receive."

I tried to prevent the blood from rushing to my cheeks with steady breathing. These were culturally sensitive matters that had nothing to do with me. At all. And never would.

Stop blushing, stupid cheeks!

"However, it was not to be. Each cycle for fifteen sun cycles my name has not been drawn in the Lottery. I have no offspring."

His voice sounded withdrawn, maybe even forlorn. I couldn't tell him that where I came from, *nobody* wanted kids.

"The day you landed was the day of my most successful hunt. Never have I slaughtered so much meat to feed my sisters on Ikshe. The food the Ikthekal provide from this planet feeds as many sisters on Ikshe as possible."

"But what about the Deadlands?" I asked him. "You had to hunt for your food."

"True. The meat from Ikthe seldom reached the poor regions of my home world when I was a child."

Oh. When he was a child. I knew with conviction he kept his mother well-supplied. He must come to this planet twice as often as others, just to provide for her as well as to the Royal Court. My admiration for him swelled, but I said nothing.

"On that day, I had mighty hopes my name would be drawn. At such time, I would choose a female to create offspring with."

I was glad he couldn't see my eyes. A part of me didn't want to hear this part, but I couldn't explain why.

"After the celebration of raxshe and raxma, we would part ways. In two cycles' time, my offspring would be born."

"Two years?" I blurted, then clamped my mouth shut. Did I mention my A *minus* in Interplanetary Relations?

"What is the gestation period for one of your kind?"

"Uh, nine months. Nine ... moons?"

His voice rose in shock. "That is no time to prepare for one's offspring!"

"I'm sure that's true," I said. "But I have no children, so I wouldn't know."

"Ah," he said in his own voice before he continued with VELMA's help. "I sent my sight-capture to the Royal Courts. My people will watch the scenes of my hunt for cycles to come."

He wasn't bragging, I noticed. Just stating the facts. *What a beast.*

"When the horde overpowered me, I thought I was a dead Theraxl."

More than familiar with that feeling, I nodded.

"My queen and the sisters of the Royal Court also thought I was dead," he said. "They would have celebrated my death as a legendary hunter of Ikshe."

I remembered his heroism, facing those monsters dead-on. And how limp he'd been, buried underneath the carcasses. I let out a moan before I could stop it. He lived. I couldn't explain why that meant something to me. I felt his hand touch my arm, then cool air replaced the sensation.

"When I climbed out of my grave, I saw something unusual in the terrain—your ship."

I would have been gone by then, hiking up to place the beacon. I shivered, remembering the rest.

"Once I found you again, you were dying. I could not hear your heartbeat. Nor could I detect the echoes of a heart-home. Your technology has since taught me humans do not possess that organ."

Heart-home? I wondered what it meant. I gestured he should continue.

"I was touched at your bravery, confused you had arrived in our isolated star system, angry you may have brought others to a knowledge of our sacred planets ..." he tapered off and squeezed my hand again.

"No," he said. "I have seen for myself you cannot be a spy." His thumb caressed my wrist. I wondered if he knew he was doing that.

"When the Royal Courts summoned me, I had no choice. I had tried to help you. There was nothing else I could do. Refusing the invitation of my queen, once they knew I yet lived?" He snorted.

I nodded. I opened my eyes a slit, as far as they would, and light seeped in.

"I am loath to tell you what happened in the Royal Courts."

The silence grew heavy. I wanted to see him, his eyes, his face. What didn't he want to tell me? What was this growing emotional bond between us? And why would it surface now, when I was at death's door?

"My name was drawn as one of the five."

"You were going to mate," I said. I wanted to see him so bad I almost lifted a hand to pry open my lids.

"Yes. After fifteen long cycles and desiring it with all my heart and heart-home." He stopped speaking for another long moment. I cleared my throat and was able to swallow a little. I also could open my eyes a sliver, so I blinked them a few times.

"Okay, so wait," I said. I clenched my teeth and squeezed my eyes shut. Took a deep breath. "Why are you here? Shouldn't you be, you know?" My cheeks burned from my impertinent question.

He scowled and stared at a panel in my ship a long time. I noticed the muscles ripple along his cheek. "I angered the queen," was all he said while avoiding my gaze. He also moved a little farther from me, like he didn't want to touch me. "In a rage, the Ikma demanded the Lottery five go on one of Theraxl's deadliest expeditions instead. Immediately."

He groaned low in his throat, but it rumbled in my chest. I turned my head away from him, sensing his discomfort. I wondered what he could have done to anger his queen. Had he told her about me? I had more questions, but I felt so tired. I tried blinking to wake myself up.

"So, this death march. That's where we were all going?" I finally asked.

"Yes."

"I don't know how I feel about that."

His expression hardened. "You are a brave female, Yasheza Mahavelt. But you could not last alone on Ikthe."

I bit the inside of my cheek. I had. For a day or two, anyway. Small comfort. "Your companions? Where are they now?"

"One of my brethren was separated from the group after we left them."

I gasped. They were all impossibly strong. "What happened?"

"They fought a pack of pazathel-nax." He paused. "Your VELMA tells me they are similar to prehistoric wolves on your home planet." His head bent a moment. Then it rose again. His red eyes glared at me. "Hivelt disappeared after facing one of the pack leaders. They had not heard from him when we last spoke."

"I'm so sorry," I said. I remembered Hivelt. He was the biggest of them all. "I wish I wasn't sick. I want you to find Hivelt." I quirked my mouth. "Although he did almost try to kill me."

Naraxthel laughed. "Hivelt has the anger of a roaring mountain. I would not have allowed him to harm you. He gave me this," he said and grazed the scab on his top lip with a claw. The scab my finger had caressed not so long ago. "But he could not hurt a female."

"What did you tell him? To make him let me go?"

He peered at me a second then caught light from the window. I could make out the tendons and musculature of his neck. He shrugged. Did he not want to answer? He met my eyes. "I spoke with my brothers when you were asleep. They are continuing on the expedition." He gestured out the window. "Underground." He stopped. "We will catch up to them when you are well. And once we have collected the Holy Waters of Shegoshel and the woaiquovelt, we will all return to Ikshe, bearers of great gifts, and legends of bravery and heroism." He pounded a fist on his chest.

My eyes lingered on his pronounced pectorals and carved shoulders and upper arms. Strange scars dotted his sage-green skin, creating patterns and designs. I wondered what they meant and what sorts of battles he had survived over the years to collect such injuries. I blinked, still feeling the effects of the medicine.

"But what about me?" I hated that my voice sounded so little.

He crouched. I stared at his hands. They were strong and lithe, the same pale-green but with black claws. His actual claws were not as long nor as sharp as on his armored gloves. He touched my face with his knuckles. My breath caught, and my heart leapt in my chest.

"I remain with you, Yasheza Mahavelt. My people will reject me once they learn you are my companion."

Um. What?

My heart galloped out of control. "Companion?"

"I will not leave your side until you are well," Naraxthel said. "This," he gestured between us, "is not done. Companionship between males and females." I watched his brow fold in consternation. He traced my hand with a claw. He tilted his head. "In my world, the males seed the females to create children. But then we part ways. Our queen, the Ikma, and her younger sister, Kama, do have consorts. But as for the rest of us, we live always alone."

My mouth worked, but I didn't know what to say. It sounded like a lonely existence.

"There is a myth about the heart and heart-home," he said, but then stopped. "It is nothing. I thought perhaps you wished to sleep. You are restless when you walk in the fields of Shegoshel."

"The fields of Shegoshel?"

"Sleeping," he explained, "and dreaming. The suns give us all. Life, water, daylight and night, waking and sleeping. And dreaming. It is why the Waters of Shegoshel are so prized. They give healing sleep, and sometimes, healing dreams."

I tried to sit up, but my restraints held fast. "Oh my gosh. The dreams."

He tilted his head and let his brows draw together. "The Waters of Shegoshel gave you dreams?"

"Um. Did they?"

He touched my temple, but said nothing, scowling.

VELMA did say there was a trace of a hallucinogenic drug in my system. Maybe it was like those ancient Native American customs where they smoked some herbs and then had visions. Except I didn't have visions. I had two vivid dreams. Hallucinations? I'd only eaten from VELMA's approved list, too.

"VELMA, is there any sign of that Salvia stuff in my bloodstream?" I assumed she would have checked it when I was out. Numerous times, judging by the discomfort at the IV port in my left arm.

"Not precisely," VELMA said. "The bacteria resembled the chemical makeup of Salvinorin A but did not act as an agonist in your neuroreceptors. Therefore, I have reclassified it as a cyanobacteria of this planet."

"When did you give me these special Waters?" I asked Red. I lost feeling in my toes and fingers, a bone-deep fatigue coming over me. I wanted to stay awake to hear everything, but I was so tired.

"In the cave after you fell asleep," he answered. "I could not awaken you. When did you have the dreams? My people hold the dreams of the Holy Shegoshel very sacred."

I swallowed. Closed my eyes. Tried to snatch at the wisps of images that haunted me.

"The first time was in the cave after the big agothe-fax attacked me," I said, pinching my eyes shut. "When I almost died." *The first time.* I needed to remember. It was more than just the peace that washed over me. There were clues and messages in there. Something about the colors and smells and tastes made me think the dreams were more than just the random firing of my neurons.

"My people believe the Goddesses of Shegoshel shine the light of life upon all creation. They esteem life as beloved and death as sacred. The worthy welcome both."

206 VICKY L. HOLT

My head shot up. "The worthy?"

He nodded slowly. "Theraxl can only hope to be found worthy before the Holy Sisters of Shegoshel. Then will their offspring be blessed."

I gasped as a memory tripped out of my limbic system and crashed into my skull. The two females said they were judging my worthiness. And then they reawakened the events I tried so hard to forget. Blood pounded behind my eyes. What did my history with Chris have to do with anything? And how dare they bring that up?

"You are angry," Red stated, interested but not troubled.

"I am. I kind of want to kick your Goddesses in the teeth."

He nodded. "A sentiment we often speak of. It is understood we do not comprehend the ways of the Goddesses. They know that, as well."

I gave a weak laugh. "You're saying they don't mind if we get mad at them?"

He smiled, his fangs gleaming in the ethereal cloud-filtered light through my porthole. "They gave birth to a race of hunters and warriors. Do you not think they are accustomed to our anger and violence?"

Good point.

He grew serious.

"Your sleep was not a peaceful one. You shed many tears for one named Chris. Is this your mate?" I saw muscles in his jaw flex and bunch, and his fangs peeked out from his firm lips. If I didn't know better...

My heart skipped a beat. Tears sprang to my eyes unbidden.

"No!" I said. "I never want to think of him." But this planet resurrected his memory.

"Yet your spirit has not let go of him."

"Oh, like you know so much about my spirit," I snapped, then clamped my mouth shut, feeling my face go hot. I avoided his eyes. My breaths quickened just remembering. I let my eyes glaze over and murmured to myself. "*No one* knows how lucky I was to leave."

I hiccoughed. Used my free hand to wipe away my tears.

I turned my head away. I couldn't bear to see disgust. Not from Red, who up until now, was my only friend in this insane place.

"VELMA, what's the status of my recovery?" I asked. The tingling in my extremities continued, and while I could open my eyes and swallow, I still felt as weak as a de-venomed wasp.

"Your body requires a full seventy-two hours to recover from the infection if my treatment is successful."

I closed my eyes.

Almost in answer, I felt a rumble in the exam table, its deep shaking making my blood vessels throb and bones tremble. I met Red's scrutiny in alarm.

"VELMA?"

Red spoke, and VELMA translated. "It is a ship from Ikshe." Red's brows deepened, and he growled, standing and reaching for a weapon that was not at his side. "How did she find us? Let us see if the Ikma enjoys the sight of *her* blood spilling upon my armor."

A spike of adrenaline stirred me. "What's going to happen? Red?"

"Stay inside," he said and squeezed my shoulder.

"VELMA, turn on the camera and release the drone," I said. "Try to stay undercover if possible."

"Deploying drone."

I watched the little drone screen inside my pod light up. A mammoth ship lowered itself into the "picnic meadow," the tall grasses flattening under its engines. I could see creatures fleeing the area, and while I still felt the rumble, my ears also popped.

I tried to gauge Red's reaction, but he was already through the hatch, meticulously applying his armor. Each piece he put in place caused a grimace to cross his face. *What?* He caught me staring and said something. The hatch closed.

The view of the ship came on my main screen. The ship was monstrous. Not just in size, but in aesthetics. Its panels boasted sharp violent angles. Horns jutted from the "top"; teeth stood in threatening rows around the bow. Spikes arrayed all over its black glossy surface. A huge round emblem was emblazoned on the side. Two suns, a red one set inside the other yellow, formed the background. Two planets, again, one set inside the other, superimposed the foreground. A single sharp tooth slashed across the image along with a drop of blood. The emblem was as clear as a cocked weapon. Don't screw with us.

I swallowed, and a little whimper escaped. Red was out there. Probably standing between the door to my pod and whoever was coming in that ship.

Breathless, I clutched at my chest with my free hand. How did I know he was standing guard? Why did that thrill me when I had only known him for a couple of days? I frowned and clenched my jaw. It was nonsense. He was nothing to me. I was nothing to him. Except … I looked at the ship's teeth and imagined Naraxthel Roika, just as he had stood the first time I saw him, full of war and blood, ready to slay a pack of slavering beasts. I found myself panting. Those teeth could be guns.

I doubted they were saying, "I come in peace." Schist. I needed a plan. *Okay*, I exhaled. First, I needed more information.

"VELMA, please patch me into any communication between Naraxthel and the ship."

"Accessing comms." VELMA scrolled words in English across my view screen.

"… come bringing word from our Ikma," a female voice said. "She noticed a woeful lack of sight-captures from Ikshe's most celebrated hunter."

"Have not my brethren sent many sight-captures?" Naraxthel said. "Surely the fight with the pazathel-nax was bloody enough?"

"It was indeed," the voice said. "But it wasn't you. Our Ikma has cultivated a … fondness, for you."

"Ikma knows I do not return her ardor, dear BoKama."

Oh. Was that how he "angered" his queen? My heartbeat picked up listening to their conversation. Did his queen … proposition him? If only I could be out there with him. I wanted to stand beside Red and face who or whatever was coming, but I couldn't lift my head, let alone a weapon. I flexed my leg muscles and clenched my hands. I felt fatigue layering over me. No! I could not go to sleep now. I might not wake up. I pinched my thigh where my hand was restrained next to my leg and blinked furiously.

"There is something else," BoKama said. "You haven't volunteered any information about this pretty little ship I spied on your earlier sight-capture. What is it?"

"I have dealt with it," Naraxthel said. "It is not a threat to Ikma Scabmal Kama."

It? Torn, I eavesdropped.

"And yet, I can see through my viewport you will not leave its side, nor will you allow anyone access to its entry, should I send my guards out to you."

"They will die, should you send them out," he said. "I suggest you return to Ikshe and tell Ikma all is well on our hunting grounds, that the Ikthekal are on her hasty *unjust* errand, and will return with more Waters of Shegoshel and woaiquovelt than Ikma's eyes have ever seen. Our work will go much faster if we do not have to send sight-captures *every other tik.*"

I gasped. Whoever BoKama was, she was getting a dressing down.

I studied the ship. I couldn't tell if any of the spikes were cannons or space guns or what. If she decided to just fire on Naraxthel, there wasn't anything I could do. My blood felt sluggish in my veins and my breathing picked up.

"Do you wish for another dose of pain reliever?" VELMA said.

"No." I squinted at the screen, fiddling with one of the wires hooked up to my suit. A thought came to mind. "Does the EEP have any kind of weapons system?"

"It is inadvisable to deploy weapons without first attempting peaceful interventions, according to Protocol #205."

I paused with a cable in my hand. "You mean the EEP *does* have weapons?"

"According to Protocol #205, all strategies of peaceful resolution should be attempted before deploying the EEP's ordnance."

Holy Hematite. Ordnance? What kind of firepower was this baby packing?

"I'm not planning on starting an intergalactic war, VELMA. Look at that ship. But out of curiosity, what kind of ordnance does the EEP have?" *And why?* I thought IGMC was all about exploration and ore discovery, not aggressive military action.

"The EEP X215 comes complete with three small surface-to-air

210 VICKY L. HOLT

missiles, a repeating rotator gun with ten thousand rounds of ammunition and a single fractionated quark bomb that can travel up to 150 meters."

I broke out into a cold sweat. Where in the EEP was this stuff even at?

"VELMA, what's a fractionated quark bomb?"

"It would have been cost-prohibitive for every single rescue vehicle to carry a full complement of ..."

"Um, never mind. So how do I fire any of it?"

"It is inadvisable to deploy weapons until you have exhausted all peaceful interventions."

"I'm not going to ..." I said and pinched the bridge of my nose. "I'm just trying to figure out what all my options are."

With my attention fading in and out, VELMA listed the EEP X215's capabilities and how to execute them.

The fatigue crept up my limbs. Even so, if Red was in trouble at all, I was going to unleash the EEP's hellfire on that big ship. And then probably die in a massive fireball. I stared at the screen, waiting. Flames of glory versus an invisible infection? No contest.

42

NARAXTHEL

I waited.

The hatch to BoKama's ship remained closed.

I felt the steady beat of my heart; its strength pushed rich blood through my veins. My breaths were even and deep. I held my hands loose by my sides, within easy reach of my weapons, and I bent my knees a fraction, ready for any movement. I would that Esra's illness would abate, but I desired she would stay hidden and compliant. As few rotiks as we had known each other, compliant was not a word I would use to describe her.

Still BoKama's hatch did not open.

The Sisters did not set foot on Ikthe, but BoKama was a formidable one. She often trained with my brethren and her own Consort and sent the sight-captures of her combat across the planet. I would not be surprised if she chose to step onto the soil of Ikthe, to be the first Sister to breathe its sweltering air.

"I spoke with Elder Sister," BoKama spoke through my comm. "I told her I have not yet found Naraxthel Roika."

I caught a breath. Younger Sister lied to the Ikma Scabmal Kama. What did this mean?

"Ikma Scabmal Kama sent an envoy to hasten your return to Ikshe. I came in its stead."

My heart slowed, and blood pounded in my ears. What game was Younger Sister Kama playing at? I had witnessed raxfathe. That was Esra's destiny if Ikma learned of Esra's existence—if Esra lived. My hands opened and closed. My mind churned with strategies. I could only think of one reason why she would lie to Queen Elder Sister. But if she were discovered, she risked raxfathe and death. Just as I did, in harboring Esra on this planet.

"I will remain on Ikthe with my brethren until we have gathered the Waters by the barrel and woaiquovelt by the barge-full," I said. "My queen shall have no reason to doubt her hunter's loyalty."

Silence a tik.

"I am coming out, Naraxthel," BoKama said. "Without my guards or weapons. Stand down."

My eyes narrowed, but I stood still.

The hatch lowered into a ramp, its gleaming black metal catching the last rays of the second sun set. I watched as BoKama's slender slippered feet and long legs appeared first, then her swaying hips draped in a leafy green tunic, followed by her navel revealed by the deep neckline, and then her angular chin. Her red eyes came into view as she walked the rest of the way down the ramp, paused at the ground, then stepped onto land. She wore the orange feathered headdress with a gleaming purple cabochon in its center. Such jeweled pieces held sight-capture technology. I saw her wrinkle her nose and contemplate the meadow before studying the gray escape pod. Then she studied me.

"I have never met an Iktheka who dared to defy my Ikma," she said. She stared at me long enough that the fading light of day receded into nightfall, but we had no trouble seeing one another. "Perhaps we might come to an agreement. You and I."

My shoulders tensed, and I clenched my hands. My gaze flicked to the open hatch. Were her guards waiting for a command? Was she not then sending a sight-capture to speak of such treason? "You are interested in a portion of the spoils of Ikthe?"

She drew back and scowled at me, fangs bared, and eyes narrowed. "Do not dishonor me with bribery!"

She took a step closer to me, and I stood taller.

"I do not care about the Waters of Shegoshel or more woaiquovelt," she said, her voice quieter. "I desire to be a weapon for the Goddesses."

I smelled the wind that carried BoKama's scent to me. It smelled of the cone trees in the Domed Mountains of Ikshe. *She spoke truth.* "I am listening." I would not promise more than that.

"You assume I agree with *Ikma's* lifestyle," she said, her voice dripping with venom at Ikma's name. "I prize my life. But Ikma has corrupted the ways of Theraxl for thirty cycles."

She took a step closer to the pod, and I advanced, my body between her and the vessel. She cocked her head at me.

"I do not know what you are protecting, but sensed truth in your words when you said it was no threat to Ikma. Do you tell the truth?"

"I do," I said. My heart beat a faster pace when she roved her eyes up and down the small ship.

She took a deep breath through her nose. "No," she said with a tilted head. "It poses no threat." She sighed and shook her head. "A pity." She circled the pod, gliding through the grasses. She inspected the ship, noting the panels and engines, its sleek lines and straight-edged fins with the tip of a finger. She peered at the round window but didn't lean closer to see inside.

I couldn't prevent my shallow breathing.

Her nostrils flared. "You are afraid I will discover this ship's occupant," she said, returning to her original spot in front of her ramp. "This puts me in an excellent bargaining position."

I growled.

Her tinkling laugh echoed in the night and launched the sawing of the nocturnal insects.

"At ease, Iktheka," she said. "I am curious, but not enough to risk being tattooed by your pretty knife." Her eyes glanced at my weapons. "Ikma will not be satisfied for long by your lack of sight-captures. If my mission fails tonight, then she will bring her entire battalion to fetch you. I will be relegated to lower-class diplomatic missions to the Deadlands for cycles. And Ikma's debauched foolery in the Royal Court will continue unchecked." She supported her chin with her delicate hand. "An Iktheka such as yourself will not be cowed by Ikma's demands, but you *will* be killed. After raxfathe, of course."

I dipped my head but said nothing.

She walked up to me and pressed her mouth to the earpiece of my helmet. "If you and I play a deep game, we might depose our Ikma and restore the true ways of Theraxl. But we need each other."

I inhaled, examining the aroma that tickled my nose. I tried to detect deception or subterfuge, but the clean scent of wind-dried linens and cone trees filled my nose through the breath ports of my helmet. She spoke the truth.

"How have you deceived the Ikma into believing your undying loyalty?" I scrutinized her.

She lifted a shoulder. "I mean what I say when I say it; it is as simple as that."

"How can I know you won't travel back to Ikshe telling tales of my treachery?"

Her eyes narrowed once again, and an unholy light shone from her red eyes. She lowered her forehead a fraction when she stared at me. "Ikma stole my Consort's affection from me fifteen cycles ago. I have not forgiven her."

The pungent aroma of burning jokal grass assaulted my nose. It was the stench of vengeance; I could not mistake it.

I folded my arms and stared at her a long tik. "What of your guards?"

"There are no guards," she said. "I came alone."

Taken aback, I tipped my head. She led me to believe she traveled with guards, but there were none. Dare I trust her? I thought of Esra, slowly ravaged by a hunter I could not taste, or smell, or defy. If she lived, Ikma would wreak her vengeance, not only upon the Younger Sister and myself, but upon the innocent traveler. I thought of my brethren, subjected to Ikma's whims, and their little hunters and sisters who would most likely become fatherless after this quest. And I thought of the Holy Goddesses. I tested my fangs with my tongue and stared into BoKama's eyes. "I will help you."

Her fanged smile parted her face. "We have little time. Confer with me now."

43

My eyes blinked rapidly. Disoriented, I searched the chamber for Red, then my sight fell upon the monitor. The EEP's drone employed night vision to make out the shapes of Red and his alien companion. I had lost consciousness and missed their conversation. Heads bent together, they colluded.

"VELMA, please translate."

"Naraxthel has removed his helmet," VELMA said. "I can only pick up scattered words through the exterior mic. Would you like me to relay the words I can hear?"

I bit my lip. "Yes."

"Very well. I will display them onscreen."

Eyes riveted to the monitor, I watched as a series of words scrolled across the screen.

"Mutually assured destruction … guarantee … discovered."

VELMA made note of who was speaking what words, but I was missing the whole picture. I glanced at the other monitor that displayed my vitals. The numbers, as well as my fading consciousness, told the story of my illness.

More words: agreement … will never … hide the alien traveler.

Alien. Traveler.

That was me. I was the alien, the interloper. And it seemed Narax-thel had just agreed to reveal my presence to his people.

Heart jumping to my throat, I swallowed a couple times.

"BPM spiking. Administering relaxant."

"Wait!" I hoped VELMA listened. "Do not allow Naraxthel or his BoKama to enter the pod."

"Hatches sealed."

I took several breaths through my nose. It wouldn't do any good to activate the camouflage. Yet. If they left the landing site, I could enable the hDEDs and bide my time. At least until I could get well and escape. There must be other cave systems. Or mountain ranges. My mind drifted to Raxthezana's map. These hunters knew this planet inside and out. Oh God, I was trapped here. With no allies except a glorified poop scanner.

"Naraxthel is requesting permission to enter the pod."

"No!" My free hand clenched. "He told the female about me. They could kill me."

"Naraxthel is requesting permission to speak."

I clamped my mouth shut. I was tied down to the exam table. Possibly dying. But I was sealed inside. They couldn't even blast me out, as the Galvanite metal was indestructible. Rumor was you could fly it into the sun.

I heard two taps on the hatch. Not pounds.

"VELMA, show them onscreen."

The one called BoKama stood away from the pod, composed. Serene. Naraxthel stood at the hatch. He had replaced his helmet, but his head was bowed at the door.

"What do you want?" I asked VELMA to translate.

"I need to discuss a matter that concerns you," he said.

I blinked away a tear. "I need for you and BoKama to leave me in peace. I will not trouble your people. Or your planet." Especially if I was dead.

"Esra, let us converse. The Younger Kama and I mean you no harm."

"We can talk through the hatch," I said. I stared at the screen, willing the suns to come up so I could see better. "You should just leave me."

"I have told BoKama of your bravery and courage facing the agothe-faxl."

I didn't reply but replayed the battle in my mind.

"A traveler from the stars is unprecedented," Naraxthel continued. "My queen would torture you before she would accept explanations. BoKama and I can see this attitude may destroy our race in the future. Please let us converse together."

I played with the fabric of my suit. A wave of nausea cramped my body, and I groaned. VELMA tightened a strap around my chest.

"Esra!" Red shouted.

"I'm fine," I said, gasping for breath. "VELMA, what's happening to me?"

"Monitoring vitals. The medicine continues to fight the infection in your system. You require rest."

I snorted. I required rest the moment I landed in this hellish place.

"I can't trust you, Naraxthel," I said through gritted teeth. "I don't know or trust BoKama. I don't know your queen. She sounds like a real piece of work."

I watched him lean his helmet against the hatch. His fists clenched. BoKama folded her arms and bowed her head, patient. Waiting.

"Esra, I understand your reluctance. I, too, had my doubts about your presence. Only the Goddesses could send one so helpless to a planet full of predators and smile upon it."

Flashes of the Goddesses from my dreams swept my mind. They were, in fact, smiling. Nearly every time I saw them.

"I can't protect myself from you, Naraxthel." My voice sounded tiny and helpless. I watched the video feed. His shoulders rose and fell.

"You will never need to, Soft Traveler," he said. I watched him lift his helmet and look in BoKama's direction. "If need be, BoKama will remain outside. We wish to make peace with you. We do not wish to make you afraid."

I laughed. "I've been afraid for days, now."

Another cramp pulled at my middle.

I gasped. Felt sweat at my temples. Creased my brows. I didn't want to be alone. A sharper cramp. Aw hell. I was dying anyway.

"I don't know why I'm doing this. But you can come back in. May as well bring your BoKama too."

On the screen, Red bowed his head and pressed his palms together in a gentle salute. BoKama made the same gesture and walked slowly toward the pod.

"VELMA, open the hatch." Then I muttered, "I can't believe I'm doing this."

BoKama entered first, her grace and beauty taking my breath away. She was the very feminine yet wiry version of the males. Long muscular limbs, spare breasts, pointy chin and high cheekbones. Her hair was up in an elaborate display of hundreds of braids. Oh. I gasped. I turned to see Red. Once again, Naraxthel paused at the opening, removing his armor piece by piece.

BoKama caught me watching him. VELMA translated for her. "Pain is a way of life for Ikthekal." She scanned Red a second. "The armor connects to his skin with barbed tendrils. To wear it causes pain. And to remove it, causes pain. But the hunter endures it without complaint."

Tears pricked my eyes, and I blinked them away. The scars dotting his body were from his armor?

"I don't want to cause him pain," I whispered. "He's done nothing but save me—almost since I arrived."

BoKama placed a bare cool hand upon my forehead. "It is our way."

I couldn't pull my eyes away from his stoic expression as he waited a second before each tough panel released. Even when BoKama spoke.

"I am called BoKama, Younger Sister to the Ikma Scabmal Kama, the Queen Elder Sister. I am second in command of these handsome hunter warriors we call Ikthekal."

"I'm Esra Weaver," I said. I felt my eyes grow round when Red's muscular body folded to crawl in. "I'm an exo-geologist and a miner." I licked my lips. His muscles. So many muscles. And so many tiny star-shaped scars. Tears pricked my eyes but I blinked them back.

Naraxthel entered. In only a step, he was standing over me. The pod was now officially crowded. His brow furrowed into a deep groove.

"You have grown sicker in a short time."

"VELMA tells me the medicine is still working."

"Sweat pours from your skin," he said. "I smell sour water. You are very ill."

I barely had the energy to chuckle. "If I knew you were going to insult me, I wouldn't have invited you in."

BoKama nudged Red back. "Hunters have not experience conversing with the stronger sex. What medicine is your technology using?"

"VELMA?"

"I have manufactured a bacteriophage using a single drop of the Waters of Shegoshel and dirt samples from your planet. The bacteria appear to be metabolizing the bacteriophage."

"What does that mean?" I asked VELMA.

"Your body may succumb to the bacterial infection."

Dammit.

"Let us take her to our ship," Naraxthel said.

"No!" I said. "VELMA is doing the best she can." Also, I knew I couldn't move. All the tubes and fluids were keeping me alive.

"The traveler should stay with her technology," BoKama said. "Our healing bays are not familiar with her physiology."

Red's shoulders sagged a little.

I cleared my throat and closed my eyes against another wave of nausea. "What did you want to talk to me about?"

"I, alone, spied your little ship on Naraxthel's initial sight-capture," BoKama said. "Sadly, that particular section of sight-capture was erased, through no fault of my own." She cocked her head. Then gave a toothy smile.

Ah. "Okay," I said.

"Being the only Sister to have seen your ship and considering Naraxthel's odd behavior on the Dais at the Lottery Draw, I came to a secret conclusion."

I nodded and fought to keep my eyes open.

"Naraxthel had something to hide. And I had something to gain.

Through mutually assured destruction, we exchanged vital information without fear of retaliation."

"BoKama desires to overthrow the Queen," Naraxthel said.

She put her hand up. "Not because I desire wealth and power." She leaned closer to me. "My motives are purer. I want revenge. And I want to change the course of Theraxl history."

My eyes grew round. I nodded.

"We will protect you at any cost," Naraxthel said.

I grimaced when more pain creased me down the middle. Panting, I huffed out, "Why?"

"We do not wish to invoke the censure of the Goddesses," BoKama said.

"But they don't care about me," I said. "How could they?"

Burning fire jolted from my chest down my left arm, and suddenly my jaw ached as if I'd been biting into Galvanite bolts.

I thought I heard BoKama say, "She dies."

Yes, I thought. I do.

* * *

"I know you," I said, looking at the Goddesses of Shegoshel. "You're Naraxthel's holy Goddesses."

They smiled, brightness twinkling in their golden eyes and glinting off their long fangs.

"Welcome, Esra," they said in unison and gestured at a table bowing under gold and purple metallic plates full of produce. Green globes with a glossy sheen, small yellow spheres with matte skins, and flat but thick purple leaves were stacked in small piles. There were red and orange berries covered with fuzz like peach skins or raspberries, and bowls filled with thick juices. The fragrances overwhelmed my nose with rich fruited scents, sweet sugary tangs that made my stomach growl, and a light aroma that refreshed me. "Please, take and eat."

I stepped out of a thick veil of white curtains, glancing back at their hazy glow. The food enticed me. I stepped forward and chose a purple leaf and bit into it, liking its dense texture and the way the flavor traveled over my tongue, sweet at first, then umami at the end. I finished and reached for another before I realized the sisters weren't eating. I felt my face redden and found a cushion to sit on.

They covered their smiles with graceful hands and watched me arrange the long white skirt around my crossed legs.

"Now that you are prepared to make your final quest, we wish to give you a token." The Younger Sister cocked her head after she spoke, examining my every expression.

Final quest? The memory of my other existence was a rocky shale. One false step, and it tumbled into the scree. What was I doing before I came here?

"The token will aid you," the Elder Sister said in her rich voice. "We desire our Theraxl people to heal. They cannot heal until the wound is lanced and the infection is bled out."

I swallowed and creased my brow.

"Here is the token," the Elder Sister said, holding it to the Younger Sister. Younger Sister took the small gleaming item and held it out to me, suspended over the overflowing cornucopia. I reached across and held my hand palm up, ready to receive the gift.

Younger Sister dropped it—a simple gray stone. It no longer gleamed, but appeared as ordinary as any river stone, granite tumbled in the water and smoothed to a flat round shape that fit snug in my hand.

"Now go. You have prepared for this your whole life. Do not fear," the Younger Sister said, her voice thickening with emotion. "Triumph." She pointed a claw at the filmy gauze veils behind me.

I stood and gripped the stone in my hand, feeling its weight in my chest, rather than in my palm. I frowned when I entered the curtains, knowing I was going to forget everything all over again. I clutched to the memory and stepped through.

44

NARAXTHEL

"She dies," BoKama said after taking a deep breath through her nose. She stood at Esra's side, her head bowed as she observed the stillness of Esra's chest. "Why do I feel an affection for this being? Could she have been a spy?"

"No," I growled and stumbled forward. "Esra," I said. I would put my hand on her, but the robotic arm whirred into position, blocking me. I backed off.

Esra's technology spoke over several blaring alarms. "Initiating sinoatrial electrolyte displacement protocol."

I did not understand the words. "What does this mean?"

"The bacteria attacking Esra's system created an inflammation response in her heart tissue, resulting in myocarditis and tachycardia," VELMA said. "The SEDP will re-establish her heartbeat."

I understood nothing save Esra's heart was damaged. I recalled my own heart's eagerness to leave its chamber whenever I was in Esra's vicinity. My heart knew where it belonged. Esra could have it.

"Why do your medicines not work?" I asked VELMA.

"The bacteria are mutating. I need another local source from which to manufacture a bacteriophage."

"The Waters of Shegoshel aren't enough?" I said. I looked around the sterile ship, as if to find something. My eyes fell on a vial resting in a compartment near a clear box. It appeared to contain the mild glowing water from a cave pool. "What of the water from the cave pool?"

"Accessing sample."

I watched as a needle penetrated the lid to the vial, and siphoned liquid into a tube. The strange figures on the monitor changed rapidly, but I had no concept of their meaning.

I felt Kama's hand grasp my bicep.

"The Goddesses brought her to you," she said. "They will save her."

I made fists. My strength was useless to help her. My anger, my bravery in the face of death: my gifts were useless to this strange soft traveler. "The Goddesses know nothing."

Kama's soft laugh held no humor. "They know all."

"Analysis of the cave pool water reveals it is a heavy concentration of the dead bacteria Esra's body succumbed to. This will prove useful in battling her illness. I have created a timeline of Esra's micro-indicators. It appears she contracted the airborne bacteria inside the cave of the agothe-faxl." A graph appeared on one of the monitors, though I could barely comprehend it. VELMA had logged every sneeze, sniffle, stumble or hiccough. I caused Esra to contract the illness when I removed her helmet. Back in the cave. *I did this.*

"VELMA, do you require more cave pool water?" I asked. "I will retrieve it."

"There is ample for my needs. It was fortunate Esra collected this for her own curiosity." The mechanical arms and clear and gray tubes maneuvered around Esra's still body. Her chest rose a tik, and I made a fist.

"Did you repair Esra's heart?"

"The SEDP was successful. Esra's heart beats on its own. I am administering the new bacteriophage directly into Esra's bloodstream. Please stand by."

I drew in a great draught of air and stepped away.

"The little one keeps your interest, Naraxthel," BoKama said. She cocked her head, peering at me. "Do you feel strange? Does your heart beat erratically?"

"Let us discuss the deposition of the Queen," I said. "It will be more helpful to you."

BoKama lifted a shoulder and looked back at Esra.

"As you wish." She met my eyes. "All we need do is lure Scabmal Kama here. When she dies, I will become the Ikma Scabmal Kama."

"Nothing will draw her out of her lair of delights," I said. I resisted the urge to spit, out of respect for Esra's ship.

"Nothing except the promise of raxfathe," BoKama said. Again, she looked at Esra.

One step brought me into Kama's face. "Do not even entertain the thought."

Kama frowned. "I do not wish to use the soft traveler as a lure." She examined Esra over her shoulder. "It would work, though. We must come up with something else."

"The Ikma Scabmal Kama travels with several guards," I said. "If I were with my other four brethren, we could overtake them."

"With my help," BoKama said. Her fingers played along the scabbard at her waist.

"How did you find this place?" I asked her. I did not like the way she continued to stare at Esra's weakened body.

"I told you," she said. "I saw the ship in the sight-capture you sent when the hoard descended upon you. One moment, all I saw was the pack of rokhura, and the next, I saw a little sparkle."

"And you're certain the Ikma did not see it?"

"Reasonably certain. It resembled a glitch in the sight-capture feed. Many would have suspected an error disrupted by star flares," she said. "However, I recognized the shimmer as a cloaking device being deactivated."

"And no one else saw or deduced this?" I frowned with folded arms. Every jotik I spied Esra to see if her skin resumed its healthful pallor or if her chest rose and fell. But now I studied BoKama's face and sniffed the air around her. "The Ikma has a keen eye and intelligent mind. She could have seen it."

"She was busy at that tik," she said with a moue of distaste. "Otherwise engaged," BoKama said. "I used my access to erase the vital moment. But suddenly all was clear," she said, smiling at me. "You weren't distracted by the pomp of the Lottery or our royal beauty," she said. "But rather by this helpless creature, all alone on the Hunting Grounds." BoKama broke into a wide grin. "When you refused the Ikma, I knew then, I had been given a gift. I have been offering sacrifices to the Goddesses to send me an ally."

I scoffed. "We are playing into the Goddesses hands?"

"You know it is true, Naraxthel."

I bowed my head. "They do not intervene," I said.

"They are not intervening," she said. "They have merely revealed the path we should take."

"Then the Ikma Scabmal Kama will arrive on Ikthe without our help," I said. I smiled.

BoKama cocked her head and smiled. "Very well. We wait."

A sigh. A cough. "Water."

Esra spoke!

45

"Very well. We wait," I heard BoKama say.

I took a slow breath then coughed. "Water." My body felt weak, but free of pain. A weight on my chest caught my attention. I opened my eyes to see Red's head resting on my chest. He looked into my eyes.

"Your heart beats strong within its … ribcage," Red said. I lifted the corner of my mouth. He must have been quizzing VELMA.

BoKama had a pouch ready. I drank my fill and stared at my guests.

Red grasped my boot with his huge hand. "Are you comfortable?"

His simple question reminded me of our little language lesson the other night, so I blushed. "Yes." I avoided his intense gaze. "BoKama? What are we waiting for?"

BoKama surveyed Red and then me before she answered. "We will speak of it later. I must attend to my ship for a moment. I advise you engage your cloaking device." With that, she exited the hatch, leaving me alone with Red.

"My cloaking device?"

"BoKama found you with ease," Red said. "Should the Queen grow suspicious …"

"VELMA, activate hDEDs."

"Activating."

I sighed and looked up at Red, who continued to stare at me. "What?"

"I almost killed you," he said.

I waved my hand. "You already apologized. It's fine." I laughed. "I'm still getting used to the idea that I'm the alien here."

His brows nearly met, and I watched muscles feather over his jaw. "When the agothe-fax struck you. I removed your helmet to assess your health. I exposed you to the pathogen."

I watched his face, noting his downcast eyes and serious expression. "Naraxthel," I said. He raised his eyes to meet mine. "I would have taken my helmet off eventually." I gestured to the outside. "I live here now."

"Nevertheless," he said. "I am sorry. I owe you a debt."

I gave a soft laugh and turned my head away. "We don't owe one another anything." I looked up at him. "If this planet has taught me anything, it's that everything just wants to live, or finally gets tired of trying."

He didn't respond but touched the corner of my eye with a gentle claw. "Dua la du maikquo?" he whispered so quietly, only I could hear him.

"What did you say?" I searched his eyes. They bored into mine. His brows furrowed and he leaned close enough I could smell pepper on his warm breath.

"Where is your fire?" VELMA translated.

Moisture pooled in my eyes. "I don't know," I said. "I thought I was going to die. And here I am. I guess—maybe your Goddesses want me to live? It's just so hard." A tear slipped out and disappeared into my hairline.

"Ik," Naraxthel said with a nod. He leaned down with his lips hovering above my own. "Ikdu?"

Was he asking permission to do what I thought he was going to do? Did I want him to do it? Goddesses help me. I did. I did want him to. "Ik," I whispered.

He closed his eyes and pushed his lips against mine, a gentle nudge. My heart rate spiked when I felt his fangs, but I was in no danger from them. His lips pressed harder against mine. I pushed back, and then he growled in his throat. I raised my free hand to touch his cheek. His smooth shark-skin was warm under my palm. I tasted salt and pepper in his kiss, and then his mouth opened just enough for the tip of his tongue to lick the seam between my lips. With my heart racing, I dared to open my mouth and let him in. Warmth, wetness, fire! Clashing sensations awakened every nerve ending, and I moaned, surrendering to the kiss.

And then he pulled away, a look of horror crossing his features, and then utter wretchedness as he crumpled to the floor of my pod.

"Naraxthel?" I wriggled my body parts, but I was still weak. "VELMA? BoKama?" I was also still strapped onto the exam table.

"Red!" He writhed on the floor, then began crawling to the hatch. "BoKama! Help! VELMA!"

He reached the hatch; it opened, and he heaved himself out. I saw him slap pieces of armor onto his chest and shoulders, and then slam his helmet on his head. The hatch closed.

"VELMA, release me!" Silence. "VELMA, unhook me," I said.

"It is inadvisable—"

"Unhook me right now," I repeated. "I'm going out."

The cables zipped back into their ports and the restraints over my left arm and both legs detached. I was still fatigued, still fighting the bacteria that zapped my energy, but I knew I would recover. Something was very wrong with Red.

"Get BoKama out here, too," I said. I fumbled with my helmet. A quick peek out the porthole revealed the pitch black of night. I still needed protection. I glanced down at my sleeve. VELMA had repaired it during my illness. Thank the Goddesses. I limped to the hatch. When it slid open, light spilled onto BoKama. She barred my way to Naraxthel, who continued to torque himself into agonized shapes.

"What—?" I reached for him, but she held me at arm's length.

"Go back inside your ship, little one," she said. "He will be fine."

I protested, but she was much stronger than I, and muscled me back inside. "I will explain all. Leave him to his torment."

"Let me go!" I fought with her, but her commanding voice urged me to calm down.

"Esra, trust me," BoKama said. "Sleep now. You need your rest so you can be strong for Naraxthel."

I laid back down on the table, craning my neck toward the hatch. "Is he okay?"

"He will be. Do you want answers?"

"Yes!" My heart beat erratically, and I felt fatigue claim my limbs again.

"Your technology informed me you require more rest," she said. "Lie here, and I will explain. Naraxthel will come to you soon."

"Okay," I said. Tremors followed my voice and my hands. BoKama's soothing voice calmed my nerves.

"Now, I will tell you a story."

46

NARAXTHEL

Agony I've never before felt coursed through my veins. Doubling over, I endured it.

Thoughts raced through my mind. Esra in pain. Esra dying. I gasped for breath.

"Naraxthel," VELMA's voice sounded inside my helmet. "Do you need medical assistance? I am unfamiliar with your biology, but I may be able to assemble a treatment plan. It appears you are in pain."

"Continue to heal Esra. My pain is a gift from the Goddesses," I grunted. "I will bear it with joy."

Silence from Esra's Technology.

"I am able to do hundreds of tasks at once. However, while processing your sentence, I cannot reconcile your apparent pain with the definition of joy."

I gritted my teeth on a humorless laugh. "I have never experienced such anguish on behalf of another." I fell to my knees, fighting the sensation of blacking out. "I am nothing. Heal Esra. I will relish the pain, to understand my Esra better."

The torment was exquisite. I fell to my side, my claws scratching the soil upon which I knelt. Waves of burning contractions rippled over my frame. I saw BoKama through slitted eyes, observing me from the pod, but not approaching. She could not hear the conversation I had with VELMA.

Through a haze of pain, I heard Esra's voice as if through a watery tunnel. "Help him!"

A burning sensation bored through my chest. It felt like it was ripping open. I went to my dream place, the place the Goddesses taught the Ikthekal to venture during times of privation.

Images of Esra flashed across my mind. Falling backward down the mudslide, lying pale and lifeless on the cave floor, her hair between my fingers, riding the great grass-eater, vaulting off its back, running through the rains without complaining, lying cold upon the table— she had done all—alone. It was the Theraxl way. And yet, what if she didn't have to be alone anymore? What if the Goddesses brought her to me, so that I might repair the errors of my people? And repair the mysterious injury done to her, as well, whatever her former mate Chris had done?

The visions of Esra stopped. The pain eased out of my heart-home, and empty of my newly enlarged heart, it settled into a state of contentment. My eyes streamed. Esra ... was my Heart Mate.

"Naraxthel Roika, your biology has undergone a fascinating change in the last hour. It appears your four-chambered heart has shifted and is now residing outside its former fibrous cavity. This change has resulted in huge fluctuations of what appear to be hormones. If I am not mistaken, it strongly resembles the human hormone called oxytocin. Furthermore, your heart is far more vulnerable in its new place. Are you well?"

"VELMA," I addressed it. "What of Esra?"

"She rests."

I closed my eyes and expelled a huge draught of air.

"VELMA, you have your invisible hands in many places."

"It is a feature, not a bug. It is in my programming to monitor the health of those with whom I communicate. Now that I have added you to my database, I cannot help it."

"I am very well, now," I said.

"The fibrous enclosure has sealed itself with scar tissue. Should your physiology attempt a return to its original state, you would experience death."

"This, I know. It is well, VELMA."

I stood and moved my joints, free of the crippling suffering that had overcome me for nearly a zatik. I approached the ship and stared through the door.

BoKama stood vigil beside Esra, holding her hand.

Would Esra agree to remain at my side as my mate? Perhaps we could have no offspring due to our differing physiologies, but I could not bear the thought of her facing her life trials alone. She already had to endure so much.

BoKama regarded me. "Your heart left its heart-home."

I dipped my head but said nothing.

"I thought it was a myth," BoKama whispered, gazing once more upon the pale soft traveler. "If Ikma learns of this, you will both receive raxfathe. She will use the Royal Court's maikshe to keep you both alive for weeks while she toys with your entrails."

I felt a hot rush of blood to my face. BoKama was correct.

"Is she—?" I gestured to Esra.

BoKama smiled. "She rests now. You frightened her."

I stepped away from the ship. My kiss frightened her? Her courage in the face of danger showed her to be an uncommon female, one worthy to bear the offspring of Theraxl, if such a thing were possible. If Esra were mine, I would never allow her to be injured again. The ritual of raxfathe would be too merciful for anyone who harmed her, including the Ikma Scabmal Kama.

My entire future danced before my eyes, here in the dark meadow.

My life-path diverged from this point. In one direction, a solitary life filled with lands and ships, frequent trips to the Royal Courts where I would be given homage and wealth, and after a time, a seat on the dais with an honored Ikma.

Or the second path: hunted by my brethren, exiled from Ikshe the home of my youth, and run to ground like the animals I now hunted without measure. But with Esra by my side, as we traveled together. And what? A small child tagging along behind, clutching Esra's clothing with one hand while sucking on the sticky fingers of the other. The child had Esra's eyes, but my tough skin and long hair fronds.

A shift in my long-held beliefs began at that moment. Ever before, treasured offspring were left with the females to raise. Theraxl hunters visited their offspring and different mothers from time to time, ensuring they were always fed and clothed. But there was no grouping of a male and female together with their offspring.

This different path suggested a life alongside the soft traveler, and if that came to be, what of my heart and heart-home? Would it then exist in this state of happiness and contentment, just as Natheka and myself had wondered many times in our adulthood? I could not imagine my life without this female.

I had endless questions about her and her people. What gave her the courage to ride the grass-eater? Why did she scrape the walls of a cave and collect water from cave pools? What did it mean when she had a question in her own eyes? These would take a lifetime to answer.

But if she feared me—my kiss, my ardor—then perhaps I should leave. I bent to restore the remainder of my armor, my pelvic and leg pieces, and my boots. If the Ikma Scabmal Kama learned Esra was my Heart Mate, she would indeed perform raxfathe on Esra.

I clutched my chest. A new pain throbbed. Fear for Esra. Longing pierced my gut and mind. I wanted to be by her side.

I cursed the Goddesses. What good did it mean to find my Heart Mate if it put her in danger of the Ikma Scabmal Kama's wrath?

With my armor in place, I trekked to my ship. BoKama would tend to Esra. I needed to think upon my future and the will of the Goddesses.

#

47

BoKama's long lashes fluttered as she blinked in the low light from the pod. "There is a myth we hear as children: The Goddesses of Shegoshel created a stone for the first Theraxl. The Theraxl could come to the stone and give it their problems, and it would swallow the problems one by one. But Theraxl began to give it every inconvenience, every trivial thing. The first Theraxl became a selfish and lazy race. The Goddesses were displeased and warned the people the stone must be reserved for those burdens that could not be born alone. Only the greatest burdens must be given to the stone. But they did not listen, and one day, a male came to the stone and complained his mate had burned his breakfast meal. In their wrath, the Goddesses came down and thrust the stone into the chest of the male. They had to remove his heart, in order to make room, and that is how the heart-home was created."

The heart-home? Red said something about that in the ship. My breath caught.

BoKama continued.

"The male returned home to see that storming out had hurt his mate's tender feelings. She shed tears as she stirred a new pot of food over the fire. All Theraxl's previous problems came rushing out of the stone and fell into the pot. The mated couple watched in horror as the problems swirled around one another in the pot and became a maelstrom. Fearing the problems would spill out and devour his mate, the male grabbed a spoon and began eating them all. From the little splinters to the greatest injuries, he tasted Theraxl problems one by one. He grew accustomed to their flavors. But his final bite was seasoned with the salt from his mate's tears, and he felt the weight of her pain in acute detail, from the tips of his hair fronds to the ends of his toe claws. Filled with regret, he left the home of his mate, to spare her the pain of all the world. To this day, the males and females avoid long relationships, to spare one another the pains and burdens of existence."

I searched her face as my mouth dropped open. A memory of a gift, the stone! I flexed my hands, but they were both empty. "What is happening to Naraxthel? Why can't I go to him?"

"I believe his heart is leaving its heart-home," she said. "We experience this in our adolescence. For three short cycles, we feel the bliss and contentment of a liberated heart. But then it slips back inside, never to leave again. This is unprecedented."

"What does this mean? You said he would be okay."

"Yes, I believe he will." She petted my arm. "He will tell you more when he returns. In the meantime, you must fully recover. We still have so much to discuss," she said. She cocked her head. "I believe the Goddesses have great plans for you."

"Why do you keep saying that?"

BoKama stared at me with her blood-red eyes. "I have been supplicating my Goddesses for two cycles. They came to me in a dream," she said, and then let her gaze drift away from me. "I saw five stars fall from the sky. And when I awoke, I felt hope." Then she smiled and turned her face to me once more.

"Theraxl people speak of the Stone Heart Myth. They say it explains our adolescence. But there is another myth." She reached out and caressed my face. I marveled that this big race of warrior-like people could be so affectionate. "There is a myth that when one finds their Heart Mate, the heart leaves its heart-home forever."

I blinked, entranced by her long lashes and sage green skin. She continued.

"The heart in its true place becomes vulnerable," she whispered. "And yet, Theraxl once dreamed to achieve such softness, if it meant they would never hunt alone again."

Another slow blink. The lights in the pod seemed to dim. BoKama hummed a melody that was at once mysterious and familiar. I wanted to ask what she meant by more vulnerable, but my mouth was lax. The pod grew darker still, and BoKama's voice was a thin strand of silky web shining in the pale light.

VELMA must have shot me a stealthy dose of a sedative, because the next thing I knew, I was waking up to a silent and empty pod. Both BoKama and Naraxthel were gone. I tested my limbs. I felt refreshed, energized. A little loopy. I inhaled deeply and found my "allergies" were gone. My body had been fighting the bacteria all along.

"VELMA, is the deadly cave bacteria exclusive to the caves?"

"No. I used the volatile emissions scanner to analyze air samples from this meadow and found evidence of the pathogen. However, I was able to use Naraxthel's DNA to genetically modify the bacterio-phage to act as a vaccine in your system. You will not contract the illness again."

"I thought the cave was antibacterial," I said. "The dead agothe-fax isn't decomposing."

"The bioaerosol is a strain that attacks living tissue."

"When did you culture Naraxthel's DNA?"

"Observe the screen," VELMA said. "This shows your oxygen levels at the time of the agothe-fax strike."

I studied the chart. "What is that influx of oxygen? And other gases?"

"It appears Naraxthel administered an adapted form of pulmonary resuscitation. I was able to collect a sample of his residual DNA from your lips."

"Oh wow." I couldn't think straight. Everything led me back to Red.

I sat up and waited for the dizzy spell to pass. A whiff of pepper entered my nose, and I touched my lips. "Red!" I hopped off the table and grabbed my helmet and machete. The air might be harmless to me now, but the predators weren't. The pod spun again, and I leaned my hand against a panel until the vertigo passed.

Exiting the pod, I peered into the darkness for BoKama or Red. Spying neither, I hiked through the grasses, checking for prints. A swatch of grass was bent leading to BoKama's ship's landing site, but the ship itself wasn't visible. *The cloaking device.*

"VELMA, where is Naraxthel?"

"Naraxthel is in his ship."

I stopped walking. "His ship?" My voice faltered when I spoke again. "And BoKama. Where is she?"

"BoKama is in her ship."

I turned to look at my pod, some thirty feet away from me, but of course I couldn't see it either, the hDEDs were activated.

The single moon rose over the meadow, its hazy blue glow washing out the colors of the featherettes and the green of the numerous trees and brush surrounding the meadow. I heard what I presumed to be insects buzzing and sawing the air. Why were they in their ships? Were they … leaving me?

I rehashed all BoKama had told me about her people's myths. She had assured me Naraxthel was fine. That he would return. But his ship was not close. He had chosen to hike there. I made fists and clenched my jaw. I needed to see him. He had been in pain. If he needed to leave, fine. But I wanted to see for myself he was okay. The kiss—well, it was breathless and sweet and held a promise I never hoped I'd receive in my life—but it was just a kiss. I tried to forget the way it made me feel.

"VELMA, chart my course to Naraxthel's ship."

"It is inadvisable to trek there during nocturnal hours due to the risk of predation," VELMA said.

"Just give me the map, please."

She inserted a map into my IntraVisor, and I studied it.

"Engage infrasonic scan," I said and lowered myself to a crouch. Already my heart raced at the thought of entering the forest jungle. I'd seen the worst daytime had to offer. What fresh hell awaited me in the dark? VELMA's scan showed small creatures dotting the area. Any of them I could dispatch easily with my machete. What lay beyond the scope of VELMA's scanners? I checked the star-spilled sky above me for black shadows. Maybe Red's Goddesses would walk with me tonight. I swallowed a lump in my throat. I almost turned back to the pod, recalling its safe haven. But then I remembered the anguish on Naraxthel's face. What had happened to him? I shook off the tremors I felt in my extremities. This was, possibly, the most stupid thing I contemplated doing so far. Red. I blinked and cleared my throat. "Bring on the darkness."

I followed the path. Rather than draw attention to myself with the headlamp, I employed night vision. The sounds of the night enveloped me, clicks, ticks, taps, buzzes and whirs that only increased in volume the deeper into the brush I traveled. I stepped on something that cracked loud in the air, and I remembered Naraxthel telling me I was too loud.

Chagrined, I tried to watch where I planted my boots, while also pointing myself in the right direction, the flat green and black night vision revealing several small animals' eye shine. I also kept looking behind me to see if I was being followed.

"VELMA, how are my vitals?"

"All within normal ranges. You have made a full recovery."

"Thank you for saving my life," I said.

"Ironically, you did. You provided the necessary virus stores from which I could splice bacteriophages to destroy the infection," she said. "The cave pool water provided ample material, as the organisms have a symbiotic relationship with a bioluminescent bacterium and a viral detoxifying mechanism. "

"Oh," I said, marveling at my dumb luck. Or my intuition. "Run a subsonic scan."

For the moment, nothing stalked me. According to the map, I had about another fifteen minutes of walking, though the route I took was thick with fallen timber and bracken. Naraxthel couldn't have walked this way; surely, he would have left trail signs.

VELMA's voice sounded in my ear. "Hostile approaching fast from your three o'clock."

A solid mass of power knocked me to the ground so hard, my helmet unlatched and shot off my head. I yelled when the creature clamped down on my shoulder and dragged me further into the wild. I kicked and tried to grab at anything with my left hand. A trunk, or the creature's neck, anything. But I couldn't take hold and ended up dragging my gloved fingers through the humus while my right hand still gripped my machete.

The pressure in my shoulder was great, but so far, my suit held strong. I couldn't see what dragged me, but the smell was putrid. Hot puffs of rancid breath blew up my shoulder into my nose. I stopped flailing, fearing my movement would cause the predator to shake me like a wolf with a rabbit.

It dragged me through the thick vegetation, leaves slapping me in the face, drips of liquids splashing down onto my cheeks and body. Skittering feet fled from the trail we cut through the weeds and bushes. The pale moonlight breached the canopy in scant slices: not enough to give me a sense of direction or memorize landmarks.

I didn't need VELMA to tell me my heart raced, and my breaths came in shallow gasps. My shoulder began to ache. The padding steps of the creature made little noise on the jungle floor. A dank smell slithered into my nose and I sneezed. The creature released me, and I lay like dead weight, blinking and trying to make out my surroundings.

My eyes adjusted enough to see a wide opening leading out into the jungle. I lay at the entrance. I heard the huge feet padding amongst dried leaves and twigs, and I also heard it snuffling and grunting. Just as with all the other big animals on this planet, it didn't make loud vocalizations. I wondered if it had one of those gross throat bags.

The dank and moist air made me want to cough, but I swallowed repeatedly in the effort to stay quiet. I inched my left hand down my outer thigh to reach the spot where I kept my multi-tool. Sigh of relief; its weight felt good in my hand. Between my tool and my machete, I could defend myself.

A strange high-pitched noise burped in the air behind me. It was joined by the little eruptions of more such noises. I couldn't be sure, but I thought maybe it was the creature's young. I still didn't know what it looked like, but apparently, I was to be its babies' snack.

Tears pricked at the corners of my eyes. I was a *geologist* for Pete's sake. I did not want to be plunged into a kill-or-be-killed scenario, but here I was.

I closed my eyes and took a cleansing breath. Gripping my tool tighter, I shifted and craned my neck to see the occupants of this shallow cave.

A huge nest of dried branches flanked one wall. I could just make out the clumsy movements of some pale-furred beasts. The mama or papa, I wouldn't know which, paced the rear of the cave. Looking for something? Waiting for its mate's return?

I forced my breaths to calm. I watched the animal—it looked like a giant cross between a hyena and a mountain lion—until it plopped down and lifted its leg to clean its genitals.

I edged away, out of the cave, sweating and gritting my teeth and praying my movements were masked by the increasing agitation of the animal's young. I had no doubt it could outrun me, and probably track me by smell or sound or whatever, too, but I had to try.

The animal lifted its head a moment and sniffed the air. It went back to licking, and I puffed out a small breath. Inch by inch, I slid myself along the ground, headed for the side of the alcove where maybe I could climb a tree or scale this hill, or something. Soon, I could no longer see the animal. I heard the babies making their burp and cough noises, and I scooted another foot to the side. I sat up, fisted my hand around my tool and uncurled to a stand. I worked to obscure every breath.

Just as I had hoped, the shallow cave lay at the foot of a rocky hill. Peach light from the east heralded the rise of the first sun. I could see the hill was an outcropping of more orange rocks. The leggy animal could easily outrun me, but maybe I could climb high enough quickly enough to lose it. It was a long shot.

I affixed the tool back onto my suit leg and grasped the nearest handholds and began climbing. I heard shuffling and grunting from the cave to my side, but nothing indicated urgency or alarm. I continued to climb, stabbing my boots into crevices between boulders, using my machete as leverage in some places and listening to raining pebbles with stark fear. Any of these noises could alert the predator to my escape.

I crested the outcropping at the same time the first sun broke the horizon. I couldn't see far, but I could see I was surrounded by wilderness. The tendons in my neck tightened. I knew Red's ship was southwest of my picnic meadow. However, I couldn't see the meadow from this pile of rocks. I had a general idea of west, and it was my best option. Swallowing my fear and dread, I made my way down the opposite side of the hill. My narrow escape was more of that dumb luck I had following me around. I wasn't going to take it for granted.

I climbed down, marking the footholds below me to prevent stumbling. It was going to be a damn long day. The first sun broke the horizon, and its sister sun followed close behind.

48

NARAXTHEL

I finished my ritual washings and reapplied my armor. I wanted to communicate with my brethren, but so much had happened, and I didn't know how they would accept my new status. *Kathe.* I didn't know how Esra would accept it.

I toggled the comm. "BoKama, how fares Esra? I will be there in a quarter zatik."

She didn't reply. I switched channels, careful to avoid the community channels that could alert others of my people that she and I had been communicating. "BoKama, how fares Esra?"

I secured my helmet, locked down my tech-slave and cloaked my ship, eager steps trekking swiftly through the ikfal toward Esra's ship.

No answer.

With a silent kathe, I ran.

With my suit's enhancements, I was able to reach the small meadow as the first sun peeked above the horizon. Neither BoKama's nor Esra's ships were visible. I enabled my helmet's wave-sight, and detected BoKama's ship. Esra's was still obscured. Good. Our technology couldn't penetrate her camouflage.

I took a step toward BoKama's ship when one of its tooth cannons slid open. "Stand down," BoKama whispered into my comm. A pungent odor assaulted my breath ports from the direction of Esra's ship. A rocket shot from the nosecone with a loud hiss, and then BoKama's tooth cannon shot artillery at the pod. I stared in horror as the pod exploded in a white fireball, its concussion pitching me backward into the brambles of the ikfal. I blinked as BoKama's ship thrust into the air, tipped in a wave to me, and then rose higher in the air.

Stunned and winded, I shook my head until it cleared. My ears rang, and colored lights danced before my darkened vision.

The spot where Esra's ship had stood so proud was now a glowing blue and white ball of ferocious flames. It roiled and billowed, like a moon of fire, and shafts of flames shot out to ignite pockets of meadow grasses. The heat from the explosion penetrated my armor.

I glared at the pod where Esra had lain, supposedly recovering from a bacterium I had caused her to contract. Could she have lived through such an explosion? There was no time. I leaped to my feet. "Esra!" I roared and ran straight into the pulsing and roiling flames.

I strode the halls of my dream place even as I entered the glowing mass of fire. There was nothing left of Esra's ship. The heat repulsed me, even as I tried to penetrate its depths. My helmet visor blared countless alarms and my suit's tendrils curled inside my body, entrenched deeper and deeper as it attempted to protect my skin from bubbling and melting off. Heedless, I circled the fireball, shouting Esra's name and looking for a weakness or rubble or the burnt fragments of the first and only female I had ... loved.

I roared again and stepped away. Perhaps her suit could protect her from such a cataclysmic fire.

I collapsed to the blackened ground, loathing the very air I breathed.

Were the flames growing larger? Would it swallow me as it had swallowed Esra? Let it.

"The myths are true," Kama's voice said in my ear. "When the heart leaves its heart-home, the male is rendered a forever idiot."

"What did you do?" I asked her and tried to crawl away, but I discovered my limbs weren't functioning. My legs splayed out, weak and useless, in front of me.

"The Queen's WarGuard approaches the planet. She may have

discovered my treachery; I do not know. I destroyed Esra's ship. She was *not* inside it."

I stared at the flaming ball, willing it to expand and devour me before her words made sense.

BoKama's voice slapped my face. "Stop looking at it, fool."

I blinked.

I heard BoKama's muttering in my helmet. "*Into* the *kathe* fire." She huffed in my ear. "Get you out of the clearing. I saw Esra leave her pod a zatik ago, heading toward your ship. I assume she knew your ship's location? The Queen's guard will arrive in two zatiks. I have led her on a merry chase of false leads."

I lay my head back against a log and closed my eyes to rest a jotik. Already I felt the tendrils releasing their chemicals into my bloodstream to hasten the healing process. Esra was alive? I felt my lips curve up in a predacious grin. Now I would hunt her in earnest.

49

I shrieked. Something was crawling behind my neck and I was seconds away from using my machete to hack it off, possible beheading be damned. I reached and grabbed, trying to find the source of the tickling, slimy wetness on my skin. Finally, I grasped a slender vine and flung it away, swiping at my neck with my other glove, trying to wipe off the goo.

I hadn't even identified it, so anxious had I been to yank it off me. I realized the tree I was under had countless dangling sticky vines. Every few seconds, another one dropped to the forest floor. I jittered and jumped a few steps out of its radius. The rising suns brought a tender glow to the green forest, and I hiked through it, trying to find Red's ship.

Sweat poured down my face and trickled down the back of my neck.

Every time my brain tried to resurrect the memory of VELMA, I shut it down. That was useless information right now. Much like the memories of Chris's fist heading straight for my nose. Or his teeth sinking into the flesh under my arm. Or his booted feet kicking me in the ribs. Useless memories that served no purpose, except to put me in a mental hammerlock.

Useful memories were how to kill a black wasp with a single swing of my machete swatter. There was one flying toward me, and I raised my swatter to hit it, but before I could swing, it veered away. I heard another one at my eight o'clock, but like the first, it swerved around and left me alone.

I stopped. That had never happened. They swarmed and stung until half of them died and the other half ate the dead ones.

A faint itching sensation on the back of my neck reminded me of the sticky vines. "Oh please, oh please, oh please," I said to myself, walking back to the tree with a flare of hope. I gathered up a handful of the dropped vines and smeared its sticky juice all over my suit and neck and forehead, and even massaged some into my hair. It smelled like cat pee, but when I saw a V formation of wasps head for the tree and then veer wide left, I was convinced.

I hiked on, paying special attention to any other details that might come in handy for staying alive. The jokal ran around my feet when I stepped through some bracken where their trails crisscrossed in the dirt. Red told me they were harmless as long as one wasn't bleeding.

The heat and the smells oppressed me, as well as the emotional work of expunging memories every other minute. Why was I still remembering Chris? I closed my eyes, but his contorted face and vice-like fists appeared. I blinked away moisture. Trudged forward.

Where could Red's ship be? I tried to concentrate on the memory of the map VELMA had shone me before.

If the picnic meadow was a bowl, then the talus-slope leading up to the beacon hill was at the north rim. The break in the woods was at the south rim. Red's ship had been several hundred feet to the south-west of my pod. I tried to calculate the suns' positions in the sky for a ballpark guess as to the time of day and the direction I was walking. If I kept at a westerly direction, I could track it within a fair radius. I hoped. Who was I kidding? I was lost in this hell-hot jungle.

The vision of finding his ship only to watch it lift off without me hastened my walk. Or maybe it was the memory of Chris's violent promises.

I swallowed and felt my face drain of blood. I gritted my teeth and kept going.

I crouched beneath branches and cut my way through the heavy jungle growth. The humidity was awful. I grew accustomed to the noises in the trees. I stopped every fifty steps or so to fix my bearings and make sure I wasn't walking in a circle. I crouched often, listening and waiting. My heart raced the further I traveled. I hoped I was closer. Something snapped behind me. I stopped.

The cacophony of twittering birds I had yet to see quieted. My heart went into overdrive and sweat rolled under my arms and down into my sleeves. I exhaled slowly, forcing a calm I didn't feel. Hyperventilating could kill me. As could standing here motionless. So could sudden movements. Another snap. Awareness stabbed my heart with a javelin. I was still on this god-forsaken planet. I was still helpless. And just like I had been helpless at Chris's hands, so I was still. Especially without VELMA to help me navigate. Or Red.

A final memory of Chris overpowered me, and I sank to a knee, unable to keep it at bay any longer. My heart went into overdrive, and I shook from the inside out, powerless.

"You sorry excuse for a woman," he sneered in my face. My plane holo-ticket lay at my feet in shards. "You thought you could leave me? Thought you could leave IGMC? I own you! I own your education, your body and your worthless life." He had me by the throat. "I should kill you right now," he said through clenched teeth. I felt pressure beneath my chin and around my windpipe, and my face began to swell. His spittle dotted my face when he spoke. "No one could indict me, you know. All I would have to say is that someone broke into the apartment." He pushed against me and released his grip. I stumbled back, gasping for breath with tears streaming in rivulets. He strode toward me, his hands in fists. "I picked you because I saw something special. And now look at you," he said, derision making his voice rise and fall in pitch. "You're nothing without IGMC. You're nothing without me. So weak you can't even stand up straight. And what's that I smell? Did you *piss* yourself?"

I whimpered, my shame bringing hot flames to my cheeks.

"You're never leaving me, Esra." He took a final step and flipped a butterfly knife open. "I'll always find you. I'll hunt you down, I'll sniff you out, and I'll *cut. Your. Heart. Out.*" He dragged the knife downward between my breasts, blood seeping out bright against my white skin. I pleaded for my life, made promises I couldn't keep, said things I didn't mean and bargained with power I didn't have. Somehow, he didn't kill me that night.

I didn't notice the sting from his blade until the next day, when nervous perspiration covered my entire body.

I waited in the call-outs room with fifty other men and women who had applied for the Kerberos 90 expedition. It had been a solid year since we'd applied, most of us having forgotten all about it. After Chris strangled and cut me, he binged on an expensive bottle of *Stardust*, and I was able to answer the phone for once. It was for me. Was I still interested? Could I be ready for a shuttle pick-up in one hour? Would I be willing to sign all the waivers? Ha.

Gasping for breath, I pressed my hand to my chest, counting the beats. Chris was far away. I had wired up a beacon. Killed gigantic serpents and amphibians. Survived a terrifying scorpion-spider. Eluded a mighty alien hunter more than once. I could do this. Kneeling in the heart of a dark-green jungle, I filled my lungs with a great breath. On the black humus, a smooth plain gray stone lay stark against the rotting vegetation. I stared at it. Where had this come from?

There were no riverbeds, no streams. Not even a rock outcropping.

I bent closer for a better look and felt the whispered breath of a slight breeze. There was one monster I hadn't faced yet. Another memory bubbled to the surface, and I dared to turn and face whatever was behind me. I was not meant to fear. To hide and disappear. I was meant to fight back. To *triumph*.

Forty paces away, one of the first creatures I'd seen on this planet stood between the wide trunks of two trees on thick muscled legs. Saliva dripped from its pointy teeth in its massive jaw, and its throat sac bulged and shrank with its breath. Or was it summoning the others?

I adjusted my sweaty fingers around the hilt of my machete swatter and rose from kneeling. Its eyes tracked my every movement.

My heart pounded in my chest and blood thundered in my ears. My vision tunneled to the scaled and taloned monster a few leaps away from me. I saw its brown talons and black and green bumpy body in harsh detail.

I had the insane thought that if VELMA were with me, she would be telling me how fast my heart was racing and asking if I wanted an Advil or something. I swallowed even though I was spitless. I couldn't outrun it. I couldn't out-fight it. I had a machete, for Schist's sake. I revived the memory of Red facing off the horde by himself. I cocked my head. And when I had been riding the hairy mammal and Red's men had flanked it. They had hamstrung it.

Without moving my head, I roved my eyes over the ground and trees, placing the lay of the land in my mind. I felt the fear gripping my heart with its every thunderous beat, but I had to do this.

You have been preparing for this your whole life.

Preparing to fight a dinosaur? No, I hadn't. I'd been trying to survive a sadistic monster.

Oh.

I widened my eyes as a vision of what I should do forced itself into my brain. I raised my machete, watching its four eyes track the slow arcing motion. And then I screeched and attacked.

Running full bore toward it, I saw it cock its head. My high-pitched keening cry disoriented it, and I dodged between trees while it shook itself from its surprise. I had seen the beasts fight in the open meadow. Their size made it difficult for them to maneuver in the forest. My advantage.

I saw its sac inflate and bulge, and I cursed. With a final burst of speed, I slid on the rotting leaves underfoot, aiming for the path between its legs. With a whoop, I scrabbled to my feet and tried to swing my machete at the same place I had seen Red's companions do, on the back of its leg. My weapon nicked something because a fountain of black blood sprang from the wound. No roar of pain. But there wouldn't be. I tried to dodge the swing of its tail, but I was too slow. It thwacked me, and I flew back, hitting a tree and cracking my head against the bark. Shaking my head until the blurred vision cleared, I tried to stand.

The beast twisted toward me, but one of the trees stood in its way.

It struggled, gnawing on the tree, its muscles bunching and flexing underneath its rough skin.

I thought of Red. He climbed up one of the monster's backs like it was a pile of dirt. I held the machete like a pickax and pushed back from the tree. Maybe I could do that. I panted, trying to get the courage to try, and then ran toward its back. Its tail swung again and hit me in the gut. My air burst out of my lungs and I hit the ground hard.

I couldn't catch my breath as the ground trembled with the beast's erratic stomping and pawing. My mouth opened and closed, and my lungs worked to snatch any air it could. I heard the bone-chilling crack of a tree splitting, and I tucked into myself and rolled away, still trying to inhale oxygen. Any second now I expected serrated blades to slice through my suit. After another few seconds, I was able to breathe in, and I rolled to my stomach. My machete was lost now. I dropped it when its tail hit me the second time.

I watched the beast as it crawled over the fallen tree toward me, its open maw resembling a sardonic grin with all the teeth. I thought I could see bones stuck between its incisors, and another breeze wafted toward me, carrying the scent of rotting meat with it.

Get up. Come on, get up.

I ripped another breath from the air with my burning lungs and narrowed my eyes at the reptile. I clenched my teeth and ground my hands into the ground as it stalked me.

I knew I didn't have a chance. This entire planet had been hell-bent on devouring me since the second I landed. It was like Chris. Stunning vistas punctuated by death falls and harrowing panic around every turn. I guessed the question I should be asking myself as the beast approached was, how badly did I want to live?

We are judging your worthiness.

My worthiness for what?

"Life is beloved, and death is sacred. The worthy welcome both."

I want to kick your Goddesses in the teeth.

"A sentiment we often speak of."

"Your boots are graded to withstand 4500 psi."

It dove for me at the same time I rolled to the side and kicked at its mouth with my boot, while I screamed at the top of my lungs.

The beast snapped on my ankle by the grace of the Holy Goddesses of Shegoshel. I felt enormous pressure, resigned to the fact my ankle was not making it out of this in one piece, even if I managed to live, which I doubted.

My hand found another rock, and I whizzed it at its head, aiming for one of its eyes. It bounced off, ineffective, and fell to the ground.

The reptile pulled at my leg and lifted me off the ground by my ankle. I swung, sick to my stomach, and felt my leg pull at my hip socket. I screamed and twisted, my heart racing so fast it felt like one continuous roll. The minute that thing shook me like a dog's toy, my neck and spine would snap, and I would be as good as dead.

This was it. This was goodnight, Esra.

"I own you. Your education, your body and your worthless life."

"No!"

Without thinking, I snatched at my multi-tool, which remained snapped to my pant leg, and jabbed it into the beast's chin, head, eye —anything I could reach. I screeched at it and howled, fighting for my life. I wasn't dying in this horrible place. I wasn't. I was worthy, dammit! My life was worthy! I had value. Life had meaning. *My* life had meaning.

Even though I dangled from its jaws, and every socket felt like ball joints were going to pop out, I angled myself to advantage, giving the beast the fight of its life. Black blood dripped from a hundred little wounds, but it still wouldn't let my boot go.

Tears streamed down my face. My muscles screamed at me to give up, to let go, to die. I let my abdomen relax, and I drooped, swinging like a pendulum. The ugly orange throat sac bulged out again, right in front of my face, and I lunged toward it with a vicious swipe.

The gush of blood baptized me, and the reptile finally released my boot as it collapsed, but we fell together, and when I hit the ground, I couldn't tell if the darkness was death and hell, or just death.

50

NARAXTHEL

I smelled her everywhere. That bush, that tree, this rock, this boot print. My joiktheka had no sense of direction, perhaps.

Urgency gripped my soul. She had no helmet, as it was hitched to my pack. I had found it, but her lack reduced her safety by a huge margin. I smelled her sign again and found the place where she entered a thick stand of trees. I ran into the ikfal, relishing the hunt. My eyes spotted the broken branches and the skids of boots on slippery leaves. Her fragrance was rich in the humid air, a pungent reminder of her humanity. Her fragile race.

"Are you searching for Esra Weaver?"

VELMA's voice almost tripped me up. "How are you speaking to me?"

"I launched a rocket that contained my Operating System. I have limited capabilities, but my memory still exists."

I slowed my run, losing Esra's scent for a moment, then finding it again on the breeze. "Your memory will live forever in the hearts of those who know you."

"I am referring to my information and data banks."

"You are a confusing entity, VELMA," I said. "Yes, I am hunting Esra."

I picked up my pace. Already I had scented the talathel and the old scat of pazathel-nax. My heart in its vulnerable place beat extra hard; I felt its pace increase with every footstep. I ran several more steps under the dropping vine tree where I lost her scent. I stopped.

"If you require assistance, I will help you."

"Thank you, VELMA," I said, tracking the ground for boot prints. It reminded me of the first time I tracked her up the hill, fascinated at a creature that emitted no trace of odor.

I found her prints. They walked away from the tree, then disappeared. In circling the area, I found her prints again, this time approaching the tree. I tracked back and saw clumps of vines had been smashed and mangled. I smiled.

"Esra discovered the secret to warding off the ikquo-daxl," I said. "Clever female."

That was how I lost her aroma. No matter. Now I would follow the cloying odor of the dropping vines. I exhaled a powerful sigh. One less danger to harbor anxiety over.

I noted the thrashed foliage as I followed her trail sign. She had her sharp weapon with her. I frowned. She very well may need it. Soon, I thought, as I glimpsed the sister suns through the leaves.

Ikthe would protect herself from encroachers. Esra was so small, she could hardly be considered a trespasser. Even now, the evidence of her passing was minimal in the grand scale of my hunting grounds. I willed the planet to leave Esra be.

Holy Goddesses, protect my mate until I can.

I ran on, until I lost the scent of the dropping vines. Because the stench of rokhura blood overpowered my nose. My heart beat painfully fast and my breaths hitched. If I could smell it, every predator in the ikfal could smell it.

How was Esra in the path of a dying rokhura? The beasts never entered the ikfal.

"Your heartbeat has increased five times its normal rhythm," VELMA said in my ear. "Do you require assistance?"

"What creatures do you detect?"

"Seven reptiles of the variety Esra calls 'dinosaur' are gathered fifty veltiks from where you stand."

"*Kathe!*" I ran full bore into the trees, tearing the foliage apart in my urgency.

"I have also detected several different varieties of excrement."

I ignored VELMA's odd nattering and grasped my weapons by their hilts. I broke through shrubs and bushes into a clearing where six rokhura fought each other over the carcass of a seventh. My heart pulsed in time with my gasping breaths.

I should circle the clearing to avoid the beasts and continue my search for Esra. I lifted a foot to step back into the ikfal when my eyes narrowed on the carcass. Its head was dotted with countless tiny wounds, like needles from the mountain trees had pricked it. No predator on Ikthe left such a mark.

My gut rolled into itself. Esra lay under the dead rokhura. I was certain. The events of the last days flitted across my memory. Playing a hunch, I activated my sight-capture to send to the Ikma Scabmal Kama.

With a roar, I launched myself at the snapping and biting beasts, slicing off limbs and stabbing bellies until three lay dead at my back. The other three leaped onto their dead, and I dropped to my knees at the ravaged rokhura before me. I deactivated the sight-capture. It was a short, bloody battle, but perhaps it would leave a false trail for the Ikma. It may buy me time.

The rokhura's bulk was nothing to me. I hefted it, ignoring the chunks of meat and offal that fell away as I lurched under its weight.

"Esra!" I hissed at the sight of her drenched in black blood. I tossed the rokhura away from me and gathered her up in my arms.

I wept when her head lolled back at an odd angle and cradled her until it no longer jostled. Then I stood and ran into the ikfal, commanding VELMA to display the quickest route to my ship.

I ran, the prayers to my Goddesses competing with the ragged breaths dragging from my lungs. No matter my pains. I bore them with joy. As I bore Esra's delicate body in my arms. I saw her chest rise. She yet lived. And would live still. Why else would the Holy Goddesses give her to me, if only to take her away? What deities would do such a thing?

Doubts assailed my mind, but I jettisoned them one by one.

BoKama's voice entered my helmet.

"I am at your ship," she said. "What do you require of me?"

"Esra has sustained wounds. Prepare the healing chamber."

"Very well."

I arrived at my clearing, the Tech-slave standing ready at the bay door. I flew past him, my boots clanging on the metal ramp as I entered my ship.

The healing chamber's bed was ready for Esra. I placed her upon it and stood back. BoKama, now wearing her light armor, placed a hand on my arm, and we watched as the machine rolled over Esra, enclosing her for a time.

"Where did you go?" I asked BoKama, anger barely concealed between my clenched teeth.

"Covering tracks, Naraxthel. You must trust me."

I ripped off my helmet and tore off my gloves, letting them fall to the floor. I approached the table when the machine receded into the wall and touched Esra's face with a knuckle. Dried blood obscured her white skin.

The healing chamber's technology announced errors. I cursed.

"VELMA," I said. "Use your invisible fingers to access my ship. Heal Esra."

VELMA said nothing, and my heart raced once more. I took Esra's hand in my own, and something dropped out. A pale gray stone. It gleamed under the healing lights.

"I have accessed your medical device. While I am currently unfamiliar with its capabilities as it is designed for your physiology, I was able to scan Esra's body. Her neck and spine are intact. Her ankle is broken." VELMA paused, then continued. "Scans indicate a significant history of forearm, wrist and hand fractures, as well as broken ribs. It appears she sustained them well before landing on this planet."

My mouth dried out, and I saw white sparks before my eyes. Heat, unclouded by guilt, boiled in my gut. What had Esra endured before she landed on my hunting grounds? I clenched my hands and took deep breaths through my nostrils.

"Put Esra's helmet on," VELMA said. "I will diagnose further injuries."

I detached her helmet from my pack and slipped my hand under her head. She stirred. I froze, unwilling to jostle her should something cause pain.

"Red? BoKama? I can smell you." Esra spoke and VELMA translated for us.

I let her helmet fall to the floor with a clunk. "Esra, what hurts? Does your neck hurt?" VELMA's voice traveled through my ship's comm as she said my words in Esra's language.

"Everything hurts, Red. That damn dinosaur almost ate me," she said and groaned. "I think my whole leg is broken. Unless it's gone. It could be gone. I was afraid to look."

"You are wearing both boots," I said, controlling the emotion threatening to close my throat.

"Thank the Goddesses," she said in a quiet voice. "Why are you holding my head?"

"You need your helmet," I said. "Can you feel your limbs? Blink your eyes or signal with your fingers?" I dared not breathe as I watched her respond to my commands.

"Everything seems to be accounted for." She peered at me through slits. "You're never going to believe this. But I killed it before it killed me."

My heart leapt and my lips curved up. "You are Iktheka Raxthe, now, Yasheza Mahavelt." *Although by the history of her injuries, she was mighty long before she arrived on Ikthe.*

"I don't know what you just said, but I hope it's good."

"It is very good," BoKama said. "Sit, if you can, child. Naraxthel will watch over you." BoKama took a wet cloth and bathed Esra's face and neck.

Esra sighed, moving her joints in turn, testing their strength. She took the helmet BoKama offered and put it on. I watched her lips move as she spoke to her technology.

"Your mate is worthy," BoKama said, giving me a sideways look. "But you deserve nothing less."

Esra deserves a worthy mate. My heart-home declares I am that mate. But would she?

"What do we do next?" Esra asked BoKama.

"We will find the Ikthekal and finish the quest," BoKama said. "I believe he promised me wealth untold." She cocked her head at me and Esra laughed.

I gave a grim laugh. "Do you think Ikma knows of Esra's existence?" I grasped her hand, and she squeezed back. My heart jumped.

"She does not. I monitored the comms from my ship. She sends the vanguard to seek explanation for your lack of sight-captures."

I gave a half-smile. "I sent her one not a zatik ago. Perhaps she will be sated for a short time." I thought of my brethren. "We have only a few rotiks before we must leave here." I opened up my comm, and triggered Natheka's channel. "Natheka, how do you fare? We are on our way to your first checkpoint."

"There is still no sign of Hivelt."

Esra gasped and furrowed her brows. Her mouth turned down. The concern touched my heart.

"We will find him," I said. I did not add we would give him a Hunter's Pyre when we did. It was understood. But I hoped we would find him alive instead.

"I have news, my brethren," I said. Esra leaned forward in her seat. I smiled. "I received a visit from BoKama." Gasps and yowls erupted through the comm. "BoKama shares our disgust for Ikma's hasty sentence. She has plotted with me to overthrow Ikma's reign. In return, she will become Ikma Scabmal Kama."

Voices scrabbled over one another. Raxthezana's came through in a slither. "You have sentenced us *all* to raxfathe and death."

I slid my eyes to see Esra's reaction. Her eyes were wide, and her mouth gaped.

"No. We will triumph."

Esra's face paled and mouth tightened. She stared at me, her blue eyes filling my vision. I could not decipher her emotion.

"BoKama will have labeled you traitor by now. Ikma Scabmal Kama will be sending the Royal WarGuard," Raxkarax growled through the comm. "I will kill you myself when you arrive, after smashing your soft traveler with my boot."

I roared and Esra curled up in her seat, a little jokal. I heard her splutter with indignation.

"Raxkarax," I said. "Esra can hear every word we speak. You will apologize when we arrive, or I will feed you the soup of the mud-beast with my raxtheza."

Silence for several tiks.

Natheka's voice entered the cabin. "We are on edge, Naraxthel. The pazathel-nax separated us from Hivelt." He paused. "And now you have made a decision that impacts the rest of us. Without our consent."

I dipped my head. Swallowed.

"You have every right to be angry with me," I said. "My attention was divided, and BoKama arrived without notice. My only thought was to protect Esra. When we land, I will explain all in detail." My eyes drifted back to her, where she listened with hands clasped together and knees drawn up to her chest. Her eyes shimmered with wetness, and the muscles around her mouth strained to stay smooth. She feared us. She feared me.

I wished I could utter the next words privately, but I wanted no secrets between her and I. I faced Esra as I spoke to my companions. "My heart has left the heart-home. The chamber is closed." I heard a gasp or two over the comm. "The myth is true. I have found my Heart Mate. You must know I would do *anything* to protect her. Anything."

The tears brimming in Esra's eyes fell down her cheek. I did not know her thoughts. Her mouth contorted and for yet another tik, I caused a female to cry. I turned away and uttered a soft *kathe*.

If my companions defied me, Esra and I would be forced to flee through the ikfal. I would not kill them, despite my threatening words. I had no desire to shed the blood of my brethren.

"Your brother has done well," BoKama broke into the conversation. Dead silence on the other end. "I was in contact with the Ikma. We have deceived her. She believes you all dead since your sight-captures have stopped. She recalled the WarGuard as Naraxthel just sent her a sight-capture. Naraxthel suggested you continue on your quest to collect the Waters and the woaiquovelt." BoKama cocked her head. "The Ikma has not detected my treason yet. After a time, I will return to Ikshe with tales of Naraxthel Roika's undying loyalty. What say you, Ikthekal?"

Silence.

My heart stilled. I dared not take a breath.

Raxthezana spoke. "May the life of Shegoshel shine upon you and your offspring, BoKama."

"May the death of your enemies bring peaceful slumber," she answered.

I exhaled. "Let us trek now."

"After we bind your Yasheza's ankle," BoKama said. She found bandages and bound Esra's ankle with haste. VELMA discouraged the use of our pain medications.

"I need to scan its properties to ascertain compatibility with Esra's biology."

Esra groaned but said nothing.

I programmed my Tech-Slave to clean the ship after our short stay and to remove trail sign in a veltik radius.

With Esra pulled close to my heart as I carried her, I ran once again, BoKama trailing behind. Ever since I had revealed Esra was my mate, Esra had not spoken a word.

"Did I offend you?" I said through dry lips.

"No, but I have a question."

I clutched her closer when I jumped over a deadfall. "Ask it."

"Why is your armor black?"

Her question nearly made me stumble, but I found my footing. I did not answer, but I heard BoKama scoff.

"I had to destroy your ship else it would be seen by the Queen's guard." She tapped my shoulder. "This fool ran into the explosion."

Esra's face went white. "VELMA. How are you functioning without the pod?"

"BoKama told me her plans. I am authorized to activate the Scram Nosecone Protocol under conditions of imminent destruction. My neural network is contained in the nosecone which now operates as a Super Low Orbit Satellite."

I watched Esra purse her lips and blow. Then her eyes found mine.

"Did you run into the fire?" Esra pushed. "To save me?"

"Yes."

"But I wasn't there," she said, her voice quiet.

"No."

"You found me anyway," she said.

"I will always find you," I replied the only way I could. With truth.

Her next question was so quiet, I was thankful VELMA still translated in our helmets.

"What will you do when you find me?"

I felt the ground beat against my boots as I ran, thinking over my answer.

"I will give you my heart, every time, Yasheza."

She whimpered.

I saw a tear trace the line of her cheek to her jaw, and I wished I could taste it with my tongue.

"What does Yasheza mean?"

"It can mean soft," I said. "Like Soft Traveler."

BoKama giggled behind us. I ignored her.

"Or?" Esra would not let it go.

I swallowed. "Or it can mean Touched Heart."

I felt Esra tremble in my arms, even through my armor. I spared a glance at her face but returned my gaze to the trail ahead of me.

She was quiet the rest of the day and into the night, but she rested her hand upon my armor, right above the place where my heart now resided. Its new heart-home, in her hands.

51

Mate?

I sat useless while BoKama and Red made a small camp. The suns set, and darkness spilled over the hills and into the forest. Every time my mouth formed a question, I dropped it. Instead, I watched him. The way he walked. The way he carried himself. The way his now-black armor absorbed light so he disappeared into the shadows when he went to collect wood for the fire.

I tried to make a comfortable place on the pallet, but chunks of feldspar, quartz, fuchsite and numerous others found the soft tissue in my body when I tried to relax. I swept them aside, a fruitless endeavor.

BoKama walked out of the dark woods and squatted next to me. "You are not uncomfortable because of the ground." VELMA translated our conversation.

I pressed my lips together a second, then lifted my eyes to meet hers. "Why were you not surprised when Re-uh, Naraxthel told everyone I was his mate?" I peered over her shoulder at his form, but his head tilted to the side, as if he slept. I was skeptical.

"Because the myth has become reality," she said. She turned to watch him. "He conceals wounds. The fire—it caused great injury to his skin beneath the armor."

My eyes burned. I shook my head at her words.

"What does it mean to be worthy in your culture?" I asked.

BoKama's eyes rounded and her brows rose. She nodded and looked between Red and I. "The Goddesses created all. I have studied the ancient words and myths," she said. "It is my understanding our worth depends upon our existence."

I chewed on that thought. "I have worth because I exist?"

She smiled. "Precisely."

My hand clutched the stone I'd found before I fought the giant beast. I didn't know how I still had it. My final quest … my eyes drifted to Naraxthel. Wounded under his armor, carrying me through the forest.

"I do not know your people." I met BoKama's eyes. "Are mates subservient?"

She grinned, her fangs catching firelight from the campfire. "The males serve us," she said. Then she sighed. "But there haven't been *Heart* Mates in hundreds of cycles."

I felt her hand push my shoulder.

"Has Naraxthel told you the name of this planet? It is called Ikthe. Certain Death."

A chill settled in my abdomen. "It's a horrible place."

"You almost died," she said. "Many times?"

"Yes." I peeped at her. She pursed her lips.

"The Goddesses view life as beloved, and death as sacred."

I sucked in a breath, remembering Red's words to me. They came to me during my darkest hour on this planet, when I almost—stopped fighting to live.

BoKama smiled. "The Goddesses favor you, child." She rested her elbows upon her knees. "Why do you not make our people your people? Stay with Naraxthel. Bear him hunters and sisters."

The blood drained from my face and my mouth dropped open. BoKama stood and walked back to the perimeter, watching for the dangers that lurked in the night. She spoke as if I had a choice. My pod was gone. I drew in a shaky breath. My pod was gone, but I hadn't used it to kill the rokhura. I had value and ability without the pod. Simply because I was alive. And by the sounds of their beliefs, I had value once I died, as well. Naraxthel and BoKama seemed to think I was worthy to be among them. What would be different if I was with Red? I thought of the song we sang together. And how we laughed. The difference was I would be happy.

I was no longer afraid of the predators on this planet. I was afraid of a life without Naraxthel.

I pondered on the myth BoKama shared with me. Why did the hunter-mate leave? The answer was so obvious. If they had only shared the soup ... My heart sped up. Shallow breaths punctuated my thoughts. The stone. I tumbled it in my hand, rolling it over and over. The token was a stone? Snippets of the dream popped up in my mind. *Triumph*. I ran a gloved finger over the stone, caressing the smooth texture.

I will cut your heart out.

But Red, with his heart on his sleeve. Huh. With his heart in the new place ...

I will give you my heart. Every time.

Red's words would stay with me forever. How could he know the perfect thing to say? He couldn't. The dreams of the Goddesses replayed in my mind. They made me pant and my chest constrict. As did the loathsome Chris's parting words to me.

I swallowed and turned away to stare into the black forest. If I could choose to give my heart to anyone, it would be to Red. I just wasn't sure if I knew how to use mine anymore. But I wanted to. I squeezed the stone until my hand cramped.

52

NARAXTHEL

"This is a horrible place."

My mate's tears tore at my heart.

Was I a selfish hunter? I declared Esra my mate before giving her the opportunity to say yay or nay. I would not push myself upon her, but she had no chance to see me in any other capacity than as a bloody warrior covered always in hunting filth. Perhaps my violence reminded her of the one who forced her to hold her arms and hands in front of her body in defense. I growled low, daring any of Ikthe's predators to face me this night.

I would not withdraw my declaration, but I could not expect Esra to run into my arms and proclaim her unending happiness. Not when she feared me more than she cared for me. *If* she cared for me.

This *kathe* planet had indeed almost killed her numerous times. It *was* a horrible place. No place for a female, let alone one of her fragile mien. And yet she had proved herself time and again. Both before she arrived, and after. I was not ashamed to call her my mate. I leaned my head against the tree and closed my eyes to pray.

Holy Sisters, what would you have me do? Certain Death is not the place to join with a mate. Ikshe is under the powerful boot of the Ikma Scabmal Kama. I cannot take Esra there. Esra belongs with her people ...

* * *

Elder Sister and Younger Sister stood before me in shimmering golden robes. Their beauty outshone the queen on Ikshe. Elder Sister did not smile, but I felt love pouring forth from her heart to mine. Younger Sister smiled at me.

"Do you dare to tell the Shegoshel where Esra belongs?" Elder Sister asked.

I felt my face darken and I was wont to take a step back, but I raised my chin. "My mate is unhappy. She was torn from the bosom of her people."

"Esra was severed from a poisonous body. She is where she belongs." Elder Sister's eyes narrowed on me until I submitted.

"What am I to do with a female on Certain Death!" My frustration burst out before I could bite my tongue.

"Bring life, of course," Younger Sister said with a smile. "The answer is in the soup."

A giant bowl of simmering soup bubbled in front of me; it wasn't there before. The Sisters stirred it with long-handled ladles. Younger Sister brought the ladle to my lips. "Sup. It will make you well."

I closed my eyes and sipped the broth. Flavors from another world burst across my tongue. I swirled them in my mouth, reluctant to swallow and lose them to my memory.

"Nay, take the flavors into your soul, Naraxthel Roika."

My eyes opened to BoKama, her hand on my shoulder.

"Take your watch."

I nodded and stood, shaking my head of the webs behind my eyes. Did I dream? I walked the perimeter, listening to the *hohipadaxl* bugs as they rubbed their spikes against their wings, begging for a mate. Their potential mates flew to them and ate them, unless each bug's body temperature matched exactly. We called them nonsense flies.

My thoughts ran to my brethren and our quest. Danger lay ahead and behind. Did Ikma believe my loyalty, we were free to travel unhindered. Did she entertain suspicions, we could expect the WarGuard to run us to ground.

Hivelt was missing or dead. And my mate could not walk.

I stopped pacing.

Was it possible she could care for me? I studied my clawed gloves. I was well-acquainted with violence and death. But my hands had never turned against a female, not even the Ikma, save to remove her hand from my face. I would never raise my hands to Esra in anger. I knew that. But did Esra?

I sniffed the air around our little camp, but all was still. The suns would rise in some jotiks from now. I observed BoKama sleeping against the black trunk tree. Esra lay on the pallet I made for her, her back to the small fire. I should let her sleep. But my dry mouth and sweating hands would not abate until I could speak with her alone. I approached her bed and sat beside her, resting my palm on her shoulder.

"Mmm. Is it time to leave already?"

I jostled her shoulder with a soft push-pull. "Wake to me, Esra."

She rolled onto her back, a soft smile relaxing her features until she bumped her ankle. Her grimace spoke of her pain.

The conversation I wanted to have with her faded away. "I brought several doses of our pain softeners," I said. "The Maikshel of our planet prepare them from the plants native to Ikshe."

"VELMA said I should wait."

My brows folded. "I understand your technology's concern, but have you eaten of the plants of our world? Have you eaten of the meat?"

"Yes," she said.

"Our Waters healed you. I am confident our medicines will heal you," I said. I pulled a pouch from my kit. "I will break the medicine cake into fourths. It will help you. Do you trust me?"

I removed my gloves and snapped the gray cake into pieces and held a quarter of it out to her. My eyes met hers, and my anxieties were replaced with a warmth in my chest. Her lips parted, and a sheen sparkled over her blue-green eyes.

I used one hand to remove my helmet, placing it beside me. Then I reached behind her and unfastened her helmet. I released it with a click and removed it.

The scent of meadow lilies once again flooded my nose. I leaned closer and inhaled. The memory of our kiss was not far from me.

Her face paled under my scrutiny. "I scent for illness, Esra." I closed my eyes and let the flavors and aromas of her essence wash over me. "You are well."

She flushed. I could detect warmth from her skin. She took the medicine fragment and swallowed it, chasing it down with water from my canister. "It taystz lik gras."

I smiled. Without our helmets, we could only communicate by looks and touch. With little thought I reached up to touch her braids. I weaved my fingers through them, feeling the silkiness of her hair. When she didn't pull away from me, I brought my other hand to her face, cupping her cheek and jaw, letting my thumb brush across her lips.

"Everything about you is soft, Yasheza," I said in my quietest voice. With ears tuned to sounds of danger, I dared to lean closer. "Your skin, your hair fronds, your very life."

I heard her breaths quicken, but still she did not push me away nor try to flee my caresses.

"Could you care for me, Esra?"

Shadows from the low firelight flickered across her expression. I couldn't discern if doubt or fear was among the emotions that also flitted across her face.

Careful of her pained ankle, I pulled her closer to me. I wanted to consume more of her. She made tiny sounds when I caressed her lips with my blunt claw and brushed my knuckle across both cheekbones. She fit into my lap when I seated her across my legs, and I brought my arms around her. I wished my suit was off, but until I healed, it would remain. I buried my nose in her neck, inhaling her aromas. She mewled and gasped when I trailed my nose along her jawline and behind her ear. I recalled the odd yearning I felt before, to taste her tears.

She was not crying now, but the urge to taste her skin overpowered me. I brought my lips to the pulse under her soft ear, and let my tongue rest there, tasting. Want, as powerful as a mountainous explosion, overtook my entire body. Consumed by heat from within, I froze, my eyes large when I searched for Esra's feelings in her eyes and face.

Her eyes grew round as well, and breaths escaped her lips in rapid bursts. She licked her lips, and my eyes darted to her tongue, its wetness catching firelight. My fingers clenched around her arms. I wanted to taste her tongue with my own. I wanted—all. I swallowed, my throat feeling as if I swallowed a rock. For some reason, the image of soup crossed my mind. I blew a gust of air and sat her back on her pallet. With shaking hands, I offered her her helmet and replaced my own.

"I do not know what to say," I said.

She laughed upon hearing VELMA's translation. "I'm just glad you didn't say you were sorry."

"Why would I say something I do not mean?"

Her laughter subsided, and her mouth drew into a line. "You are special to me, Naraxthel." Her gaze didn't waver. My heart beat erratically, yet joyfully, in my chest. Warmth spread from my chest to my neck and face and wrapped around my ears. I felt my smile widen and my fangs break free of my mouth. And it wasn't from the suns cresting over the horizon.

"You are special to me, Esra."

Her smile widened. "We should probably discuss what it means to be mates," she said. "You know, in your culture versus mine. Where I come from, the mates live together. They go out and work and do their jobs, and then they come home at the end of the day. The same home." Her face reddened, much to my fascination. I did not know why.

I tilted my head in the other direction. "This is done on your world?"

She nodded with vigor, a small smile curving her lips. "Yes!" Then her features softened. "BoKama told me the mates don't live together. But you said we were." She swallowed and gestured between us. "Mates."

I put my gloves back on as I pondered her words. "I thought it was a silly tale spun at my bedside as a child." My eyes caressed her face, watching the flames reflect in a happy dance upon her helmet and her sparkling eyes. "But it is said that once two Heart Mates find one another, they can never be parted. Not by enemies, nor by death. They are one."

I was startled to see a tear brim in one of her eyes. Fascinated, I watched it build then spill over and mark a path down her cheek. When she said nothing, I reached for her hand. She put it in mine.

"Your mate raised his hands to you."

Her eyes shot to mine. "Who told you that?"

My eyes narrowed but I squeezed her hand in a soft pulse. "The healing machine on my ship saw many past injuries in your body's bones."

More tears fell from her eyes. I would hold her close, but our helmets were crucial to this conversation. "I didn't know how to get away once I realized he would never stop," she said. I couldn't hear her voice, only VELMA's translation. "The chance to leave Earth practically dropped into my lap. I took it and never regretted it." She looked up at me. "Landing here was a mistake. I was supposed to be headed to a mining colony with a bunch of other employees of IGMC. It was a new life. But all this? It's still better than my life with Chris, and," she laughed, but it sounded hollow. "I'm here in the middle of ..." She swung her hand to include me and BoKama and Ikthe. "I'm a lost soul now."

I exhaled and nodded when she searched my face. I did not understand all she said, but one thing. "You are lost to your people," I said. I placed my hand on her shoulder. "But you are not lost to the Goddesses. They know you. And I believe they sent you, not only to me, but to my people."

Her eyes filled with more tears. My heart ached at the sight, but I would endure my mate's tears. My mate's *tears*.

A flash of the Holy Goddesses sprang to my mind.

The answer is in the soup.

What am I to do with a mate on Certain Death?

Bring life, of course.

My hand clamped upon Esra's. "I will taste your tears."

She turned her head. "What?"

"I will taste your tears. And should I cry, you will taste mine."

Her brows furrowed, and the corners of her mouth turned down. "I don't ..."

I smiled and leaned forward, grasping her other hand. "We will create life. Together. I will bear the burdens this Chris gave you." I recalled the long scar down the center of her chest, and fire burned bright in my gut for revenge. "And you will bear my burdens. We will build this life from here. From Certain Death."

"You want us to bear each other's burdens?" she asked.

"You are a mighty hunter, like me." I gestured to the wilds. "We will create a life here, and it will be very difficult. But the strength between us is great. We will endure it together as equals."

BoKama's voice broke through my fervency from behind me.

"And the Goddesses said, let Life spring from the ashes of Certain Death, and let the joy of Our People spread from Death to Life and Life to Death throughout all the ages of Time."

I watched as Esra's eyes widened. Her gaze pierced my heart, but she exchanged a look with BoKama next. "The story you told me. The hunter tasted his mate's tears and ran away."

I admired her profile as she shared a look with BoKama.

"If he had stayed, they could have eaten the soup together," Esra finished. Her eyes met mine. "And he could have shared his heart-home."

She held her hand out to me. I reached for hers, but she didn't take my hand. Instead, she dropped the stone into it.

"The Goddesses gave me a gift in my last dream," she said. "A simple stone. And then I found it in the jungle. Right before that thing almost ate me. I remembered the dream, and the gift, and everything." She pressed my hand around it. Her face turned pink again. "This planet is terrifying and deadly. But you already figured out my last life was just as terrifying, and just as deadly. If I have you by my side, I think I can handle it." She pursed her lips and blew out a breath, then raised her eyes to me. "My quest and my triumph—is you."

"Ah, Yasheza," I said, taking her hand. "Then we will hunt together."

BoKama smiled and took Esra's hand.

I put my hand out for BoKama. She kissed it. "May the life of Shegoshel shine upon you and your offspring," I told her.

"And may the death of your enemies bring peaceful slumber," she said. "I will run ahead to meet your brethren." She squeezed my hand and caressed Esra's cheek. "We will see each other again." BoKama loped off into the woods.

"Your brethren," Esra murmured. She faced me. "What did you tell Hivelt to make him let me go?"

"Ah," I said. "I told him, *zama do ikrax*. It means something like, "The woman is *my* gift"."

"Oh," she said in a whisper.

I lifted Esra into my arms.

"I'm sorry you have to carry me everywhere," she said.

"I am not sorry. This way I can run through the ikfal in silence. Your footsteps are as loud as a birthing scabika in the middle of a mountain burst."

She yelped and hit my armor with a weak fist. I smiled.

"When you are healed, I will teach you how to move silently through the forest. You will be my Mighty Hunter."

"And then I can run and hide so you never find me."

I scoffed. "I will always find you, Esra. Do you know why?"

I watched curiosity and skepticism play across her face through her helmet. "No."

"Because you have my heart, and I cannot live without it."

Her smile lit her entire face, and its light warmed me like the love of the Holy Sisters of Shegoshel. She and I forged ahead, the suns bright at our backs, and our shadows leaping into our future on Certain Death. A future that promised abundant, if not easy, life.

EPILOGUE

"Wake up, Yasheza," Red whispered in my ear. "I have a gift for you."

"Mmm, unless it involves a chocolate tree, I'm not waking up," I mumbled into his naked chest. Weeks of constant company and VELMA's help allowed us to have simple conversations in his language. We slept on Red's pallet in the ikfal. His peppery aroma surrounded me. My body hurt from our relentless trek to catch up to his brethren. My ankle slowed us down, but it was almost healed thanks to his people's medicinal herbs.

I blinked my eyes in the second sun's morning light, tracing the intricate scarring on his skin. "It doesn't hurt?"

"Nothing hurts, Yasheza," he said to me, like he had said the last few weeks. I didn't believe him. BoKama told me those many weeks ago that both taking off and putting on his armor caused pain.

The burns he suffered from mistakenly trying to rescue me from my exploding pod had healed, and on the night he finally removed his armor, we sealed our love for one another. But I was obsessed with his scars. Maybe because most of mine were internal. He carried his battle wounds on the outside.

Even though we came from different worlds, we fit together where it mattered, and Red brought me joy I never imagined.

"Wake up," he growled and caressed my bare skin. "You will be angered if you do not receive your gift."

I grunted. "I've received a lot of your gifts," I teased, closing my eyes again. "That's why I'm so tired."

A deep chuckle.

"Very well. I will tell your Technology you do not wish to know about the signal."

I sat up, suddenly wide awake.

"What signal?"

His eyes burned with desire when he looked at me, but instead of carrying me away, he reached across and handed me my helmet. "Listen."

"This is a recorded message. My egress pod landed on a lush planet full of dangerous animals. I'm tracking something big. If you can hear this message, come find me. I'm at 41.9020 N and 86.5958 W. I'm human, and my name is Pattee Crow Flies."

"VELMA," I said. "Send her IntraVisor this message: "Do not remove your helmet. Airborne pathogen fatal to humans in atmosphere." My stomach roiled. "Send the files on what you need to make her bacteriophage vaccine." I paused. "Shouldn't she already have this information?"

"I have been unable to access the AI in her pod. It seems she has disabled me. Once she unlocks Overseer Mode via the Handler chip, she will receive the messages. I will keep trying."

"Oh no," I said. "We have to find her fast, Red." I held his face in my hands. He pulled my hands away and kissed them then stood.

He began applying his armor before he spoke. "We are mighty hunters, Esra. We will hunt. Together."

A pang crossed my features when he turned away, but I knew he protected me from his pain. We were going to have to work on that. But his strength, his immensity, took my breath away every day. He was my hunter-warrior; he treated me as an equal, and if any partnership could endure hardships and setbacks, ours could. We were mightier together, and together we would find her, before it was too late.

ACKNOWLEDGMENTS

She doesn't know me, but I read Ruby Dixon's Ice Planet Barbarians a few years ago and fell in love with hunky aliens and spunky space exploring colonists.

At the time, it never occurred to me to write my own science fiction fantasy series. I was busy working on other projects at the time such as my sweet romances and cozy mystery novellas. Fast forward a few years, and I had an idea for a swashbuckling romance that takes place on a savage planet where death lies in wait around every ikfa, er, tree. So, I'd like to thank Ruby Dixon for being a true inspiration as I attempted to write in one of my favorite genres to read.

I'd also like to thank Victoria Clapton, who is a never-ending source of encouragement. Tara Niekamp is another unfailing cheer-leader who helped me amp up my writing.

May, your book, "Hack Your Writing: 7 Search Functions to Instantly Elevate Your Manuscript" was invaluable. Also, I edited adverbs out of my acknowledgments. Thanks. 😊

Paul, you're ruthless. But this is a better book because of you.

My family goes without at times when I am wrapped up in a book, and I appreciate their patience during these times.

Finally, I have to thank God for this one. 2018 and 2019 were rough years, and I spent more than a few hot minutes shaking my fist at the sky. My belief in His unconditional love and desire for me to grow stronger was inspiration for the ordeals that my beautiful but dented heroine had to endure, but also for the benevolent, yet non-interfering Goddesses of Shegoshel.

Writing a language to go along with my alien race was both a challenge and a fulfilling activity. I hope you enjoy flipping through the dictionary coming later in the series, and if you'd like more taste of the

Predator Planet, visit my website for Earth-inspired imaginings of Ikthe at: www.lovevickyholt.com.

ABOUT THE AUTHOR

Vicky Holt is the proud mother of six children, one daughter-in-love, and a grandmother to one darling boy.

She keeps houseplants and one naughty big puppy, and still gets a thrill when her husband reaches out to hold her hand. She believes most people are good, and that love and romance are worth fighting for.